Mary E. Pearce was born in London but moved
out of the city as soon as she could, working for
a number of years in a library in Cornwall
before settling in the beautiful hill country
of the Malverns some thirteen years ago. She
now lives in a delightful three-hundred-years-old
cottage in the village of Kempsey, devoting her
time to writing and gardening, her two great
passions. It was this lush farming area of the
West Midlands that she chose as the setting for
Apple Tree Lean Down, the first novel in her
moving rural saga – and, astonishingly, her first
published book.

Apple Tree Lean Down

Mary E. Pearce

Mayflower

Granada Publishing Limited
Published in 1977 by Mayflower Books Ltd
Frogmore, St Albans, Herts AL2 2NF

First published in Great Britain by
Macdonald & Janes Ltd 1973
Copyright © Mary E. Pearce 1973
Made and printed in Great Britain by
Cox & Wyman Ltd
London, Reading and Fakenham
Set in Linotype Pilgrim

For Barbara

CONTENTS

Part One

Ah! I do think, as I do tread
Theäse paeth, wi' elems auverhead,
A-climèn slowly up from Brudge,
By easy steps, to Broadoak Rudge,
That all theäse roads that we do bruise
Wi' hosses' shoes, or heavy loads;
And hedges' bands, where trees in row
Do rise an' grow aroun' the lands,
Be works that we've a-found a-wrought
By our forefathers' care and thought.

– William Barnes

CHAPTER ONE

To Beth, as a child, grandfather Tewke was merely a strange old man who sometimes passed through the village, driving a smart little pony and trap.

'There goes your grandpa!' Kate would say. 'The old ramrod!' And John Tewke, returning from Capleton or Chepsworth, would sometimes say he had passed the old man on the road. 'He gave a nod and I gave a nod and that was all we said between us!'

Once, when Beth was sitting on the front doorstep, shelling peas, grandfather Tewke went by on foot, across the green and up to the church. He passed so close that Beth could hear the squeak of his boots and could see the white hairs that sprouted from his long fine nose. But even then, passing so close that his shadow fell across her, he took care not to glance her way.

'Seems grandfather Tewke don't know who I am,' she said, indoors.

'*He* knows!' Kate said. 'But he's queer with us. He likes to pretend we don't exist.'

'Why does he?'

'Ask your father. He's the one for stories, sitting there, doing nothing.'

Kate was always too busy to stop and talk, but John Tewke would always make time, and now, having dropped his newspaper, he drew Beth on to his knees.

'Your grandpa and me fell out,' he said. 'Years ago. Because I left the carpenter's shop. I wasn't happy there, you see, whittling away at bits of wood. – That went against the grain with me.'

He looked at her with a little smile, but she remained solemn, waiting for him to continue his story.

'Mind you,' he said, 'I served my time and could tackle any carpentry job you care to mention.'

'Well,' said Kate, rattling spoons and forks on the table,

'there's scores of jobs here in this house, waiting for you to show your skill.'

'Ah, I'll do the lot when the spirit moves me.' And he winked at Beth. 'Your mother don't understand,' he said, 'But that's murder to me, having tools in my hands, after all them years in the workshop.'

'It's a shame about you!' Kate said.

'Now horses is different ... I've got a feeling for horses that I never had for timber ... But I'm sorry the old man's as sore as he is.'

'The old man's silly,' Beth declared.

'He likes his own way, that's all. I'm the same, but I get my way with the horses, see, and that keeps me happy. Which is just as well, 'cos I don't have no say at home, do I? Your mother's the gaffer here, ent she?'

He liked to pretend he was under Kate's thumb, but the truth was, although she nagged and grumbled, Kate rarely had her own way. He was the one who made the decisions, and she obeyed his slightest wish.

There were often quarrels between them because she, according to him, had no sense of fun, and he, according to her, had more than his share.

'Kate! You look as though you'd swallowed a cockroach!'

'So I might, my husband coming home market-merry, stinking of beer and refusing good food.'

'Dammit! A man's entitled to celebrate, surely, after a day's business? Guess what I got for Dolly and her foal?'

'I hope it's more than you've spent on feed, that's all.'

'Here, take this silver, woman, and make it last.'

'Where's the rest, I'd like to know?'

'Ploughed back into the business. – I bought three ponies off a Welshman. And here, Kate, guess who I saw at Ross?'

'Who?'

'Everybody I looked at!'

'Oh, get away, you tipsy fool!'

'Beth! Your mother's as grave as a churchyard. Why did I marry a woman like her?'

'Nobody else would, I don't suppose.'

'So now my daughter's siding against me? That's a pity, that is. She won't want the present I've bought her.'

'What present?'

'Only a work-basket with coloured threads and a little tambour . . . I reckon I'll give it to Hetty Minchin.'

'No!' Beth said. 'You must give it to me.'

'What d'you give in exchange, then? Do I get a kiss? And what'll my wife give for this nice plaid shawl? Ah, smiles all round now, ent it?'

'All the same, you should save your money,' Kate said. 'Shawls indeed! No wonder I'm grey!'

Always, on market-days, the scene was the same. Kate knew she would never change him, yet continued to scold. But Beth, although she began by echoing all her mother's complaints, soon learnt instead to accept him. He was her father and that was enough. He brought warmth and colour into her life, and comforted her when she was sad.

'Where's the sun today, then? Gone behind the clouds? I'll soon make you laugh! How much d'you bet? Sixpence on the nose or a penny for every nail in a shoe? There, that's better! That's the face I like to see!'

When the weather was bad, he stayed at home and was lazy. He sat in his chair, his feet on the hob, his hands tucked in the waist of his breeches, while Kate struggled past with pails of water or bundles of wood. But out working his horses, he drove himself to the point of exhaustion, and Beth often had to fetch him home, to prevent his falling asleep on the way. Often, he walked twenty miles to a sale, and returning with a couple of raw new colts, perhaps, his arms would be bruised black and blue to the shoulders. 'The beggars led me a dance,' he would say, 'but I'll do the same for them tomorrow.'

His honesty and judgment were well known: farmers round Huntlip asked him to buy horses for them, and called him in to doctor their cows. Beth often went with him on these errands, and once, when they were taking a cart-horse to Middening, he showed her where her grandfather lived and had his business.

'That's Cobbs, where I was born, and there's the carpenter's shop, like I told you.'

13

He preferred to avoid meeting his father, so he stood in a place where the hedge grew high, but Beth, on the horse, could see right over. She could see the house, with its black timbers and red-bricked panels, half in sunshine, half in the shade of surrounding oaks and elms; the big workshop yard, with its stacks of planking all around, the sawyers at work in a cloud of dust in the sawpit, and the carpenters busy in the workshop.

'Goodness! What a din!'

'That's music to some,' her father said. 'Specially your grandpa. Can you see him anywhere?'

'No, but he must be there somewhere, 'cos the men are hopping about like crumbs on a griddle.'

'Can you see the big oak tree in the yard?'

'I could hardly miss it, the size it is.'

'It's been there since domesday, that old oak. Since ever the house itself was built and that's going back a year or two.'

'Grandfather Tewke's just come to the door.'

'Time we moved on, then,' her father said, and pulled at the bridle. 'We don't want him to think we're snooping, do we? Even if we are!'

'Does he live all alone in that great house?'

'Yes, and must be very lonely sometimes.'

'That's his own fault,' Beth said, shrugging.

When not at school, she was always on the common, watching her father as he worked. But she had to be good and keep away from the horses; be very quiet and not cry when he used his whip. She must sit like a little mouse, he told her, and then, when they ate their oneses together, she should share his beer.

As she grew older, he gave her a few little duties to perform, such as cleaning the harness and beating the rugs. He allowed her to mix the horses' feed. But he would never allow her to ride them, even when they were broken to the saddle.

'One of these days I'll get you a pony all your own. Ah, when my ship comes home, that's right. Or when my lucky star is shining. One of these days! You'll see!'

He was always a great believer in luck.

Every day, before school, she went up to the green to fetch water, and one October morning, early, while she was waiting her turn at the pump, grandfather Tewke drove by in his trap. Young Freddie Lovage, whose father worked in the carpenter's shop, stopped pumping and gave the old man a smart salute.

'There's your grandpa. Ent you bobbing him a curtsey?'

'I'd sooner bob to that gander!'

'Your dad's daft, cutting loose the way he did. That's a tip-top business old Tewke's got at Cobbs.'

'My dad's got a business all his own.'

'Horses!' scoffed Freddie. 'That's a gipsy game!'

'My dad's his own master. That's more'n you can say for yours.'

When Beth returned home, her father was brushing his boots on the doorstep.

'I heard all that, and you done right, sticking up for your dad.' He took the pails and carried them for her into the kitchen. 'I shan't always be working my horses on commoners' rights. Oh dear me no! One of these days I'll buy some land and build stables and then I shall start a good stud.'

'What'll you use?' his wife asked. 'Shirt-buttons?'

'Money'd be better. All I need is a bit of luck.'

'There's no luck on Chepsworth race-course.'

'Who mentioned the race-course? It's the fair I'm going to, woman! Though as it happens, there *is* a couple of runners I fancy ... Now which d'you say, Rufus or Penny-Come-Quick?'

'Safe-in-the-pocket,' Kate said.

'Beth?' he demanded. 'Which horse d'you fancy?'

'Rufus,' Beth said.

'Rufus it is, then!' And he held a crown-piece for her to kiss. 'With a bit of luck, that'll soon be fifteen pounds, and one of these days I'll be breeding horses that's famous throughout the three counties. One of these days! You'll see!'

That afternoon, he was killed by a stallion he had bought in Chepsworth. His body was found on Huntlip common and carried down by the haywarden's men. They said he must have died in an instant, caught unawares, hammering a hobbling iron into the ground. His eyes were wide open and he had one big black wound in the back of his skull.

Beth heard the news while she was at school and ran home at once through a heavy rain-storm. Kate sat in the darkened kitchen, rocking backwards and forwards, arms crossed over her chest, hands clutching her hunched shoulders. She seemed not to notice when Beth came in. She was locked inside herself, like a stranger. But when at last, putting out a hand, she found that Beth's clothes were sodden, she came to life again sharply. She stirred and got up and began to scold.

'You'd better strip! You're like a drowned rat. Why didn't you shelter instead of coming through all that rain!'

Standing naked on the hearth, Beth had a violent fit of shivering. Her flesh would not be still however hard she clenched her muscles. She rubbed herself with a rough towel and scrambled into warm clean clothes. The warmth and comfort made her feel guilty, for she had thought, running home through the storm, that nothing could ever matter again. But her body, it seemed, had a will of its own: she could still feel glad to be at home; to be warm; to be safe; to be alive.

Kate lit the lamp and her face as she stooped to blow on the flame looked suddenly old. The lines that puckered her mouth were deeper. She moved about, drawing the curtains, setting the kettle to boil again, warming the teapot and making tea. But now and then she would stand quite still, staring before her with hurt, angry eyes. And then, coming to, she would say: 'I'm glad he was found before that storm. I'd hate to think of him lying out there, all smothered in mud.'

Later, she said: 'Parson Wisdom was very kind. He took your father into the vicarage.'

'What became of the horse?' Beth asked.

'They catched him and put him in the pound. I suppose he'll be sold . . . if anyone's mad enough to buy him.'

'There's a mare, too, up there somewhere. And saddles and bridles . . . things like that.'

'Yes, well, I must see the haywarden. Maybe he'll fix a sale for us. God knows we shall need the money.'

'Queenie Lovage called in. She asked if your dad's coffin was to be made at Cobbs. I said no. – I'd sooner deal with the man in Chepsworth.'

'That don't seem right,' Beth said. 'Grandfather Tewke makes coffins for all Huntlip. He should surely do the same for his own son?'

'I don't want dealings with *him*,' Kate said. 'Though nobody's stopping him coming to the funeral, of course.'

But grandfather Tewke was not at the funeral, and they heard that work had gone on as usual in the carpenter's shop that day.

'It's what I'd expect,' Kate said. 'An unforgiving man, your grandpa.'

The horses and gear were sold by auction, and the undertaker was paid on the nail. Then accounts were settled with the Chepsworth corn-chandler and the smith at Collow Ford.

'Leaving precious little!' Kate said. 'But we're shut of debts, finally, and I aim to keep it that way.'

'I could go into service,' Beth said.

'There's no need. I'm taking up the gloving again. I've still got my old wooden donkey and I hope I've still got my skill too. I can surely do as well as the other women hereabouts, anyway.'

The gloving materials were brought, and the finished gloves collected, by a man who came every week in the carrier's cart from Chepsworth. His name was Arthur Roberts, but because of his lisp and his smart clothes and the scented handkerchief he held to his nose when entering a cottage kitchen, he was known in Huntlip as Lily-Milly-Bobs. Beth disliked him because, although her mother's work was good, he always found excuses for reducing the payment.

'This quirk's rather clumsy, don't you think, Mrs Tewke?'

'I don't cut the patterns, Mr Roberts.'

'Even the stitching is not what it might be.'

'There was no complaints when I worked in the factory. Mr Ganty called me his best glover.'

'One-and-nine the dozen pairs. That's the best I can offer today, Mrs Tewke.'

'It's not enough!' Beth said, before her mother had time to accept. 'Leave the gloves and we'll take them in to Mr Ganty ourselves.'

The young man looked down his nose.

'Shouldn't you be at school?' he asked.

'I came home early on purpose to see you.'

'Indeed! Little meddlers are ripening early these days. But you'll get no change from Mr Ganty.'

'We'll see about that.'

'One-and-eleven,' he said, wearily. 'A special concession, you being so poor.'

When he had gone, Beth took a duster and fanned the air.

'What sort of man is that, I wonder, going about, smelling of violets?'

'You were very sharp,' Kate said. 'I don't hold with a scrap of a girl speaking up like that. Supposing he'd took a huff against us?'

'How can he?' Beth said. 'When he pockets the coppers he knocks off folk's earnings? All Huntlip knows he does it. You have to stand out like old Mrs Topson.'

Kate worked hard, but poor sight made her slow, and although Beth helped, the weekly earnings were never more than seven shillings. Often, indeed, they were a good deal less.

One day in January, when Beth came home, her mother was lying on the settle, grey-faced and in pain. A neighbour, Mrs Wilkes, was with her, and the kitchen smelt of burnt feathers.

'Your mother's sick,' Mrs Wilkes declared. 'And it's not to be wondered at, seeing she don't eat enough for a sparrow! Yes, you can stare, miss, but I'd be ashamed if I was you. A girl of eleven, going to school when you should be out earning.'

'Annie, be quiet!' Kate said. 'It was only giddiness, that's all.'

'What did you eat for your dinner?' asked Beth.

'I ate what I wanted,' Kate said.

'You ate a cup of tea!' Mrs Wilkes exclaimed. 'I know

18

what dinners you have!' Fiercely, she rounded again on Beth. 'There's two eggs and half a loaf in that cupboard. But it ent to be touched! Oh, no! It's for *your* tea and *your* breakfast.'

'Rubbish!' said Kate, struggling to sit erect on the settle. 'I just ent had time to get to the shop. Besides, it's none of your business, Annie Wilkes, and I'll thank you to keep out of my cupboards.'

'Then I'll be off!' Mrs Wilkes retorted. 'That's what I get for being a good neighbour!'

As the door rattled shut, Beth went to look in the jug on the dresser. She found it empty.

'A man came,' her mother said. 'A stranger to me, but he said your father owed him a debt. Thirty shillings, he said it was.'

'And you gave it to him, without question? A man you'd never seen before?'

'Seemed to me he was speaking the truth. And I don't want debts hanging over me.'

'No, you'd sooner go hungry and make yourself ill.'

Beth brought in sticks and made up the fire. She boiled an egg, cut thin slices of bread and lard, and persuaded her mother to sit up and eat.

'All this fuss!' Kate said. 'Just because of a giddy turn!'

'How d'you feel now?'

'Fit as a flea. Never fitter.'

'Then you won't mind if I go out for a little while?'

'Why, where you off to all of a sudden?'

'I told Hetty Minchin I'd help her with her sums. I shan't be gone long. You take things easy till I come back.'

'Here! It's a sight too early for lighting that lamp.'

'It's a nasty dark evening, that's all I know. And it's cold and damp, so see you keep a good fire.'

'See this! See that!' Kate exlaimed. 'You're getting too bossy by half, my girl.'

'Somebody's got to keep you in order,' Beth said.

With the dusk, a mist had risen from the Derrent brook and was creeping, cold and grey, all along the village. Always in winter the mist came up from the Derrent like this, and the villagers called it the Huntsman's Breath. According to old tales, Huntlip had once been a place of evil, for the Devil's Hunt had ridden there. The hounds had savaged little children, and sparks from the horses' hooves had blinded anyone that stood in the way. According to some, the riders were heard even now on certain nights in winter, leaping the brook at Collow Ford. The smith, it was said, had heard the crack of the Huntsman's whip and the baying of the hounds outside his forge.

Beth wore a coat of her father's, its upturned hem thick and heavy, sweeping her heels at every step. She had to thrust her hands in the pockets to keep the folds wrapped close around her. The collar stood up high at her throat, and when she snuggled down inside it, the warmth of her body rose in comforting waves to her face.

Huntlip was deserted. Her footsteps echoed along the Straight. She passed the Minchins' and kept on, over the bridge and along the other side of the Derrent. At the Middening turn, having left the last light far behind her, she had nothing at all to guide her on the way. Night was fully come, and mist surged against her face, and she felt she walked at the edge of the world, about to fall into everlasting darkness. But she kept on, groping her way along the hedge, and came at last to the gates of her grandfather's workshop yard.

The workshop was lit from end to end, every window casting its shape on the squirming mist. The twin doors stood open, and Beth looked in, the warmth and lamp-smoke stinging her eyes.

Four men worked at a bench beneath the windows, backs bent, ankles deep in shavings. Another two worked on the centre floor, driving home the slats of a sheep-crib. One was Sam Lovage, a born gossip, and as he whispered in his neighbour's ear, grandfather Tewke, who stood with his back to the stove nearby, making notes in a notebook, turned around and saw Beth. He hesitated; then came across.

'Who might you be?' he asked with a frown.

'I reckon you know who I am,' she said.

'Maybe. Maybe not.'

'I want to talk to you,' she said.

'Talk away! I'm all ears.'

'So's the rest of the party here.'

'All right. We'll step outside.'

Outside in the yard, against the mist, he seemed enormous. His shoulders, although rounded because of his trade, were thick and broad and his bearing stiff. In the light from the doorway, his face, under the peak of a tight-fitting cap, had the sharp edges and smooth planes of a statue carved in clean pink wood. His mouth had a strong curve downward. His nose was very straight and fine.

'Well? What d'you want with me, miss?'

'My mother's sick,' Beth said. 'She ent getting enough to eat.'

'Whose fault is that? It surely ent mine! But maybe your mother thinks it is?'

'She didn't send me. She'd sooner starve.'

'Kate's got her pride. I know that. But what about you? D'you know the meaning of that little word?'

'Pride won't feed us,' Beth said.

'You don't look all that hungry to me.'

'My mother's the one that's been going without. I only discovered that today.'

'And you came straight to me?'

'There's nobody else to go to.'

'Ent you heard of the row I had with your father? And how I turned him out of my house? Well, then! – What makes you think I'd be willing to help you?'

'I just thought you would, that's all.'

'You've got definite notions for a girl of your age. You have, that's a fact! Here, hang on a minute. I'll come with you and see your mother.'

He went to the door and called to the men.

'I shan't be here at knocking-off time, so see you turn out the lamps and lock the door, will you? And don't go jumping the clock, neither. – I shall soon know if you've skimped your work!'

He came back, buttoning his jacket to the neck, and set off with Beth. The mist and the darkness seemed nothing to him. She was the one who tripped and stumbled.

'Here, take hold of my hand, before you go tumbling into

the brook,' he said. 'You want to eat carrots. Then you'd be able to see in the dark.'

In the cottage kitchen, Kate was busy stitching gloves, and her eyes, sliding up, blind at first from the close work, sparked into sharp little points of light as she saw the old man standing before her.

'What's all this? I wasn't expecting company that I know of.'

'It'd be more civil if you asked me to sit.'

'Since when have we been civil together?'

'Damnation! It's *your* daughter that's fetched me here, Kate Tewke!'

Kate turned and glared at Beth, who was bringing a chair for the old man to sit.

'My daughter's a sly little toad! She'd no right, sneaking away behind my back.'

'The girl's got sense. She says pride is a poor provider.'

'I'll have something to say, too, when her and me is by ourselves.'

'Listen,' he said, sitting stiff and upright in his chair. 'You ent thriving on a feed of pride, so why pretend you are? A good puff of wind would send you floating up that chimney! Well, I ent prepared to see my son's widow going on the parish, so let's get down to brass tacks.'

'A lot you cared for your son! Cutting him off the way you did!'

'That's ancient history. I'm concerned with here and now. The best thing for you is to come and live at Cobbs. I ent short of a shilling or two. I can provide for you and the girl.'

Kate sat perfectly still, her lips pressed together, her eyes set in a hard stare. Beth moved quietly about the room, taking off her coat and scarf and hanging them on the hook on the door. Then she went and stood at the table, within the circle of yellow light, and the old man glanced from her to Kate.

'Well?' he demanded, making them jump. 'I'm still waiting for some sort of answer!'

'Charity,' Kate said. 'I'm not stuck on charity, whether it comes from you or the parish.'

'If you come to me, you'll earn your keep by running the

house, taking over from Goody Izzard. That ent charity, surely, is it?'

Kate looked at Beth. She was no longer angry. She seemed resigned.

'Ah, you think of the girl!' the old man urged. 'She's the one you've got to consider.'

'All right,' Kate said. 'All right. I'll come.'

'Good! Good! That's settled, then. That's all in the book!' He got up and moved to the door. 'I'll send Izzard down with the cart on Friday. Ten o'clock in the morning, sharp.'

'Here!' Kate said. 'You're rushing me, ent you? I must get sorted out and see Mr Bates about quitting the cottage.'

'Well, you've got three days, and Izzard will help with your bits and pieces. As for Bates, you leave him to me.'

The old man went. Kate sat and stared at the door.

'I suppose it's all for the best,' she said. 'But I dunno! I'm all of a heap!'

'At least you can stop straining your eyes with the gloving,' Beth said. 'Now! This minute! Mrs Topson'll take this lot.'

'Living at Cobbs!' Kate said. 'The ways things change! All in a twinkling! Out of the blue! I dunno what your father'd say, I'm sure.'

'He'd be pleased. You know that.'

'Seems you started something, girl, going behind my back like that.'

'Seems I did,' Beth agreed.

Promptly at ten o'clock on Friday, Walter Izzard knocked on the door. The pony and cart stood outside, the cart covered because of the rain.

'I'm glad of that rain,' Kate said. 'It'll keep the neighbours indoors where they belong, instead of poking about among my belongings.'

'Yes, they're a neighbourly lot in Huntlip,' said Walter. 'I'm always glad I live away out at the Pikehouse.'

He was a thin streak of a man with a narrow face, all nose and cheekbones, and frizzled grey hair cut close to his skull. Beth had seen him often, tramping the lanes with his bag of tools over his shoulder, and she knew his son Jesse, a boy of nine, always in disgrace at school for failing to learn his lessons.

Walter loaded the furniture on to the cart, and, with Kate and Beth sitting up beside him, drove round the green and into the Straight. Some neighbours came out to wave them off, and Kate nodded, sitting sedately, dressed in her best black hat and coat, with the clock, swathed in sacking, on her lap. As they went through the village, the clock chimed, and a few people, hurrying past in the rain, turned to stare.

'That's a nice clock,' Walter said. 'I like a clock with a nice chime. Did you see Peggy Marvel gawping as we went past? She'll be full of tales when she gets home. She'll say she actually heard the time passing!'

They drove past the workshop, turned down a track, and rattled into a cobbled fold at the back of the house. Goody Izzard came out to help them. She humped their belongings up the stairs, showed them their rooms, and helped Beth to set up the beds. Kate was listless, moving about as though in a dream, and Goody had to make the decisions. When they were finished, she herded them down into the kitchen and gave them hot cocoa.

'You must be shravelled, riding that cart in this freezing rain. Come to the stove and steam yourselves dry.'

'We're pushing you out of a job,' Kate said. 'I'm sorry for that, Mrs Izzard. I am truly.'

'It's only right,' Goody said, 'that old Tewke should have his family to live with him.'

'Don't worry about Goody,' Walter said. 'She's never liked traipsing in from the Pikehouse every day. She'd just as soon work in the fields.'

When Walter had gone, Goody took a last look round the kitchen, and put on her coat.

'There's a stew of sheep's corsets on the stove and baked apples in the oven. The old man'll be in at twelve. Oh, yes! Just one thing more. That's the cows.'

'Cows?' Kate said.

'Two of them. Out in the pasture. The old man milks them hisself in the mornings and he leaves it to me in the afternoons. That's your job now so beware of that Cherry. She'll lean on you if she gets the chance.'

'Cows!' Kate said, left alone with Beth. 'I never milked a cow in all my life!'

'I have,' Beth said. 'Oftentimes, at Henry Mapp's. I'll manage all right.'

At twelve o'clock, grandfather Tewke came in for his dinner. He went straight to his chair at the table, still with his cap on his head, and sat waiting for Kate to serve him. While he ate, he kept eyeing the helping on her plate.

'You should eat more'n that. You need to put some flesh on your bones.'

'I've lost my appetite,' Kate said. 'It's all this upheaval. I'm upside down.'

'You'll buck up in time, I suppose. You better had, 'cos I don't hold with pecking at food.' He looked across the table at Beth. 'You're playing hookey from school, I see. I don't hold with that neither.'

'I'm not going to school in future. I'm staying at home to help my mother. There's too much work for her in this big house.'

'Dammit! Goody Izzard always managed!'

'My mother's not as strong as Goody Izzard.'

'You stop at school and. be a proper scholard. I've got ideas about you. I want you to help me in the business, keeping the books and things like that.'

'I'm scholard enough,' Beth said. 'I'm top standard in reading, writing, and reckoning.'

The old man glared.

'Top standard, eh? Well, we'll see what sort of scholard you are!'

At the end of the meal, he got up and went to the dresser. He brought paper, pen, and ink to the table, and set them out in front of Beth. He returned to his chair and opened a newspaper.

'Now, then!' he said. 'You write what I read and we'll see what janders you make of it. Are you ready? Right so! "Mr Thomas Lissimore, Esquire, of Clay Hall Farm, near Kitchinghampton, noted for his foresight in matters pertaining to the weather, the yield of crops, etc., having made certain predictions for this, the year 1886, has asked us to publish the said predictions in the hope that they may prove useful to fellow farmers throughout the western midland region." '

'Is that all?' Beth asked.

'All and enough,' the old man said.

He took the paper and blew on the ink. Beth waited, biting her pen. But when he had finished, he seemed pleased enough.

'You've made a pickle of some of the words, – there's no x in predictions for a start – but you write a clear hand, that's the main thing, and you don't skitter blots all over the place. So now let's see what your reckoning is like.'

He leant back in his chair.

'I buy a chisel at tenpence, a hammer at one-and-six, a saw at a florin, a gimlet at fourpence, and eight pounds of brads at twopence a pound. How much change shall I get from a crown?'

'Nothing,' Beth said. 'You owe a shilling.'

'I build a shed for Arthur Kyte, costing me eighteen pounds in labour and materials. I aim to make a profit of fifteen per cent but Arthur pays cash so I give a discount of one and a quarter. How much do I charge in all?'

'I'll need pen and paper to do that.'

'That's all right,' the old man said. 'I needed pen and paper myself when Kyte called and paid this morning.'

Beth wrote for a few minutes, then looked up.

'Twenty pounds, eight shillings, and tenpence.'

'Who got the best of that split farthing?'

'You did. It seemed only fair, seeing you was giving the discount.'

'Are you being pert, miss?'

'I'm waiting to see if there's any more problems.'

'Just one and that's the lot! Which is the heaviest – a pound of feathers or a pound of flour?'

'You don't catch me with that old trick,' Beth said. 'A pound's a pound whatever its compound.'

The old man rose and pushed his chair in under the table.

'You're as cocky as a dog's hind leg,' he said. 'You're certainly top standard in sauce.'

'Then I can stop school?'

'Suits me,' he said, with a shrug. 'But mark this! I'm the

master in this house and I'm the one to make the decisions. Is that clear?'

'Clear as glass,' Beth said.

'You should've been a boy,' he said. 'It vexes me to have nobody following in the business. Still! It can't be helped now. And I've got plans about that too!'

CHAPTER TWO

Kate, at first dismayed by the big house, was soon enjoying the importance it gave her. She dealt with tradesmen at the door now, instead of shopping in the village. She took pride in her cooking and made great batches of puddings and pies. And she kept Beth busy all the time, scrubbing the floors in kitchen and dairy, cleaning the rugs in the hall and parlour, burning lavender to sweeten the air in the disused rooms; dusting, polishing; hunting for moths and mice and ants.

Later, she took to inviting old friends from the green, giving them afternoon tea in the parlour, with the best Worcester china, the silver spoons, the pearl-handled knives, and the dainty napkins edged with lace.

'Your grannie Tewke must've been a lady, judging by some of the things in this house. It'd be a pity not to use them. It gives pleasure, you know, to simple people like Annie Wilkes and Mrs Topson.'

'And simple people like us,' Beth said, slyly.

Beth had a bedroom at the back of the house, looking down on the buildings surrounding the fold, and out over the fields beyond. She woke every morning at half past five, when her grandfather clomped across the cobbles, on his way to milk the cows. The rattle of pails, the lowing of the cows, the answering whicker of the pony in his stall: these sounds were the start of her day; and, winter or summer, she sprang from bed in a single bound.

Every morning, while washing, she looked out of her window and guessed the weather. Dew on the cowshed roof meant sunshine. Martins flying in low from the fields meant change. Excitement among the pigs at Anster, the farm adjoining Cobbs, meant wind on the way. And a clear view of Houndshill meant a soak of rain.

But whatever the weather, the weathercock on the workshop roof was always pointing northward. The workshop had once been stables and had a clock in a little turret on the roof. Every morning, going downstairs, Beth looked out of the landing window to check the time: the clock was in order, but the weathercock was stuck fast, and she often wished she could reach out and set it spinning true to the wind.

Every morning, she and Kate were in the kitchen, with the stove alight and bacon frying in the pan, when grandfather Tewke came in to breakfast. His temper was always bad in the morning, and if they dared to speak together, he silenced them with a sour look. Just before seven he went to the workshop and soon afterwards, when the men arrived, the hammering and sawing would begin, filling the whole house with noise.

For Beth, the workshop yard had a deep fascination now that it was part of her life. The butts of oak and elm and ash waiting to go to the sawpit, and the planks and beams stacked up to season, all chalked with their dates, gave her a sense of provision and richness. And she shared the carpenters' pride in their work; their satisfaction when a new gate or door or ladder went to stand in the store-place.

Often, when Beth went to gather the chips and shavings for use as kindling in the house, she stayed in the yard to watch the men. Her grandfather disapproved at first: if he found her there, he would drive her out.

'But I want to know what's going on,' she said. 'I want to understand what I write in your ledger.'

'There's sense in that, I suppose,' he said. 'Yes! Yes! There's sense in that.'

By the end of her first year at Cobbs, he had ceased to grumble. Within two years, he was leaving her to cast up accounts without his supervision. He never praised her but little by little he gave her freedom to come and go as she pleased.

One of her duties was to collect the notes of work done away from the workshop, but some of the men were unable to write and had to give her the details directly, and this caused some resentment at first, because she was only a half-pint girl. After a while, however, they came to accept her, though a kind of sly warfare continued for years. They liked to tease her and were always trying to catch her out.

'Three days at Norton mill,' said Steve Hewish. 'Forty feet of elm planking. Five pounds of tenpenny nails. That was repairs to the granstead luccomb.'

'Luccomb?' said Beth. 'How d'you spell it?'

'That's your problem. Not mine. We're only the wooden knows.'

'Poor old numskulls, that's what we are,' said Timothy Rolls. 'We ent much use except to labour.'

'The hardest work you do is with your tongues,' Beth said.

'Here, Beth,' said Sam Lovage. 'You must get young Kit to show the misericord he's making for the church. That'll make you open your eyes! He's carved old Adam and Eve and the apple, all as naked as can be.'

'So what? – I've seen a naked apple before!' said Beth. 'And I certainly ent running round after Kit Maddox, telling him what a clever boy he is. I've got better things to do with my time.'

'Lumme!' said Sam. 'D'you hear that, Kit?'

'Ah, I heard,' said Kit, working.

Kit was the youngest carpenter in the workshop. He was at this time about eighteen. His father had been killed by a fall of rock in the quarry at Springs. His mother had thrown herself under a train. Kit had been raised in an institution, but now lived with his widowed grannie at Collow Ford. He was dark-haired and dark-skinned, with the sharp good looks of a gipsy. He liked to be different from everyone else, and he always dressed in a showy way. Even at work he wore a crimson velvet waistcoat.

At times he was merry, playing tricks on the older men, and telling them stories picked up at the barracks in Capelton Wick. At other times he would be silent, absorbed in his work, and in this mood, if anyone teased him, he would turn on them with savage contempt, dark eyes alight with temper, fists ready to hit out. His work was good, which made him a favourite with grandfather Tewke.

'Kit's a tip-top craftsman,' the old man was always saying. 'He'll go far, so long as he keeps his mind on his work.'

'He's wild,' Kate said, 'and a sore trial to his poor old grannie.'

'Who says so?'

'All Huntlip says the same. – Too free with the girls and too free with the little brown jug.'

'Tittle-tattle!' the old man said. 'I'm deaf to that.'

Between Kit and Beth there was constant conflict, and her battles with him were different from those she had with the older men: the conflict was sharper, more tinged with spite.

Once, when she went to the yard as usual to collect the chips and shavings, she found them burning in a heap, and Kit standing by with a rake, watching.

'What d'you think you're doing?' she demanded.

'I'm tidying up. Making everything smart and dandy.' He leant on his rake-shaft, smiling at her, enjoying her rage. 'I reckon I could get work as a charcoal burner if I was ever at a loose end, don't you?'

'You've got work already. You should stick to that and not waste time annoying me.'

'You should stick indoors, then, instead of poking about out here.'

'The chips is mine. Just leave them alone in future!'

'You should get out of ribbons before you start giving me orders!'

Grandfather Tewke came out of the workshop to see what all the noise was about.

'Who lit that fire? You, Maddox? You ought to know better'n that. – The chips've always gone to the kitchen.'

Kit went red in the face. Then he laughed. He pushed the rake into Beth's hands and walked away.

'Seems you like provoking that boy,' the old man said. 'You're like all the girls! – Can't keep away from a handsome chap.'

'Handsome!' Beth said. 'I'd sooner look at Timothy Rolls!'

But grandfather Tewke would not believe her, and made a great show of searching the sky.

'I fancy I heard a cuckoo!' he said.

Whenever the old man was driving out on business, Beth would hang about the fold on the chance of an outing. She polished the trap. She beat the cushions. She fetched the harness and backed the pony between the shafts. But the old man, though he must have known what she wanted, would never invite her. And so, since she could be obstinate, too, she dressed herself up one afternoon and arrived as he was mounting the trap.

'Where are you off to, then, so smart?' he asked.

'I'm going with you,' Beth replied.

'Hah! Is that so! Very well, you can nip and fetch young Maddox as well. Say I'm looking at a stand of timber on Lodberrow farm.'

'Why take him? He'll only spoil things.'

'You nip along and do as I say!'

Beth went to Kit, who was splitting stakes in the yard.

'Suits me,' he said. 'I'd sooner be out larking than splitting these damned stakes.'

It was mid June, and a hot day. They drove down rough lanes, raising a dust that whitened their clothes, the trap, the pony, and the hedgebanks on either side. The pony, Jakes, would not be hurried that day, but jogged along steadily, blowing through his nose because of the heat and the flies and the dust.

On every farm, the hay had been cut early, and its scent was with them all the way. In some fields, men were already carting. In others, men and women were turning the swaths. The hay looked yellow, spread on the aftermath of live green grass. The women's pinafores were patches of dazzling whiteness, and the kerchiefs on their heads were blobs of red or blue.

Beth sat back, looking from left to right all the time. She liked to see what went on in the fields. Kit, beside her, was peeling the bark from a twig of hazel. Today his mood happened to be friendly and he wanted to talk: he dropped bits of twig into her lap to attract her attention; he hummed a tune; he sneezed loudly.

'Bless me!' he said. 'It's all this dust. I'm like a miller, except that I'm honest.'

Beth was silent, removing the bits of twig from her lap and throwing them out into the road.

'Nice bit of sun, ent it?' he said.

Beth still refused to be drawn, and after another little silence, her grandfather spoke over his shoulder.

'You seem to be talking to yourself, boy. If Beth fell off in the road back there, you should've told me.'

'No such luck!' Kit answered. 'She's here all right. But the cat's got her tongue.'

'You're making her shy, then, for her tongue is busy enough at home.'

When they drove into the farmyard at Lodberrow, the farmer, a red-faced man named Charley Blinker, came from the stackyard to meet them and led them to a hillock on high ground. They crossed a stretch of pasture and skirted great sloping fields full of corn. In the pasture, the cattle moved as though enchanted, or stood in the brook in the shade of the willows. In the cornfields, the corn stood motionless in the heat. The ears of wheat stood erect, out of the fountains of grey-green blades, and the barley bowed its awns to the sun. Beth pulled a fern from the hedge to wave away the flies that buzzed round her head. With her other hand, she kept her skirts from sweeping the corn.

The neat round hillock was crowned with oaks, the trees growing wide apart, spreading their boughs and making a green twilight below. Blinker led the way to the foot of the mound, and they all stood in the outer shade.

'There's your timber, Mr Tewke. You can make me a bid.'

'You never said it growed on a hill,' the old man said. He went to a tree and kicked it with the toe of his boot. He opened his knife and stabbed the bark. 'They're sound enough if this is a sample, but hill-grown timber ent all that useful. It's too twisty. Still, I'll pay fifty pounds for this little lot.'

'Get away!' Blinker said. 'You'll make that on the bark alone.'

'That's my bid, – take it or leave it,' the old man said.

'All right. When d'you pay?'

'When I fell the trees. Next winter or next spring.'

Going back, Charley Blinker walked with Beth, while Kit and her grandfather went ahead.

'I remember your father. The best man with horses I ever knew. I liked him a lot.'

'I liked him myself,' Beth said.

'You wouldn't happen to have his touch?'

'What, with horses? Good gracious, no!'

'I wondered, that's all. Your dad had a sort of magic about him. I thought it might've got handed down.'

'He always said it was just common sense.'

'Whatever it was, I wish I had it,' Blinker said. 'I've got a mare that's slinked two foals and I'm blessed if I can fathom why 'cos she's healthy as beans.'

'That's nothing,' Beth said. 'Mares is often awkward that way.'

'But she gave me a foal the first time, easy as falling off a log. Here, come and see her, just on the chance. You never know! She'll be coming in season again directly and you might work a charm.'

Beth smiled.

'All right. No harm in looking.'

In the farmyard, Kit and the old man sat on a bench, and Emily Blinker brought them beer. Blinker took Beth through to the stackyard, where a load of hay was being transferred to the stack. The hay was low down in the waggon, and the carter was sweating, pitching high to the man on the stack. Both men stared as Beth approached the mare in the shafts. Then they went on working again. But the carter kept a watchful eye.

The mare was as black and as sleek as treacle, gleaming sweatily in the sun. She was big but docile, standing at ease between the shafts, one rear hoof tilted on edge on the ground, one great haunch relaxed sideways.

Beth offered a knob of cowcake, and the velvety lips tickled her palm. She moved to the mare's side and ran her hand down the hot, moist flank. The sweat dripped from her fingers, and she put her hand to her nose and sniffed.

The carter stopped pitching and came to the off side of the waggon.

'What d'you think you're doing?'

'I was admiring your mare's shiny coat.'

'Oh, ah!' the man said.

'She's nice and quiet, too, ent she?'

'Hah! She wasn't always. She was nervy as a bird when I first had her. But I soon cured that!'

'Why, what d'you give her?' Beth said.

'Give her! I never said I gave her nothing.'

'But you *do* give her something,' Beth said. 'I can smell it in her sweat.'

'I dunno what you mean,' the man said, and half turned away.

'I've heard mistletoe's good for nerviness,' Beth said. 'I remember my father telling me that. But he said he never used it hisself 'cos that'd make a mare abort.'

'What!' said Blinker. 'God almighty, I'll have his guts!' He went to the waggon and shook his fist at the carter. 'Great flaming fool! Risking my mare with muck in her feed! Wasting two lots of stud fees! I've half a mind to heave you in the horse-pond!'

The carter was sullen. The man on the stack stood gaping down. And the mare looked round, her ears twitching as Blinker bawled at the top of his voice.

'I've got to go,' Beth said. 'My grandpa's waiting.'

'Hang on!' said Blinker, following her. 'I owe you something for helping me. What'll it be? – A flask of cider? A few eggs?'

'You owe me nothing,' Beth said.

'You got hens of your own at Cobbs? No? Then I'll give you some pullets to start you off.'

He lumbered about the stackyard, chasing the pullets into the barn. He caught two and thrust them, flapping and squawking, into a basket with a lid. He caught a third and then a fourth.

'There! How's that? They've been with the cock so let them go broody and you're all set up!'

In the farmyard, grandfather Tewke was sitting alone, his beer-mug on the bench beside him.

'Chickens?' he said. 'Who said you could keep chickens?'

'Why shouldn't I?' Beth said. 'We've got the ground.'

'All right. If you do the work.'

'Where's Emily?' Blinker asked.

'Gone off with Kit,' the old man said.

'What? I ent having that! I've heard a few things about your young mitcher. Which way did they go?'

'Search me! I ent their keeper.'

'Hell's bells! This is my day!' Blinker said. 'I'll smash that boy if he's trying it on with my daughter. I'm just in the mood!' And he lumbered off.

Grandfather Tewke sat at ease, looking at Beth in a thoughtful way, as though he were guessing the weight of a pig.

'Kit seemed struck with Emily Blinker. You'll have to get a move on, growing up, if you want to catch him your own self.'

'I'd sooner catch cold,' Beth said.

'How old are you now? Nearly fourteen? Ah, well, you're coming on in your own way. You've got a bit of a shape now, and you ent too bad to look at, neither.'

'Thank you, I'm sure.'

'The trouble is, that tongue of yours. The chaps don't like the taste of sorrel.'

'They must look elsewhere, then,' Beth said.

Kit came sauntering into the yard, his hands in his pockets, his velveteen cap on the back of his head. Emily Blinker came behind him, looking tearful and flushed, and at that same moment, her father returned from the other direction.

'What d'you mean by running around with my daughter? Eh? She's a lot too young to be pestered by you, so just keep away or I'll tan your backside for you, big as you are!'

Kit said nothing, but looked away, bored and superior.

'Well?' Blinker shouted. 'D'you hear what I said?'

'No,' Kit said. 'I heard nothing.'

Blinker turned to his daughter and took her arm.

'Did he lay hands on you? Eh? Did he? Answer me, girl, or I'll shake you apart!'

The girl looked up with frightened eyes.

'No,' she whispered. 'We went to see the kittens, that's all.'

'Very well! I'll believe you! Now get back to your mother in the dairy.'

Blinker subsided, mopping his brow; Emily hurried into the house; and grandfather Tewke stood up to go.

'If the entertainments is come to an end, we'll get along home! Mr Blinker, I'll bid you good day. Kit, give Beth a hand with this basket of poultry.'

Now, as they drove along the lanes, the sun was aslant in the open sky, and the workers in the fields had long shadows. Now, in the pastures, the cows were moving with more purpose, eager for relief at the hands of the milkers, who were calling them home.

Kit sat wedged in his corner, resting an arm on the side of the trap. He was looking at Beth in a way she hated, with a dark bright stare like that of a lizard watching a fly. Suddenly, he thrust a hand before her face, showing a deep scratch on his knuckles.

'That's what I got, looking at kittens. One little cat had sharp claws.'

'Good,' Beth said. 'Emily Blinker's got some sense.'

His hand dropped like a stone to her lap, and he squeezed her thigh with vicious fingers. Her foot shot out, kicking the basket containing the pullets, and it skidded across the floor of the trap, the pullets squawking and fluttering inside.

'Keep your hands off me,' she said, through clenched teeth, 'or you'll get worse than a little scratch!'

From grandfather Tewke came a loud snort of laughter.

'If I was you, boy, I'd wait till the girl's grown up full size. She'll have more nous than to grouse then!'

In the morning, she asked if one of the men could make her a hen-hut, and her grandfather promised to send Walter Izzard.

'The one man I can spare and not know the difference!'

Walter came and worked in the orchard. He built a hut from old bits of timber, up off the ground on stone blocks, with a ramp at the door. Beth soon perceived the truth of her grandfather's sneer. Walter was clumsy. He handled his tools in a haphazard way and ruined a great many nails and staples. But he had a peaceful, easy-going temper, and Beth liked him.

'I reckon you're laughing at me,' he said. 'I reckon you

knowed I was splitting that fillet. You saw it coming a mile off!'

'I thought you wanted to split it,' she said.

'Glory, no! I'm club-handed and that's all-about-it. Just look at that hut! Did you ever see such a tarnal botch-up?'

'It looks all right to me.'

'Why, that rocks like a see-saw. I shall have to put a wedge in somewhere. Now where's my pencil disappeared to?'

'Behind your ear,' Beth said.

When he had finished and was packing his tools, a cloud of bees flew into the orchard and began to look for a place to swarm.

'Lumme!' he said. 'A swarm in June is worth a silver spoon. – That's what Goody always says.'

'There's some old skeps in the barn somewhere.'

'Ah. Your grannie kept bees at one time of day. You run and fetch a skep, then, and I'll see about settling the swarm.'

Beth ran to the barn and fetched a skep. When she returned, the bees had swarmed in the crutch of a plum tree, and Walter, below, was beating the blade of his saw with a hammer.

'They're settling,' he said. 'Laws, I never saw anything like it! Now you take these and keep up a good ran-tan while I get a ladder.'

She took the saw and hammer and kept up the noise, while more bees, coming into the orchard, zoomed past her to join the swarm. Walter brought a ladder and set it up against the tree. He climbed up, with his cap in his hand, and eased it gently under the bees.

'Come on, little beggars. Gently does it, that's the style. They like the music you're making down there. They're humming to it, can you hear?'

The clamour had brought the men from the workshop. They stood at the orchard fence and watched, and one or two offered mocking advice.

Walter came down with the swarm in his cap, but some of the bees were flying about, buzzing wildly, and many crawled on his arms, face, and neck. Beth dropped the tools and took up the skep. She held it at arm's length while

Walter lowered the swarm inside. He shook his cap and pushed at the bees with his free hand.

'Mind! You'll get stung!' Beth said.

'What, with my tough hide?'

He picked the bees from his face and hair as though they were nothing but butter-burrs, and when they clung to his fingers with sticky feet, he flicked them off, gently, into the skep.

'The queen's in, so the odds and bobs'll soon follow.' He took the skep and turned it over on to the box he had used as a workbench. 'They'll soon cool down when we find them a nice little place in the shade.'

Kit Maddox called from the fence:

'Are you stung yet, Walter?'

'No, not me! Not that I know of, anyway.'

'No sense, no feeling, – that's what they say.'

'They say so best who say so knowing,' Walter retorted.

He carried the beeskep on its box and set it down by the orchard hedge, where the damson trees hung over and gave it shade. He turned the skep till the bees' doorway faced south.

'Not east,' he said, 'or they'll get up too early and catch a cold in the morning dews. Just southward, that's best.'

'How do I take the honey?' Beth asked.

'Glory be, you're in a hurry, ent you?'

'No. I just don't know about bees at all.'

'Well remind me in the back-end of the year and we'll see what's what then, shall us?' He leant down and put his ear close to the skep. 'They're all right. They're right as ninepence. It's nice to have bees about the place. And Goody always swears they're lucky.'

Always, after that day in the orchard, Walter and Beth were close friends. Whenever she wanted anything done, however trivial, Walter would always do it for her. He cut her a prop for the clothes-line. He made little feeding-troughs for the hens. He helped with the bees. And he made her a ladder, small and lightweight, for her to use when picking the fruit in the orchard.

Often, when Walter was with her, grandfather Tewke would work himself into a rage.

'Izzard! Come here! You're wanted in the workshop.'

'All right, gaffer,' Walter would say.

'Running round after that blasted girl! Who's paymaster here, I'd like to know?'

'Why, you are, gaffer. You surely know that.'

'Then look slippy, you glib streak, or I'll turn you off.'

'You'd better go,' Beth would say to Walter. 'Don't get into trouble on my account.'

'Don't worry. Your grandpa's been threatening to turn me off for twenty-odd years and it ent happened yet. Now, then! See if you can carry that ladder without a sweat. All right, is it? Nice and easy to lug about? Good! You'll be round them fruit trees in no time at all.'

The orchard at Cobbs had never done well, and grandfather Tewke was always threatening to fell the trees. 'Same old story, year after year! Plenty of blossom! Plenty of show! And no more fruit than'd fill an old wife's apron!' And it was true. Beth had seen it during her first three summers at Cobbs. But the year 1889 brought a great change, for the bees had been at work on the blossom, and the fruit had set, both the plums and the apples.

In August that year, Beth worked hard to pick all the plums in due time, and Kate worked, too, bottling and jamming. In October, Beth was busy again, picking apples day after day. Her grandfather knew she was working at it from dawn to dusk, but he never sent help, and she was too obstinate to ask him. Walter was working away at Norton. Kate was too nervous to climb a ladder. So all the picking fell to Beth.

When picked, the apples filled every shelf in the hayloft, and Beth was proud, taking the credit because of her bees. There were three stalls in the orchard now, for she herself had taken two casts. She no longer feared them, for, having been stung once or twice, she knew it was not such a terrible thing after all. She liked to see them coming and going about the garden, working away, hum and suck, in the scarlet runners under the wall. She would stand and watch them squeezing in and out of the flowers.

When Walter helped her to take the honey, she would not allow the bees to be killed. She preferred to save them, setting a new skep against an old one, tap-tap-tapping, quietly, patiently, with her fingers, until all the bees had moved from the old skep into the new. And she made sure they had enough honey to last them through the winter months. 'They do the work. It's only right they should be cherished.' Her own harvest was rich enough even then. The crushed combs hung in a muslin bag in the kitchen, and the honey ran, pale and clear as golden sunlight, into the big earthenware bowl.

That winter, Walter was ill, and because he was often away working in distant places, a month went by before she knew. Then, as soon as Timothy Rolls had told her, on a wet day near Christmas, she put some things into a basket, and borrowed her mother's waterproof cape. On her way out, she met her grandfather crossing the fold.

'Why didn't you tell me Walter was ill?'

'What've you got there? You taking my food to give to Izzard?'

'The eggs and honey are mine,' Beth said. 'And as for the jam – I picked the fruit so I reckon that's half mine as well.'

'Is that so! And whose grain feeds the hens?'

'Yours. But you get free eggs every day.'

'And whose damned trees gave the fruit?'

'They only gave it because of my bees.'

'Hah! I wonder how I got on before you came! I wonder how I struggled along!' He looked at her with a sudden sly gleam. 'I'm going to Upham to fetch a load of deal. You can come along for the ride if you like.'

'No,' she said, 'I must see Walter.'

'It's three miles out to the Pikehouse. And a mucky day for walking.'

'I shan't melt for a drop of rain.'

'Suit yourself. Though why you should trouble about Walter Izzard is a mystery to me.'

'But he's one of your men,' Beth said.

'Not any more. He's licked for good.'

'What d'you mean?'

'Just that. He's coughing his guts out. He's making his will!

A pity, I know, but I can't pretend he's much loss to me. A ham-handed hedge-carpenter, that's all he was, fit only for work on the farms.'

'You made good use of him all the same,' Beth said angrily, 'squeezing extra hours out of him every week without a penny extra on his wages.'

'Dammit, you're too fond of chipping me!' the old man said, showing her a threatening fist. 'Your tongue is too sharp, as I've told you before.'

'I keep it sharp for speaking the truth,' Beth said.

It was open country out past Norton fork, and the Pikehouse stood at the edge of the old pike road, its garden cut neat and square from a sweep of wasteland known as the Chacks. Eastward, the road ran with the woods of Scoate House Manor. Westward, the wasteland rose gradually, and Eastery church looked down from the ridge. 'The church mice are our nearest neighbours,' Walter had said. 'Them and the folk in the churchyard, sleeping.' The Pikehouse, built of brick and whitewashed with lime, was a tiny place with a thatched roof. 'A queer shape,' Walter had said, 'like a little oblong with two of its corners sliced off.'

He was sitting up in a narrow bed in the downstairs room when Beth went in. His face looked bonier than ever, and his skin was grey. His breathing came in jagged gasps, and when he coughed, his chest emitted a dreadful noise, like bellows blowing under water.

'Fancy you coming through all this rain!'

'I'll soon dry off by this nice fire.'

'The kettle's on. You can make some tea. The pot's in the hearth and the caddy's up on the mantelpiece. Make it good and strong. There's plenty more in the cupboard there.'

But Beth, who knew the price of tea and what it meant in a household such as Walter's, merely put in a single spoonful.

'I brought a few things,' she said. 'Eggs and such.'

'We've got hens of our own,' he said, 'though they ent exactly shifting themselves to lay at the moment, it's true. Honey!'

'How's Goody?' Beth asked.

41

'Right as ninepence,' Walter said. 'She's working at Checketts full time now. And so is Jesse.'

'What's Jesse doing?'

'Chopping roots at a few pence a day. But we're all right. Goody's a Trojan. And the house is our own, that's something.'

'I shouldn't let you talk,' Beth said. 'It's making you tired.'

'It cheers me up, having someone to talk to. I was always one for a good yarn.'

He told her how he came to own the Pikehouse.

'My dad was pike-keeper here till the tolls was lifted twelve years ago. Then it looked as if we should be homeless. But he went to Scoate and asked if we could stay on and pay rent. Well, old Mr Lannam had shares in the new road going round by Hallows, and it seems he wanted it finished double quick, so he said we could have the Pikehouse for our own if we put in some time breaking stones at Brinting. Me and my dad had jobs to go to. — We could only manage a few hours each day. But Goody and my old mother! — They was at it sunrise to sunset! They used to take food in a big basket, and when me and dad went down in the evening, we had a proper picnic together, all among the heaps of stones.'

'And the Pikehouse was yours after that?'

'Deeds of possession, signed and sealed! And I'm glad Goody's got the place to call her own when I'm dead. She's worked hard enough all her life.'

'Don't talk of dying,' Beth said. 'You'll be better when the spring comes round.'

'I shan't get better. I know that. Goody had the doctor to look at me. But it's no use. I'm all rotten inside.'

'Wait until you see a bit of sunshine. You'll feel a lot different then.'

'I might,' he said, just to please her. 'I'll send up a prayer and see what happens.'

He began to cough, holding a towel against his mouth. He doubled over, hunching his shoulders and folding his arms across his chest, as if only force could keep his lungs from bursting. Watching him, Beth felt the strain and pain in her own body, and when he coughed, she smelt corruption on his breath.

'What can I do?' she asked, frightened. 'Shall I give you some medicine out of that bottle?'

'Don't mind me,' he said hoarsely. 'I'm used to these bouts. I've got them beat as you might say.' He lay back, exhausted, against the pillows. There were dark smudges of blood on his mouth, and his eyes had a haunting brightness. 'You ought to go,' he said. 'It ent good to be shut up with me too long. But there's one favour I'd like to ask.'

'Ask away,' Beth said.

'I'd like Jesse to go in the workshop. Maybe you'd put in a word with the gaffer.'

'Yes, of course,' Beth said.

But that evening, when she spoke to her grandfather about it, he laughed her to scorn.

'I've just got rid of one Izzard. – I surely ent going to saddle myself with another! That boy Jesse's as slow as snails.'

'He could do odd jobs about the workshop.'

'The answer's no. And that's all-about-it!'

Walter, when Beth went to see him again, tried to hide his disappointment.

'Oh, well! Never mind. It was just my foolishness, that's all, wanting Jesse to take my place.'

Beth went every week to the Pikehouse, taking little custards and jellies and cakes. She took her grandfather's old newspapers and read to Walter for a couple of hours at a time. As the weather improved, he grew stronger. He sat in a chair at the open window, watching the larks rising from their nests in the nearby wasteland, and the spring changes coming over the distant fields.

One day at Cobbs, when a cow was calving, grandfather Tewke came into the kitchen and ordered Beth out to the cowshed. The cow, Minnie, was a young one, and this, her first calf, was giving trouble. She stood in the shed, her legs splayed out, her body contorted, screaming and bellowing all the time. The calf had begun to come, awkwardly, head in advance, and was now stuck in the neck of the womb.

'See what you can do to help her,' the old man said, 'I've

43

tried, but I'm too big, and we'll lose her if we don't get a move on. You're small. You should be able to manage all right.'

Beth stood still, her hands in her pinafore pockets, and stared at the cow.

'I'll help on one condition. – That you give Jesse Izzard a job in the workshop.'

'God in heaven! You dare to make bargains with me?'

For a moment, it looked as though the old man would strike her, but when he made a threatening move, her stillness checked him, and his hand fell against his side.

'You damned wicked bitch!' he said, baffled. 'You'd let that beast suffer just for some crotchet like this. You'd let her holler! You'd let her die!'

'It's you that's letting her suffer, wasting time while you swear.'

'Swear! I'd swear right enough if I knowed enough words. Here, where d'you think you're going to, eh?'

'It's no use my stopping if we can't come to terms.'

'Hell's bells? Ent you ashamed? Just hark at that cow! Don't that mean nothing to you, hearing her holler like that?'

'I reckon it means she's near her end. If I'm to help her, you'd better say the word pretty quick.'

'All right! All right!' the old man said. 'I ent stone like you, young miss. I've got some feeling for poor dumb beasts. Now get a move on and give her a hand.'

Beth pushed up her sleeves and went to the cow. She eased her hand, her wrist, then her forearm, into the folds of hot throbbing flesh that pressed on the calf. Her fingers, exploring its shape and posture, groped and found a slippery hold, and little by little, while bearing down on her other hand, she turned the calf within the womb. The cow gave a heave, screaming hoarsely, and went rigid, arching her spine. Beth spoke in a quiet voice.

'Come on, Minnie, there's a good girl. One more try and it's all over. That's the idea. There's a daisy. One more push and it's all done.'

The cow had a spasm, contracting her sides, and the calf was suddenly squeezed from the womb. Beth received it, a hot moist weight, and drew it away. She let it down on to the litter and rubbed it hard with a wisp of straw.

Her wrists burnt with a melting weakness. Her face and body were prickly with sweat. Her clothes clung under her armpits. She went to the doorway, and the cold fresh wind blew into her lungs.

'Are you feeling twiddly?' her grandfather asked.

'I'm all right now. It's passed off.'

The cow was moving, tottering about on shaky legs, leaning one shoulder against the wall while she twisted herself round to lick the calf and nibble the cord.

'Seems you've got a nice new heifer.'

'Seems I have,' her grandfather said.

'All due to me, so remember your promise.'

'What's to stop me taking it back?'

'You're supposed to be a man of your word.'

'All right. Get back to the house and clean yourself up. And when you see Izzard, tell him to send his half-baked son on Monday morning, seven sharp.'

She went to the Pikehouse the following day, in a changeable wind that bloated her skirts with one gust and wrapped them close round her legs with another.

'A loopy old day,' Walter said, as they sat looking out of the Pikehouse window. 'March has got all tangled up with April. But glory, there's naught like good news for putting a shine on the day, is there? How'd you do it, I wonder? Did it rain upside down? Or was there a ring round the moon on Sunday?'

'Seems my grandfather changed his mind.'

'Jesse'll be all of a heap when he knows. He's out there scaring birds in the Uptops and he comes to the hedge sometimes to wave. Supposing you nip out and tell him?'

'Why not wait until he gets home?'

'Ah, go on. It won't take long, nipping down there.'

'All right, if that's what you want.'

'Tell him he'll have my bag of tools. And my watch with the strap on it. Tell him—'

'No,' Beth said. 'I'll leave a few little items for you to tell him.'

She went out again, onwards along the old pike road, and into the lane that led to Checketts. There, a little way along, she stopped at a gate and looked into a big brown field that sloped down from the edge of the wasteland. It was newly sown; the birds were there in great numbers; and the boy Jesse ran to and fro from headland to headland, whirling a pair of wooden clappers. Sparrows and starlings flew up and were tossed about like leaves on the wind. Rooks and jack-daws flew up and cruised in circles, dipping their wings.

When Beth called out, Jesse stopped in his tracks, looking around as though puzzled. His face was a fiery red, whipped by the wind, and his fair hair stood up in spikes from the crown of his head. He looked across to the field running up from the far side of the ditch, where a man was ploughing, followed by gulls. He cocked his head, listening intently. Beth called again, and this time he came, plodding across the field towards her.

'Laws, it's you!' he said, relieved, and his chapped lips cracked in an awkward grin.

'The way you gawped, you seemed to think it was some old seagull calling your name.'

'I was flummoxed, that's all.'

'You was always easy to flummox. You used to get tied in knots at school.'

'Don't remind me of school! I'm finished with that, I'm thankful to say.'

'And what've you got to show for it? Did you reach standard four?'

'No, nor never would if I stopped till domesday.'

'Can you read and write?'

'I ent bad at reading. I read all the papers you bring my dad. The almanacs, too. – I like them a lot. Ah, and I like them custards you keep bringing, too.'

'They're meant for your dad, not you.'

'He shares them with me all the same.'

'I reckon you're greedy,' Beth said.

'I reckon I am,' Jesse agreed. 'I'm generally nearly always hungry. Goody says I must have a hole in my belly.'

'Why d'you call her Goody? She's your mother. You should be more respectful.'

46

'I ent never called her anything but Goody.'

'Well, I didn't come to preach you a sermon. I came to say you're to start in the workshop.'

'Laws! Am I to be a carpenter after all, then? And drive the timber-cart like my dad?'

'You'll have to grow a bit before you do that.'

'I'm growing like grass. I am truly!'

'You'll have to spruce up a bit by Monday, too.'

'I ent got but this one suit of clothes.'

'You can keep them tidy, can't you? And give your boots a taste of blacking. You'll hear from my grandpa otherwise.'

'Will he go for me? I've heard he's a terrible man in a temper.'

'You'll have to mind your p's and q's, surely.'

'I dunno as I want to come,' Jesse said, his blue eyes very wide and frightened. 'I think I'd just as soon stay on the farm.'

'Never mind what you want,' Beth said. 'Your dad's sick. It's up to you to do something to please him.'

Jesse was silent, looking away to the far field, where the ploughman was ploughing the rising slope, cutting a clean brown furrow through the acid-green turf. The wind brought the jingle of harness, the blowing of the horses, and, in snatches, the sound of the ploughman singing.

'I had a mind to go to plough myself,' Jesse said, 'just as soon as I got the chance.'

'Well, you can't,' Beth said. 'Your dad's set his heart on your being a carpenter so just you buck up and look cheerful about it.'

'All right,' Jesse said. 'I'll be there Monday.'

'Seven sharp,' Beth said.

When she went back to Walter, he could talk of nothing but Jesse.

'He ent too bright, it's true. He takes after me. But he's a good boy in his way and there ent a ha'porth of harm in the whole of his body.'

'He'll have to wake up a bit when he gets to Cobbs.'

'Ah. I only hope the men'll give him a fair chance. They're a funny lot sometimes.'

'Don't worry,' Beth said. 'I'll keep an eye on him for you.'

CHAPTER THREE

She was out in the yard on Monday morning when Jesse arrived, carrying his father's bag of tools. He was late, and grandfather Tewke, confronting him outside the workshop, pointed up at the clock on the roof.

'Can you tell the time, Jesse Izzard?'

'A bull got out in the road,' Jesse said. 'I had to go back and tell Mr Mixt.'

'Bulls is no concern of mine. Nor yours now you're working for me. Is that clear?'

Jesse nodded. He stood red-faced and sweating, moving his tool-bag from hand to hand. He looked at the men, who had stopped work and were gathering round him, and he looked again at the workshop clock, where the weathercock, as always, pointed northwards.

'I see you're squinting at our old cock,' said Sam Lovage. 'I reckon it's got you properly moithered.'

'It has, that's a fact, for I could've sworn to a soft southwester as I was coming along the road.'

'Ah, we always get different weather in Huntlip. It's always a couple of waistcoats colder here than anywhere else.'

'I see you've got your dad's tools, Jesse,' said Bob Green. 'Have you done much in the carpentering line?'

'A bit now and then, that's all.'

'Well, if you're half the craftsman your dad is, we'll have to look out for ourselves,' said Sam, turning to wink at Kit Maddox.

'Oh, I ent a patch on my dad!' said Jesse, and stared in surprise as a shout of laughter went up all around.

Beth, stepping forward, elbowed her way into the circle.

'Take no notice,' she said to Jesse. 'They'd laugh to see a maggot crawl!'

She glared at her grandfather, standing by, but the waste of time was nothing to him so long as it offered some entertainment, and, perceiving his mood, the men were quick to take advantage.

'Here, Jesse, you ent like your dad to look at, are you?'

'I dunno,' Jesse said.

'Well, you're fair-haired for a start, boy.'

'I was born at harvest time, that's why.'

'I ent seen a head of hair like that since Whitey Newby was round these parts,' said Sam Lovage, 'and that's funny, really, 'cos Whitey was shepherd at Scoate for a while, wasn't he?'

'Yes,' Jesse said. 'He was there till last Christmas.'

'Laws! That Whitey! The randiest chap in the three counties. They say he was busy, all round Scoate and the Pikehouse and all.'

'Yes,' Jesse said, utterly guileless. 'Specially when the lambing was on.'

'Is that so? And Goody was kind to him, being neighbours, eh?'

'I dunno about that,' Jesse said. 'She wasn't too keen on Whitey. She said he had fleas.'

'How'd she know?' asked Bert Minchin.

'She got bitten, perhaps!' said Steve Hewish, and they all laughed.

'Oh, you're so funny!' Beth exclaimed. 'Yes, laugh yourselves silly, you great fools!'

'What's up with you?' her grandfather said. 'Clucking around like a hen with a chick?'

'Ho, so Jesse's a favourite with Beth, is he?' said Steve Hewish. 'Fancy a strapping great girl like her, picking on a little poor little hob like Jesse! Why, he's only thirteen. I bet he don't even know what girls are for yet.'

'That's enough!' said grandfather Tewke. 'Time we got down to a bit of work. Izzard, you can put your tool-bag away for today. Your first job is stacking timber. Hopson here will show you how.'

The men dispersed, returning to work, and George Hopson, a man of few words, motioned to Jesse and led him away. Beth went indoors, aware that her promise to Walter had proved worthless. She could never stop the men making game of Jesse. He would have to learn to fend for himself.

The following day, when she was cleaning out the dairy, he came to the door to look for her.

'Sam sent me. He said to ask for a bag of holes. Assorted sizes. Urgent, he says.'

'Jesse Izzard, you're a born fool!'

'Eh?' said Jesse. 'Oh, glory be!'

'They can wait for their laugh,' Beth said. 'Seeing they sent you, you can help me here.'

She kept him busy for nearly an hour, running to and fro with pails of water till the whole dairy was clean and cool and sweet-smelling. Then she gave him a dipper of creamy milk and watched him drink it.

'Why, I ent had such a treat since we lost our old Clover,' he said, with a sigh.

'Don't you get milk from Checketts, then?'

'We get a quart, but it's blue beside this. My dad has a pint of that, cos Goody makes him. Then there's a gill goes to feed our pig, and a gill for us to have in our tea.'

'I'll put out a pint for you every morning,' Beth said. 'You can nip round and drink it at dinner-time. But don't tell the men, else there'll be ructions.'

'A pint to myself every day? I'll soon be as fat as a land-lord, shan't I?'

'You'd better go now. And wipe your mouth or the secret's out. Here, hang on a minute. I've got an idea.'

She went to the barn and rummaged among a heap of sacks. She pulled out one that was full of holes and gave it to Jesse.

'They asked for a bag of holes, didn't they? Well, there you are. – You can take them that.'

Throughout that spring and summer she visited the Pike-house twice every week, and Walter was always pleased to see her.

He was growing weaker again now, wasting away to a frail husk. Yet life still burnt fiercely in him, as in a bird with a mortal wound, and on fine days he sat in a chair at the open door, eager for every last sight and sound the earth had to offer.

'I ent going yet!' he used to say. 'Not while the summer

50

holds so fine. I was always a great one for sunshine. I shan't go underground yet if I can help it.'

That summer, the plum trees at Cobbs gave a heavier crop than ever, and even when the workmen had taken all they wanted, Beth had a surplus of seventy pounds. So she took them in two big baskets, one on each arm, and went to the green to catch the carrier's cart into Chepsworth.

She sold all her plums in the open market and walked home, the empty baskets creaking against her thighs, her pinafore pockets jingling with coins.

'Have you got something to tell me?' her grandfather asked, at supper time. 'Or is it a secret, your nipping to Chepsworth to sell my plums?'

'Secret? When Timmy saw me boarding the cart?'

'Traipsing to market like some little badger! Folk'll be thinking I'm on the rocks!' He pushed his mug across the table and watched her struggle to raise the big stone flagon of beer. 'Well?' he demanded. 'What did you get for the plums, then, dammit?'

'Eight and sixpence,' Beth said.

'Is that all? For seventy pounds of best belindas?'

'I'm quite happy with what I got.'

'And where is it, what you got?'

'I've put it away,' Beth said.

'Along with the pennies you make on your eggs? Did it slip your mind that the fruit was mine?'

'I did all the picking so I reckon the bit of returns is mine. Something put by for a rainy day.'

'A little old miser, that's what you are! A grannie skinflint, like old Mrs Bunt.'

He finished his supper and sat leaning back in his chair. He watched her narrowly, reluctant to demand the money, yet hating the thought of it in her possession.

'There ent going to be no rainy days for you,' he said. 'You're safe as the Bank of England with me and that goes for your husband and family when they come along too.'

'My stars!' said Kate. 'You might give the girl a chance to grow up before putting notions into her head.'

'She don't need notions! She's as forward as nuts in May

and if I'm any judge, she'll have a couple of brats by the time she's twenty.'

'Only a couple?' Beth said.

'You needn't get hoity-toity with me, miss. I'm not against your settling early. The sooner the better as far as I'm concerned, and I'm making my plans accordingly.'

'What plans?' Beth said.

'Just you wait!' he said, happy now that he had the last word. 'You'll know what they are soon enough.'

The next day, at twelve o'clock, when Jesse came to the dairy for his milk, Beth was waiting and gave him a little bag full of money.

'What's this?' he said.

'It's to buy a few special things for your dad.'

'It feels like a fortune. I dunno as I should take it.'

'If you don't take it, I'll drop it in the drain there.'

'You must be powerful rich, Beth.'

'No, I'm not.'

'Then I reckon you're good. I do! Honest John! A proper Samaritan, that's what you are.'

'I've known what it's like to be poor, that's all. And I reckon I'll know what it's like again one day. Then I might be coming to you for help instead.'

'Why should you ever be poor again, Beth?'

'It's just a feeling I get in my bones.'

She was feeding the hens in the orchard one morning when a clamour arose in the workshop yard. Grandfather Tewke was out on business. The men were therefore in holiday mood. They had smeared the mortising-stool with glue, smoking hot from the pot on the burner, and were forcing Jesse to sit astride it. Only George Hopson and Timothy Rolls stood aloof. The rest were crowded about the stool, pressing Jesse down on the seat, and tying his boot-laces together under the crossbar.

'Don't you kick, boy, or we'll do to you what we always do to donkeys!'

'Loose him now and see how he rides!' said Liney the pitman.

'Stand back! He's threshing about like Old Nick with two

52

nails. How're you doing, Jesse? Ent you still got nothing to say?'

'He ent talking. He's too stuck up!'

'Whoopsee! He don't look too safe for all we've give him a holdfast saddle.'

Jesse swayed, throwing himself forward to keep his balance, and clutching the narrow seat of the stool. His hands were instantly fouled in hot glue, his fingers stickily webbed together, and his skin scalded. He swayed again, rocking about from side to side, and then, as his knotted boot-laces snapped apart, he toppled and fell in a heap on the ground.

Beth, with her skirts hitched up, climbed the fence and ran to help him. She took the stool by two legs and pulled it away. Jesse got up, unfolding slowly like a hurt crab, covered all over in filth and sawdust.

'Oh, he's dirtied his britches!' said Sam Lovage. 'What a dirty hound it is to be sure.'

The men roared, and Beth, in a fury, hurled the mortising-stool into their midst.

'You'll laugh the other side when my grandfather hears how you waste your time! The feathers'll fly pretty smartish then!' Still in a fury, she rounded on Jesse Izzard himself. 'As for you! It's time you woke up and kept a ha'porth of wits about you! Laws, if I was a boy, I'd take a mallet and mash a few skulls before they made a monkey out of me!'

Jesse just stood, stricken dumb. Under his filth, his face was white, and he stared at Beth with anguished eyes.

'Jesse, what is it? Has anything happened? Is it your dad?'

'Dead!' Jesse said, and could say no more.

The men were silent, looking ashamed. Timothy Rolls removed his cap and one by one the rest followed suit.

'Oh, that's pretty, that is!' Beth said. 'If only the wind could change now!'

'The boy should've told us,' Steve muttered.

'Poor old Walter,' Sam said. 'I'm sorry about it. I am, that's the truth.'

'If you're so sorry, you can think about making amends,' Beth said.

'What d'you mean?' asked Bob Green.

'Walter's widow, that's what I mean.'

'You're right!' said Sam. 'I was thinking along them lines myself. But what had you got in mind exactly?'

'I leave that to you,' Beth said. 'Only don't be scared of letting the light get into your pockets.'

She led Jesse out of the yard, across the fold, and into the scullery adjoining the house. She filled the copper and lit the fire underneath.

'Tell me about your dad,' she said. 'Did he go easy at the end?'

Jesse gave her a look of horror. He shook his head, refusing to speak.

'You should talk if you can. It does no good to stopple things up.'

'I can't!' he said. 'Oh, Beth, I can't!'

'All right. Nobody's going to make you.'

'It was bad!' he said. 'Bad as bad. All the night through. He was too weak to sit up and cough. We had to hold him, Goody and me. He couldn't breathe, yet he coughed and coughed, and the blood came up all over us, him and Goody and me.'

'Here, take a hold on yourself, Jesse.'

'I never saw anyone dying before. It oughtn't to be like that, Beth.'

'There's a lot of things that oughtn't to be.'

'Goody gave him some drops . . . He was quieter then.'

'Did he die while he slept?'

'No, not till morning,' Jesse said. 'He woke up for a while and turned his head towards the window. It was just first light, with bits of pink coming up in the sky, and he lay quite peaceful, watching them shining in on the wall. Then he suddenly said, "I'm off now, Goody.– I'll see you anon." In a quiet voice, like he always said it, going to work. "I'm off now, Goody. – I'll see you anon." And the next thing I knew, Goody was covering his face with the blanket.'

'It's better he's gone,' Beth said. 'He's earnt his rest.'

'I know that. But I dunno! It seems like nothing'll ever be the same again.'

'It won't be the same. It'll all be changed. But things don't hurt for ever and ever. That's the one little mercy, I reckon.'

'I feel a lot better, talking to you.'

'You'll feel better still when you're rid of that dirt,' Beth said, opening the copper and dipping her fingers in the water. 'It's getting warm. You can start scrubbing. But as for that glue, – only grit and grind is going to shift that.'

'Don't I know it! My britches feel like they're made of glass!'

'The next time they start tormenting you, just stick up for yourself, d'you hear? Great fists and knuckles like you've got there! You should be able to uncork a nose or two, so see you do it!'

'I'll try,' Jesse said. 'But I ent much of a fighter, Beth. You ask Goody. She always says my dad and me couldn't knock the skin off a rice pudding.'

When her grandfather heard that Walter was dead he ordered the men to make a coffin and take it out to the Pikehouse.

'Tell Goody Izzard she can pay when it suits her. Week by week if she chooses. Beth here will make out the bill.'

'No need for bills, gaffer,' Sam Lovage said, with a large gesture. 'Me and the chaps've clubbed together and we're paying for the coffin our own selves.'

'Hah! What's up with you all of a sudden?'

'Well, we want to do right by an old butty, don't we?'

Walter was laid in the churchyard at Eastery, up on the ridge, half a mile from the Pikehouse. The village of Eastery lay in a dip, hidden away among the elms, but the little church stood up by itself, its timbered tower a famous landmark, its one cracked bell a famous disgrace. In spring, the steep churchyard was yellow with cowslips; in June and July, it was blue with sheepsbit. The place was a wilderness. Larks had their nests in the long grass, and lizards sunned themselves on the flat stones. The surrounding low walls were covered in ivy, and in the autumn, wasps and hover-flies came in great numbers to the creamy-green blossoms. Wizzlewings, Walter had called them, and the day he was buried, the churchyard was filled with their quiet hum.

The following Sunday, when Beth went to the Pikehouse, Goody was busy cleaning. She had carried the furniture out to the garden and had scrubbed every stick and stitch at the pump. The kitchen table, the chairs and cupboard, the bedstead and settle: all stood steaming dry in the sun. Strips of matting hung from the apple tree. Curtain and blankets were spread on the hedge. The house itself had been swept and scrubbed, and all the windows were open wide.

'I'm glad Walter's gone before me,' Goody said. 'He wouldn't have liked it if he'd been the one to be left behind. Him and the boy would've moped theirselves silly without a woman to molly for them.'

There was no change in her when she talked of Walter. Her dark little eyes were as quick as ever; her frown was as fierce; her voice as rough. And while she talked, she darted about, swooping to pick up the windfallen apples, sorting them in her apron, setting the good ones on one side and throwing the maggoty ones to the pig in his run.

Jesse sat on a bench, blacking his boots, and Beth, beside him, was mending a rushwork mat with bast.

'D'you believe in heaven, Beth?' he asked.

'I dunno. D'you believe in heaven, Goody?'

'I dunno neither,' Goody said. 'But if there is, Walter'll be there, I'm sure of that. And that's good, 'cos it means he can put in a word for me. I reckon I'll need it, with all my sins.'

'Are you such a terrible sinner, then, Goody?'

'I'm just about loaded if anyone is. Snuff for one thing! I get through a paper of snuff in no time. And sometimes sooner!'

'You've got to have some bit of pleasure,' Beth said.

'Then there's my temper. I swear and cuss and get in a terrible paddy sometimes. I do! That's a fact.'

'You've got to say what you feel, ent you?'

'Then again I ent exactly nice when it comes to pickings. I often help myself to bits and bobs off the farm.'

'You've got to live,' Beth said. 'What else after that?'

'Nothing else. That's just about the sum and total.' Goody shooed a chicken from the settle and sat down with her hands in her lap. 'There ent a lot of choice for a woman past fifty.'

'It's a funny thing,' Jesse said suddenly, 'but whenever my hands are covered in blacking, my nose itches!'

Beth, having finished repairing the mat, was putting Goody's bodkin and scissors away in their bag.

'You go ahead and scratch,' she said. 'It won't make no odds 'cos your face is skittered with blacking already.'

She took up the hank of bast and began smoothing out the tangles.

'Why're you looking at me like that, Goody?'

'I'm looking at you and the boy there, sitting together so right and tight, and I'm wondering if your grandpa knows you're such good friends with my Jesse.'

'I reckon he knows right enough.'

'And does he like it, young woman?'

'I've never asked him,' Beth said.

That year, 1890, Beth began picking the apples at Cobbs on a day in mid October. It was bitterly cold at eight that morning and the ground was covered in a dense white mist, but when, on her ladder, she climbed into the cage of branches, she climbed up out of the mist, into a gentle brightness above. The leaves were a bright, pale yellow; the apples a bright, dark red; and the drops of water were splinters of light pricked out like silver on the twigs.

She worked quickly, picking with both hands at once, dropping the apples into her poke-pocket apron, descending to the ground to empty them into a big basket, then shifting the ladder and climbing again.

She was high in a tree, reaching up to the topmost branches, when the ladder was shaken rudely from below, and she had to throw herself forward quickly, clutching the rungs. The tree rocked as though in a gale, its branches springing and bouncing and creaking, sawing together wherever they crossed. Leaves and twigs came down in a shower, and apples bounced about her head.

When the shock had passed, and the tree became steady again, she turned to look downward, but the mist was still thick on the ground and hid the lower half of the ladder completely. There was no dark shape in the whiteness. There was no sound in the long grass. Beth, however, was not deceived. She took two apples out of her pocket and threw them into the mist below. The first thud brought a grunt. The second brought a burst of laughter.

'I'll pay you for that!' a voice promised, and, the ladder

yielding under his weight, Kit Maddox came shouldering up through the mist beneath her. 'You very nearly spoilt my beauty.'

'Stay still,' Beth said, 'or I'll dot you again.'

'Ah. I can see you've got plenty of ammunition.'

'What d'you want?'

'The gaffer sent me to give you a hand.'

'I've got two hands already, thank you.'

'Shall I start picking up here with you?'

'No. Get your own ladder and start elsewhere.'

'All right. You're the one with the say-so here.'

He climbed down, vanishing into the mist again, and a little while later she saw a ladder go up in a neighbouring tree. At first he was quiet, but quite soon he broke into song.

'Oh, a lad and his lass they went fishing
On a misty morning in May
On the banks of the Naff in the fair Vale of Scarne
Somewhere down Cropley way.

'Now the lad he fished with a lobworm
And his labours came to naught
But the lass she fished with a daintier bait
And alas! the lad was caught!

'Oh, the sun was just about setting,
The shadows were long on the hill,
And Jack his basket was empty,
And Jill her basket was full.

'But that lass she never grew weary;
She said to the lad "One more cast";
But the lad he folded his rod away
And vowed he had fished his last.

' "Then go sling your hook!" she cried proudly.
"Take your floater, your plumb, and your gaff!
There's plenty more lads in the fair Vale of Scarne
And plenty more fish in the Naff!" '

Kit's singing was one of his vanities, and in the silence that followed, Beth knew he was waiting for her to praise him.

'There now!' he said, disappointed. 'At The Rose and Crown I'd have got a pint of Chepsworth for that. Hey, Beth, can you hear me?'

'You'll bruise them apples if you throw them into your pail like that. You should put them in softly.'

'All right! Whatever you say!'

'What's up with you, all sops and milk all of a sudden?'

'The gaffer said I was to make myself agreeable.'

'Oh, did he, indeed!'

'That's right. His very words. And I'm game to try it, so what say you?'

'I'd say you was wasting your time,' Beth said.

By ten o'clock the mist had gone from the orchard and the sun was warm. The air was soft and still and filled with the sweetness of nibbled fruit. Wasps, having gorged themselves to repletion, lay curled in the hollowed-out shells of apples, or flopped drunkenly out of the trees.

Kit had shed his jacket and rolled up his shirt-sleeves, and now, instead of using his ladder, he swung about from branch to branch, a showy figure in red waistcoat and black corduroys. Beth, as always, tried to ignore him, but now, whenever she came to empty her apron into the basket, he was there to empty his pail. If she hung back, he waited for her; if she went first, he leapt to the ground and hurried to meet her. Whatever she did, he was always there, leaning across the big basket, smiling his moody, meaningless smile.

'A great help *you* are!' she said, provoked at last. 'You've only got two or three apples in that pail.'

'I'm trying to be friendly. That's what your grandpa sent me for.'

'I prefer to choose my own friends,' she said.

Kit laughed, and, leaning forward across the basket, put out a hand to touch her face. She recoiled at once, and he let his hand fall in such a way that his fingers brushed the front of her dress, lightly tracing the shape of her breasts.

'You're growing up . . . Nice and comely.'

'Keep your hands to yourself!' she said.

'Ent it time we took these apples up to the hayloft?'

'Yes. You can start now. You know the way.'

'Ent you coming? Well, why not? Don't you trust me?'

'No. I don't.'

'Seems to me you've been listening to gossip.'

'I know what happened to Rosie Lewis, if that's what you mean. And I know about Lillibel Rye, too.'

'You come up to the loft with me,' he said, and his fingers closed on her bare arm.

She pulled herself free and hurried past him, but he ran to the ladder to block the way, and so, in exasperation, she snatched up her coat and walked off, leaving him alone in the orchard.

At twelve o'clock when grandfather Tewke strode in to dinner, his face was like a thundercloud. He came to where Beth was ladling pot-soup into a plate and dropped his fist with a crash on the table. The plate bounced, and the hot soup slopped from the ladle, spattering into Beth's face.

'What're you playing at, leaving Kit by hisself like that? God almighty! You grumble to me about picking the plums yet when I send someone to help with the apples you start a morum like today!'

'Kit wasn't helping. He was wasting time.'

'Looking you over, do you mean? Well, so what? He's a boy, ent he?'

'Beth's right to keep out of his way,' Kate said. 'That boy spells trouble.'

'Gammon! I've no patience with cant of that sort.' The old man's fingers poked Beth's spine. 'You get back to the orchard this afternoon and not so much of your dammed nonsense.'

'I'm not going if Kit's there.'

'God in heaven! Other girls would be pleased as Punch.'

'Not me. I don't like him.'

'I don't believe it. Not one little jot!'

'You don't *want* to believe it,' Beth said, 'But you can't make me go, so the apples will just have to stay unpicked.'

The old man sat down, scowling at her as she passed to and fro. He could not understand her, but he had to give in.

'All right. Kit's too good a workman to waste to no purpose. But you'll try my patience too far one day, miss, and then there'll be ructions!' He broke a crust into his soup and stirred the pieces round and round. 'I can be pretty nasty when I like, so you watch out, miss. You just watch out!'

The oak trees at Cobbs, and especially the big oak growing in the workshop yard, seeded abundantly that year, and when, at the end of October, there were several days of high wind, it seemed the acorns would never stop falling.

Beth, returning from church on Sunday morning, was surprised to see Jesse at work in the yard. She went in, and found him shovelling acorns into a barrow.

'What're you doing, working on Sunday?'

'The gaffer's paying me a whole shilling extra to work today. He says the acorns attract vermin.'

'What're you doing with them?'

'The gaffer said burn them. I wanted to feed them to the cows, only he said no, it'd curdle their milk, But I'm certainly taking some home to our pig, 'cos Goody says acorns make the sweetest, tastiest pork and bacon ever. And she should know, the pigs she's raised.'

'There's enough acorns here to feed your pig for a month of Sundays.'

'There is, that's a fact! I've took a load from the sawpit alone. But there! I can't carry more than a sackful.'

'No. We'll have to borrow the pony and cart.'

'Glory be! Will your grandpa let us!'

'I shan't ask him. He snoozes in the parlour after dinner on Sunday, and I shall be back by the time he wakes up.'

At two o'clock, when Beth slipped out of the house, Jesse was waiting in the fold, the cart in the shed already loaded with sacks full of acorns.

'Golly, I'm frightened to death, I am,' he whispered.

'You needn't be. My grandfather's snoring like a hedgehog. Spread this straw and he won't hear a murmur.'

'Look,' Jesse said, and pointed up at the workshop roof. 'I climbed up there and fixed the vane.'

Beth looked up, and, sure enough, the weathercock was pointing westwards, moving gently in the wind.

'Are you pleased?' Jesse asked. 'You said you wished the

vane would work so I climbed up and done it and gave it some grease. Are you pleased, Beth?'

'Yes,' Beth said, looking into his eager face, 'Yes, I'm pleased.'

While Jesse scattered straw on the cobbles, she went to the paddock to fetch the pony, who came suspiciously, lured by a carrot, and had to be coaxed between the shafts.

Cautiously, they drove round the fold and under the archway, hooves and wheels moving almost noiselessly over the straw. Slowly, they creaked along the track that circled the house, and came at last to the village road.

'Whew!' said Jesse, wiping his forehead. 'That's the first breath I've drawn in ten minutes. I wish I could be calm and courageous like you, Beth.'

'You're all right as you are,' Beth said.

As they were crossing the Derrent at Collow Ford, Kit Maddox came sauntering out of the cottage next to the smithy and sauntered down to the slip to meet them. He stood at the edge of the water, blocking the way, and took hold of the pony's bridle.

'I saw you from the window. I wondered what you kids was up to, gadding about in the gaffer's cart.'

'Get out of our way,' Beth said.

'Does the gaffer know you're out with his yard-boy?'

'Get back to your kennel and leave us be!'

'What's in the sacks? The gaffer's money?'

'Laws, no!' said Jesse, frightened. 'It's acorns, that's all. We're taking them home to feed the pig. There's no harm in that. You won't split on us to the gaffer, will you, Kit?'

'I might,' Kit said. 'Or I might not.'

'Get out of my way,' Beth commanded.

'Surely! Whatever you say!'

He released the bridle and stood aside, but as the pony and cart moved past him, he reached for a hold and hauled himself up onto the runner.

'Shove over kids! – I aim to drive.'

'Oh no you don't!' Beth exclaimed.

'Ent I welcome on this here jaunt?'

'You're as welcome as fleas!'

'Ah, well, you don't get rid of fleas that easy.'

'We shall see!' Beth said.

She gave the ribbons a sharp twitch, and the pony trotted, swinging round at the top of the slipway and into the lane that ran for a mile or so with the Derrent. The wheels jolted over the roots of willows. The cart bumped and shuddered. Yet Kit retained his place on the runner, hands grasping the edge of the buffboard, body lightly riding the bumps.

'Whoopee!' he shouted. 'I've had rougher rides on the Porsham ferry!' And he waved one hand to show how sure he was of his balance. 'Now then, you kids! I've had enough of riding first class. I'm coming up to sit in comfort.'

'Not while I'm here!' Beth said.

She pulled the near ribbon, and Jakes responded, trotting in. The near side wheels mounted the bank, and the cart lurched steeply sideways, just as Kit got a knee on the buffboard. He was jolted backwards and this time he fell. Beth brought the pony and cart to rights again and drove on without a check.

'Christmas!' said Jesse, looking back. 'He's gone a most terrible awful whomper. I reckon he's hit his head on a rudge.'

'Good,' Beth said. 'I hope he has.'

'He ent so much as stirring a peg. D'you think he's hurt bad?'

'Hurt? Not him!'

'Ent you going to stop and see?'

'No, not me.'

'But he might've gone and bost a bone. He might be bleeding. Or even be dead!' Jesse put a hand on the reins and looked at her. His blue eyes were distressed but stubborn. 'If you don't stop, I shall just have to jump,' he said.

'Oh, very well!' Beth said crossly, and drew rein.

Jesse got down and started back along the lane. Beth remained, nursing her temper. She would not trouble herself to look behind, but watched the pony cropping the bank, the wagtails bustling about by the brook, and the willow leaves falling into the water.

After a while, Jesse returned and climbed up beside her, and she flipped the ribbons and drove on.

63

'Well?' she said, glancing at him. 'What's the weather like back there?'

Jesse turned with a sheepish grin, and she saw that his lip was bruised and swollen.

'You was right,' he said. 'Kit ent dead after all!'

When they got to the Pikehouse, Goody came from the garden to meet them.

'You're putting on style, ent you, boy, driving up like Puss in Boots? I suppose it's tuppence to speak to you today?'

'Fourpence,' said Jesse, jumping down.

'How'd you get that lumpkin on your lip?'

'A gatepost hit me,' Jesse said.

'There! Fancy! And did you happen to hit it back?'

'Here, Goody, guess what's in them sacks?'

'I can't,' Goody said. 'I'm blessed if I can fathom it out.'

'Acorns!' said Jesse, looking important. 'Bushels of 'em! To fatten our porker.'

'Would you believe it!' Goody said. 'And only this morning I was telling that poor pig he needed a couple of tucks in his waistcoat.'

They carried the sacks to the lean-to, and with every sack that Goody emptied, she uttered her own rough blessing. 'There's another couple of rashers!' she would say, or, 'There's a nice tasty joint of pork!'

Jesse took the last sack direct to the sty, and they all stood around, watching the pig as he ate the acorns and spat out the husks.

'If we die this winter,' Goody said, 'I *shall* be surprised.'

When Beth got home, Kit Maddox was waiting for her in the fold. He sat on the bench, in a patch of sun, at work with a clasp-knife, carving an elaborate wooden spoon. Beth drove around the enclosure, stopped directly in line with the pump, and backed neatly into the cartshed. Kit called out a word of praise, but she ignored him, going briskly about her chores. She took the pony out of the shafts and led him through into the paddock. She put away the sacks that had held the acorns and swept the litter of straw from the cobbles.

'Ent you speaking to me no more?' Kit asked.

'I'm surely not in a hurry,' she said.

'Well, don't be too long thinking about it or I might've upped sticks and gone for a soldier. Here, look at this! How's that for a bit of carving?'

He held up the spoon, which was cut from a piece of sycamore wood, very clean and light, the colour of oatmeal. Its bowl was round and shallow, its handle carved in a barley-sugar twist, with a knob on the end shaped like an apple, and all so smooth that the marks of the knife could scarcely be seen.

'That's what I like to do,' he said. 'Work that a man can put his stamp on, so that folk'll always know it's his. Take that screen I done for the church. — Now there's something folk is always seeing and they say to each other, "That there screen was done by Kit Maddox." '

'And the day they stop, you're as dead as mutton, ent you?'

'They don't stop. That's just it. It's always there for them to see. It's like this work going on at Spailes. Just imagine! — Restoring the whole abbey from scratch! There's masons and carpenters there from all over England and the work they do will last forever. Not like the stuff we've been doing lately — all tubs and pails and blasted ladders!'

'Them things is useful,' Beth said. 'They're a part of life.' She gathered up the last of the straw and threw it over on to the midden. 'I've got more thanks for the man who makes me a pail than for him who carves grapes and such on my pew in church.'

'Get away! Nobody notices a pail from one year's end to the next!'

'I never notice my eyes or my ears but I'm thankful I've got them all the same.'

'You don't understand,' he said, shrugging.

'But I do!' Beth said, standing before him. 'I see into you like a cup of water. It ent enough for you to be clever. You have to be told it over and over again and again. And that'll be your trouble all your days 'cos folk've got other things to do besides fussling over you.'

Kit smiled, looking at her through his lashes.

'You don't fussle me, do you, Beth?'

'No, not me!'

'Too much sense, I suppose you'd say?'

'Why so smooth and lardy all of a sudden?'

'Your grandpa thinks a lot of me. We're like a couple of snails in a cabbage. And you know what he says? – The moment you and me get together, he'll make me his partner, with my name on the board at the gate and all.'

'There now! Fancy that!'

'It's sense, really. What good is the business coming to you if you ent got a husband that knows the trade? Your grandpa's thinking well ahead. A partner for him and a partner for you, all neat and tidy, like nails in a row.'

'Oh, it makes sense, right enough.'

'Then why not get on and fix things up? Your grandpa said you needed coaxing, so here's a courting spoon for a start. Go on, you take it. I made it for you.'

'I don't want it,' Beth said. 'You'd better give it to Lillibel Rye.'

Kit's face went dark.

'I made it for *you*. Don't you understand plain words?'

'Listen to me! I'll give you plain words! I don't want you. I don't even like you. And it's no use your wheedling me with your come-to-bed eyes and your nonsense with spoons 'cos you're not getting into my grandfather's business by marrying me! Is that plain enough?'

Kit sprang up as though she had struck him. His face was rigid and his eyes looked blind. To Beth it seemed his temper must break out at any moment, but then, abruptly, he turned and walked away, dropping the spoon in the gutter as he passed.

The next morning, while Beth and her mother were in the kitchen, the door burst open and grandfather Tewke stamped in.

'Have you seen Kit Maddox?'

'Not since yesterday,' Beth said. 'Why?'

'The lock's been forced on the workshop door and all his tools is gone from the bench! I've called on his grannie and she says his bed ent been slept in all night. So what's he playing at? You got any notion?'

'That's easy,' Kate said, before Beth could answer. 'Jeremy

Rye's been threatening to haul Kit under the town clock for getting Lillibel into trouble. And Jeremy's sons've been saying they'll tar him.'

The old man scowled and turned back to Beth.

'So you saw him yesterday? A Sunday outing together on the sly. Is that it?'

'No, it ent. I met him by chance.'

'And did he let on he meant to scuttle?'

'Not exactly. But he talked a bit about Spailes Abbey.'

'So that's it! He's gone off adventuring, seeing the sights and spreading his wings, and without a fairy fan to me. I suppose he thought I'd stop him going. Well, well! It might do him good to knock about in strange parts for a bit. He'll see what a damn good pitch he's got here at Cobbs.'

'You seem pretty sure he'll be back,' Beth said.

'Hah! I give him six months! Maybe a year, if he waits for things to die down with the Ryes. Then he'll be back, large as life and twice as saucy.' The old man's anger seemed to have cooled. He was even pleased with the turn his thoughts had taken. 'The boy's got nous, going off for a while. It'll maybe bring you to your senses.'

Later that day, Beth retrieved the carved wooden spoon from the drain in the fold, and burnt it in the kitchen stove.

'Kit's gone,' she said, in answer to Kate's look of surprise, 'and I don't want no little remembrances hanging about.'

CHAPTER FOUR

But although Kit had gone, Beth was not allowed to forget him. Grandfather Tewke made sure of that, always finding excuses for speaking Kit's name. 'Seems grannie Maddox has took a lodger. Kit won't like that, finding a cuckoo in the nest when he gets home.' Or: 'Tell Mr Horton he must wait for that panelling he wanted doing. – My best craftsman is helping out at Spailes.'

And later, when Sam Lovage was allowed to bring his son into the workshop, the old man said to Beth: 'Don't get smitten on that boy Fred. I've took him on to keep up the numbers but he can't hold a candle to Kit for skill nor never will from now to domesday.' Beth, although indifferent to Fred Lovage, was pricked into making an answer to this. 'I shan't choose a husband by how he shapes as a carpenter. I'll choose by how he shapes as a man.' But her grandfather had the last word. 'Either way, Kit's the best bargain you're likely to get!'

That winter, the long hard winter of 1890-91, the Derrent was frozen for weeks on end. The young people were well pleased. So was the blacksmith who made their skates. The pool at Slings Dip, having broken its banks before freezing, became an enormous ice arena, attracting skaters from Middening, Eastery, Norton and Blagg. Every Saturday night, a big fire was lit on the ice, and a few rabbits or hares or even pheasants were roasted there.

Sometimes, Beth went down to join in the games, and once her grandfather went too, taking a bundle of elm loppings and feeding them to the fire with a great deal of show. But even there, watching the skaters, he found an excuse to speak of Kit. 'Look at them all, tumbling over, arsing about! No more idea than a pig in pickle. Now if Kit was here, he'd soon show them figures of eight. There's nobody here can't skate like Kit.'

The following April, Lillibel Rye's baby was born, and Timothy Rolls, who lived in the cottage next to the grocer's, brought the news to the workshop at Cobbs.

'A daughter,' he said. 'A bonny thing, though merrybegot, and I for one shan't hold it against her.'

'What's she look like?' asked grandfather Tewke.

'Just the usual little lump, with a dumpling face, like they mostly are.'

'But who does she feature, you damned fool?'

'Well,' said Timothy, scratching his head 'I reckon you'd better go and see the child for yourself, gaffer, seeing you're so interested in her.'

'Interested!' the old man said. 'I've got no interest in Lillibel Rye and her mischancements. I'm a busy man.'

But later on, one day at the end of summer, when he and Beth were driving home from Chepsworth, he showed his interest all too plainly. The weather was hot, and Lillibel

Rye, nursing her baby, sat on a stool at the door of her father's shop. Grandfather Tewke drew rein before her and stared at the baby in her arms.

'Here, hold it up!' he commanded, 'I want to see!'

The girl, scarcely more than a child herself, obeyed without question, holding the baby for him to see, and meekly enduring his open contempt. The baby's hair was a golden floss; her skin was fair; and her eyes, dreamily watching the pony's movements, were deep violet.

'H'mm! If that's Kit Maddox's child then I'm an Egyptian!' the old man declared, and drove on, leaving the girl no time to answer.

He was pleased with himself, as Beth could see, and he smirked and nodded to himself all the way home. But then, as they were passing the workshop yard, he became sober and gave an exasperated sigh.

'You know what I think?' he said abruptly. 'I think it's high time that boy was home!'

And the following Saturday he went to Spailes.

He returned on Sunday, empty-handed, for Kit, it seemed, had vanished from the abbey after a fight with a fellow carpenter.

'Three little weeks! To think I missed him by three little weeks! I could kick myself for that. I could, that's a fact.'

But although his mission had been in vain, the old man was perfectly cheerful.

'It's plain to me the boy is making his way home. If he's been in trouble, well, he'll come a roundabout way, won't he, to shake off any nosy parkers?'

And having, as always, ordered events as he thought they ought to go, he spent that Sunday evening clearing the dust and cobwebs from Kit's old place at the workshop bench. He set up new chops and brockets, took out the carved oak chest that Kit had left unfinished, and set it ready on the stocks. 'My dockerment chest,' as he called it. 'My dockerment chest that Kit was making to my speculations. Seems I'll have it finished sooner than maybe.'

But as the weeks and then the months went by, he became tetchy.

'Dammit! What'n hell's name does he think he's doing, playing the fool all round the landskip? And to think I missed him by three little weeks! Three little weeks! It makes me render!'

The chest remained on the workshop bench, the dust collecting again in its unfinished carving. The men were not allowed to remove it. They were not allowed to use Kit's place. And when, after a while, they joked about it, referring to their 'invisible mate in the corner' and saying, 'I wonder what wages he gets paid?' grandfather Tewke would scowl and swear. 'Kit'll be back!' he kept saying. 'Kit'll be back, sure as domesday!'

During the gales that winter, a great bough broke from the oak tree in the yard and smashed right through the workshop roof. It happened at night, which was fortunate, for several rafters and even a crossbeam had fallen in, and the stove-pipe was smashed to smithereens.

Timothy Rolls said the time had come for the oak to be felled, but grandfather Tewke, having climbed up and made an inspection, pronounced the tree safe and sound. The one broken bough was a fluke, he said, and he sent Jesse up to saw off the splintered stump and paint the cut with Stockholm tar.

Repairs began first thing in the morning. The wreckage was all cleared by noon, and the new crossbeam, rafters, and laths were all up before nightfall. Tiling began next day.

It was bitterly cold, with a murderous wind cutting straight from the east, and Beth, going out that afternoon, felt shravelled through to the very bone. Up on the roof, the men worked in the teeth of the wind, handling tiles that were sticky with frost. There was no warmth coming up from below, for grandfather Tewke had not yet returned from the forge with the new stove-pipe.

'Nippy, ent it?' said young Fred Lovage.

'Ah, cold enough to be winter,' Jesse agreed.

'It is bloody winter, you fool!' said Sam Lovage.

'Why, so it is,' Jesse said, surprised.

'Ent you cold, Jesse?' Fred inquired.

70

'Laws,' said Jesse, 'I'm that cold I don't hardly know which fingers is mine and which is George's.'

'Well, I votes we stop!' said Sam, nursing his hands inside his coat. 'What say you, Timmy?'

'Not me!' Timmy answered. 'I'm cold enough, working, but if I was to stop, I reckon I'd freeze to death where I stand.'

'Christ!' said Sam. 'I never knowed such a bleeding wicked wind.'

'It's an uncivil wind,' said Steve Hewish, his mouth full of nails. 'It don't step aside for nobody.'

'Christ!' said Sam, rocking backwards and forwards. 'Oh, oh! Sweet Jesus Christ.'

'Are you getting warmer, swearing like that?' Timmy said severely. "Cos we've got female company down below.'

Sam looked down and saw Beth.

'I think we should stop. It's murder up here. Nobody should have to work in this.'

'I reckon he's right,' Beth said to Timmy. 'You'll be froze to daglets up there.'

'There's only a bit more to do,' Timmy said. 'We'll be finished by dark-fall if we press on.'

Beth went indoors and took three bottles of cognac brandy from her grandfather's cupboard under the stairs. She emptied them into a big stoneware jug and set it on the stove to heat. She put in the juice and rind of six lemons, a grating of nutmeg, a few sprigs of ginger, and a few cloves. Then, as soon as it grew steaming hot, she stirred in a pound of clover honey.

'D'you want a tot of my punch, mother?'

'Me? My goodness! You don't catch me drinking stuff like that!'

'Then I'll take it out to them that need it.'

'Well, a taster, perhaps,' Kate said quickly. 'It's a cold old day, sure enough. I'll have just a taste to warm my tongue.'

It was getting dark, and when Beth took the jug of punch and twelve mugs on a tray to the workshop, the men were all down from the roof, stamping about on the hard ground and swinging their arms to make themselves warm.

'Here, Beth, what you got there?" Sam Lovage asked.

'Come in and see and light the lamp.'

'Glory be, but that smells good,' said Bob Green. 'It smells like Christmas at Howsells Hall when I went singing carols as a boy one time.'

'Is that there jorum for us?' asked Timothy, coming and sniffing at the jug.

'Ah, she's got some good in her after all,' said Sam Lovage. 'What say you, our Fred?'

Fred nodded, clenching his teeth to stop them chattering. He received his hot mug between his hands and breathed into it, warming his face in the rush of steam, watching intently as Jesse was served.

'Jesse's too young for this,' he said. 'He'll be falling over his own feet.'

Fred, aged sixteen, was only a year older than Jesse, but liked to give himself grand airs. He was a good enough boy in his way, but spoilt by jealousy.

'You got a slice of lemon in yours?' he asked, trying to look into Jesse's mug.

'Yes, and I aim to keep it,' Jesse said.

'What name d'you call this drink by?' asked George Hopson, looking at Beth.

'Punch, I reckon,' Beth said.

'I call it jorum,' said Timothy Rolls.

'I call it toddy,' said Liney the pitman.

'Posset!' said George. 'Ah, posset! That's what it is.'

'Whatever it is, it's certainly loosened your tongue, George,' said Bert Minchin. 'That's twice you've spoke in as many minutes.'

'It ent posset,' said Steve Hewish. 'Posset is made with curdled milk.'

'Bishop, it's called.' said Bob Green. 'I had it that time at Howsells Hall.'

'Here,' said Fred, presenting his empty mug to Beth, 'let's have a fill-up.'

'Is the roof finished?' Beth asked.

'Every cresset!' Timothy said. 'There's only the hole for the stove-pipe will want jointing up, that's all.'

'That reminds me!' said Fred, and, taking his father's

hammer and chisel, he climbed on a stool and began making marks on the new crossbeam.

'What're you doing, our Fred?'

'You'll see in a moment, our dad.'

'Don't bring the whole lot down again for God's sake!'

'There!' said Fred, and raising the lamp, showed them the date he had cut in the beam: Jan: 15: 1892. 'How's that?' he said. 'I ment be such a wonderful carver as Kit Maddox, God rest his wandering soul, but I've made a good job of that date, now, ent I?'

Sam, like the rest, was silent, for grandfather Tewke had come in at the door.

'God almighty! What's all this? The aroma in here fair knocks you down.'

'Well,' said Timmy, in a mellow voice, 'we finished the roof in double quick time, you see, gaffer, and the young miss saw fit to make it a proper occasion, as you might say.'

'And is that brandy mine you're all so busy pouring down your throats?'

'Yes, gaffer, and I dunno as I ever tasted better.'

'Well, if I ent presuming,' said grandfather Tewke, with heavy irony, 'perhaps I might be allowed to join the party?'

'Why, here's your mug set ready, gaffer, and now you must do the same as us – toast your new roofbeam, wishing it a long life and a long watch over all the good work going on underneath it.'

The old man was pleased, and drank with relish, but he still looked darkly at young Fred Lovage, who had taken the name of Kit Maddox in vain.

'Here, Fred!' whispered Sam, in the boy's ear. 'Say something right-putting, quick sharp.'

'Gaffer!' said Fred, with a loud hiccup, and raised his mug high in the air. 'Your very good health and damnation! Amen!'

Every year after that, when January came round, the men would draw Beth's attention to the date on the beam and say: 'That's nearly time for our bit of celer-beration, ent it?' And every year, Beth would make up the jug of punch. Grandfather Tewke always grumbled about it, but in fact the little custom pleased him, and he took care never to miss it. Anything that marked the stability and importance of the business was pleasing to him, and he liked, also, to throw his generosity up to the workmen, as when, in the spring of 1894, Timothy Rolls came into the office and asked for a rise in wages.

'Rise? Good God, man, you're getting tip-top wages already. Not to mention perks. You get free kindling. You get plums and apples every autumn. *And* there's the brandy-drinking every new year. So don't speak to me about rises in wages!'

Timothy went, and grandfather Tewke sat scowling at Beth, who was entering figures in the time-book. He snatched up a pencil and began to sharpen it with quick, savage cuts, sending the shavings across her page.

'As for you!' he said, annoyed by her silence: 'I s'pose you think I should give it to them?'

'Not if you can't afford it,' Beth said. 'That'd be daft, to my way of thinking.' She blew the pencil-shavings away and turned the page. 'I hope they won't blab about it all over the place, however, 'cos it won't help the business if folk get to hear it's feeling the pinch.'

'Pinch? Who said we was feeling the pinch? I never said so! I'm damned if I did!' The old man fell silent, frowning into his open cash-box. 'Pinch!' he muttered, after a while. 'A well-run business never feels no pinch.'

He got up and went out, and Beth heard him speaking to Timothy Rolls.

'About that rise. You can tell the men I'll think it over.'

The following Saturday, when they came to the office for their pay, he announced his decision: each man's wage would be eighteen shillings and each boy's would be seven-and-six; and, with a great deal of frowning concentration, he began to count out the piles of coins.

'It's what I expected,' Timothy said, 'for a good little business like you've got here is always bound to look after its men.'

'I suppose,' said Sam Lovage, watching as his money was counted out, 'it'll all pass to Beth, gaffer, when you're dead and gone?'

'A lot'll depend on her finding a husband.'

'Fred,' said Sam, 'there's a chance for you, son.' And he pushed the boy against the desk, where Beth was writing up the wage-book. 'I know you're sweet on the young miss.'

Grandfather Tewke leant forward and planked Fred's wages into his hand.

'If you can win her, she's yours!' he said. 'And my blessings upon you both.'

When the men had gone, Beth shut her book with a loud thud.

'You know I don't care tuppence for Fred Lovage, so why encourage him like that,'

' 'Cos it makes me laugh,' the old man said, 'watching him and his great sheep's eyes!'

'He's nothing but a nuisance to *me*,' Beth said.

Fred was always wanting to help her in the house or garden. 'I'll beat your mats,' he would say, or, 'I'll come and water them taters for you.' But when, with some cunning, she asked him to take a cast of bees, swarming wildly in the garden, Fred was alarmed. 'Lumme! I ent much of a hand with bees.' And later, when she wanted someone to deal with the rats in the outbuildings, Fred fought shy yet again. 'Rats?' he said. 'I shouldn't know how to start to begin.'

Beth was scornful.

'You're no help to me. I shall have to ask Jesse after all.'

'It's about all he's good for!' Fred said. 'He ent no carpenter, I tell you that. Jesse Slowsides, we call him in the workshop, 'cos he's as thick as Double Gloster.'

'At least he ent scared of a rat!' Beth said. 'Nor a bee-sting neither.'

It was true that Jesse was a poor carpenter. He took after Walter, and his fingers were all thumbs, as he said. He had no judgment, and once, making a dolly for Beth to use in the wash-tub, he whittled it clean away on the lathe. 'Fred's right,' he would say. 'I'll never be nothing more'n a hedge-carpenter, jobbing about on the farms and such.' And Beth, seeing his look of sad surprise whenever some cherished piece of work flew to pieces in his hands, would try her best not to laugh. 'Somebody's got to do them jobs, fencing and mending stiles,' she said. 'And as for Fred, he's just jealous. – You know that.'

Fred was jealous even of Jesse's strength and was always challenging him to some contest, such as raising a ladder with one hand, or dragging an elm-butt by rope to the sawpit. Jesse had grown, especially broadways: at seventeen, he was the strongest man in the workshop; and when he won these contests, as he did always, Fred would pretend to be contemptuous.

'You're beefy, you are! All beef and no brain!'

Jesse would merely nod and agree. No one could ever hope to provoke him.

'It was milk that made me the man I am,' he would say, with a little smiling glance at Beth. 'Yes, it's milk that's done it, building me up so broad and strong.'

But although a poor carpenter, Jesse, again like his father, was good with the bees, and Beth was glad to have his help, making new skeps and taking the honey, housing and feeding the bees for the winter, and making hackles to keep them warm. He was good with animals, too, and would hold the pony's head while Beth poured a drench down its throat, or would wean an obstinate calf from the cow.

And he had his own way of killing the rats in the outbuildings, setting traps of his own making, each containing a heavy block that fell and crushed the rat in an instant. He would never use poison because it was slow and caused suffering. 'And besides,' he said, 'if the rat goes and dies in some hole in the wall, you've got blowflies and all sorts infesting the place.' He preferred to use his big, clumsy traps. 'My ratting engines,' he always called them.

Fred Lovage could not understand why Beth should make such a favourite of Jesse.

'Such a duff sort of chap, with nothing up top – I dunno why you bother with him.'

'Because,' Beth said once, 'he happens to be worth a dozen of you.'

Fred gave a grin. It never occurred to him that she seriously meant it.

That summer, the summer of 1894, Kit Maddox returned

to Huntlip. It was in July, early one morning, and Beth was sharpening the kitchen knives at the grindstone in the work-shop yard. A dark shadow fell across her, and when she turned, Kit was standing against the sun, his bag of tools slung over his shoulder. It was four years since he had left Huntlip, and his face was thinner, heightening the look of gipsy sharpness. There were shadowy hollows under the cheekbones, and deep lines in the brown skin, and although he had grown a drooping moustache, it could not hide the hard, bitter cast of his mouth. He was twenty-four but looked much older. His glance was withering. His smile was sour.

'Well?' he said. 'Ent you pleased to see me?'

'No,' she said. 'But there's one who will be, and that's my grandpa.'

'He damn well should be. I've come a long way.'

From across the yard, the men had seen him. They were gathering round.

'The invisible craftsman . . . In the flesh!'

'Glory be! The spook hisself!'

'Here's the old gaffer,' Timothy said.

The old man stood at the edge of the circle, looking Kit over from top to toe, and then, aware of his audience wait-ing expectantly, he took out his watch and compared it with the workshop clock.

'Maddox!' he said. 'You're just about four years late for work this morning. – You'd better look slippy if you're going to make up for lost time.' He put away his watch with great deliberation and turned directly to face Kit. 'And your first job,' he said, 'is to finish that dockerment chest I need so badly!'

CHAPTER FIVE

Every evening now, when she went to the orchard to shut up the hens, she knew that Kit was watching her from the darkness under the trees. Sometimes she heard his soft tread in the long grass, and sometimes, out of the corner of her eye, she caught a movement among the shadows.

Tonight, the air was very soft and still, and as she went about, she could feel the prickle of dew on her forehead. Under the trees a great many moths were fluttering, pale presences in the darkness, and overhead the bats were out, peeping and squeaking. Otherwise, the orchard seemed perfectly silent, perfectly still. And yet she felt certain that Kit was there.

She shooed the last chicken into the hut and let down the door. She took the pail of eggs and walked back, lifting her skirts from the long grass. Just before reaching the gate of the fold, she stopped to place an egg among the nettles growing alongside the cowshed wall, and as she stooped, she heard soft footsteps close behind her. She straightened and turned, and this time, as she moved towards the gate, it squeaked on its hinges, swinging slowly open before her.

'Kit?' she said sharply. 'Is that you?'

'The same,' he said, and stepped forward out of the shadows.

'You and your tricks!' she said angrily. 'Brevitting about! Always mysterious!'

'What was you doing, putting an egg down there?' he asked.

'For the rats,' she said.

'No trap nor poison nor nothing?'

'A rat's suspicious if a trap appears in his run suddenly. But he ent so wary if he's had the gift of an egg once or twice.'

She crossed the fold and went into the dairy. She groped for the matches and lit the candle on the pricket. Kit followed, lounging about, watching her as she wiped the eggs and placed them in crocks on the cold slab.

'You look a bit bothered. Did I give you a scare just now out there? Laws! You don't never need to be scared of me.'

'Don't I?' she said.

'So that means you are? What a lark! To see you scared! That's a flaming marvel.'

'What d'you want, hanging around every night? Why don't you clear off and leave me alone?'

'Same old Beth,' he said, laughing. 'Up in the air at the slightest thing,' and he slouched about restlessly, kicking the floor. 'Same old place!' he said. 'Same old work going on in the workshop!'

'You was glad to come back to it even so.'

'I thought I'd give it another chance ... See if you'd maybe changed your mind.'

Beth, drying her hands, swung round to confront him.

'I haven't!' she said. 'You can think again.'

'Now I wonder,' he said. 'Just look at you! The way you're built. And not yet married at nineteen.' His glance flickered darkly over her body. 'Or maybe it's twenty? – I've lost count.'

'Get out,' Beth said. 'I don't want you. Can't you get that into your twisty brain?'

'I'm going to change your mind,' he said. 'It should be easy enough, I reckon. No girl's an angel, especially you.' He reached past her and douted the candle. 'That's better,' he said, and spoke so close that his breath was warm against her face. 'The dark's a lot better at times like this.'

Beth turned and ran, out of the dairy and across the fold, but he followed close, catching her skirts and pulling her backwards.

'I'm just about out of patience with you!' he said savagely. 'The gaffer's right. It's a waste of time. You need to be took in hand and showed what's good for you once and for all!'

He drew her backwards against his body and dragged her, stumbling and kicking, into the barn. There, in the darkness, he put a knee against her spine and sent her sprawling on to the straw, and as she rolled over, trying to rise, he threw himself heavily full-length upon her, covering her body and spreading his thighs against hers.

'There was never a girl yet that didn't want me to love her!' he said. 'You'll see! You'll see! Just shut your noise and stay still and you'll soon find out what you've been missing!'

'I'll kill you!' Beth said. 'Swine! Swine. I'll kill you for sure if you don't let me go!'

She arched her spine and threw him over on one side, straining against him and clawing at his face and head. But his grip on her arms only grew more cruel, his fingers grinding her flesh on the bone. He was very strong, forcing her down again, underneath him, his body hard and heavy on hers, his booted feet kicking her ankles to keep them still. He laid his forearm across her throat and leant on her with all his weight.

'What's the odds? What's the odds?' he kept saying. 'It's got to happen sooner or later so what's the odds? You're a woman, ent you? You're no different from all the rest!' His arm moved away from her throat, and his hands moved down to pull at her clothes, fumbling between his body and hers. 'You're no different! So what's the odds?'

She twisted and writhed, and his arm came down on her throat again. She was being choked. Her head was full of splintering pain. But now, as she fought for breath, she became aware of a yellow light growing and blossoming out of the darkness high overhead. The light took shape, revealing the ladder going up to the hayloft, and there, peering down through the open trapdoor, with a lantern in his hand, was Jesse Izzard. She turned her head, painfully, and tried to cry out. Her voice was just a whisper, but Jesse heard, and called to her that he was coming.

Kit sprang up and ran to the ladder. He gave it a jerk and dragged it from the trapdoor, letting it fall while Jesse was only half-way down. Jesse jumped, backwards and sideways, kicking the ladder out of the way, and the lantern went flying through the air. It fell in the straw and Beth swooped, snatching it up before the oil could spill from the can, and setting it on the wall for safety. When she turned, Jesse was rising on all fours, dazed and shaken. She went to help him, but Kit ran forward, shouldering her to one side, and swung his boot at Jesse's head.

'Spying on me!' he said through clenched teeth. 'Spying and prying! Hanging around where you ent welcome!' He caught up a batten of wood and swung it at Jesse's head and shoulders. 'Great lumping clod! You always had a habit of getting in my way.'

Beth went forward again, but he pushed her back, swinging the batten till it broke in splinters on Jesse's head. But Jesse now was on his feet, moving forward with arms upraised. He hit out clumsily, both fists together, and Kit went stumbling, falling against an old heap of lumber and bringing it crashing down about him. When he rose, he held in his hand an old-fashioned barking-spud, rusty but sharp, with a spear-pointed head.

'You!' he said. 'You make me heave, the way you come crawling, letting her use you as a foot-scrape!' He began to advance, the barking-spud pointed at Jesse's face. 'I'll teach you to get in my way!'

Beth reached for the hayfork stuck in the straw and swung it hard, knocking the barking-spud out of Kit's hand. She stood before him and levelled the prongs at his chest.

'Get out!' she said. 'Before I spike you like a cockroach!'

Kit was nursing his bruised fingers, looking at her in pain and loathing. He hated any harm to come to his craftsman's hands.

'I mean it!' Beth said. 'Get out this minute, else I'll spike you!'

'D'you think I'd stay?' he said shrilly, and spat on the ground at her feet as he passed.

She fetched lint and iodine from the office and a dipper of water from the pump, and returned to the barn where Jesse waited.

'Sit down,' she said, 'under the light where I can see you.'

She knelt before him and cleaned his face, wetting the lint and mopping the blood from his forehead, his eyes, his lips, his cheekbones.

'Can you still see?' she asked him.

'Ah, just about,' Jesse answered.

'And can you breathe through that swollen nose?'

'I reckon I can,' he said, sniffing.

'Is your heart still beating?'

'Why, that's ticking away like an eight-day clock.'

'Then it seems you'll very likely live.'

'Golly, yes, I'll live to be ninety!'

'What was you doing up in the loft? Setting your rat-traps? That's late, surely, if you've been there since the workshop closed.'

'I've been working at Anster and didn't knock off till after seven. Then I cut over here to see to the traps before going home.'

'You took your time letting on you was up there.'

'Well,' Jesse said, not meeting her eye, 'the gaffer's been hinting that you and Kit would soon be getting teamed up.'

'And you believed it? Knowing how I always hated him?'

'Well . . . Girls've got a way of changing their minds.'

'Not this one,' Beth said, and began, with a new piece of lint, to dab iodine on his cuts. 'Hold hard. I'm going to hurt you.'

'That's all right. You go ahead. You're doing me up humpty-dinker.'

'Now give me your hands,' she said, and winced as she saw them. 'You're a mess and a wreckage. You are truly.'

Under the dirt and the dried blood, the flesh was scraped back, red and raw, from his knuckles. The skin came off in shreds on the lint.

'Seems to me it's time we got married,' she said quietly. 'I've been looking after you one way and another ever since I can remember. – I might just as well be your proper wife.'

Jesse was looking down at his hands, where they rested in hers. He was perfectly still, and his eyes, half hidden under their fair, almost colourless lashes, seemed emptied of all thought.

'Laws,' Beth said. 'That little notion's fell on stony ground and no mistake.' She folded his fingers into his palms and pushed his hands together into his lap. 'I never heard such a silence before in all my days.'

'You're having me on,' Jesse said.

'And why not indeed? I was always one for a good joke.'

'Married!' he said. 'I must be twiddly in the head.'

'You ent too keen? Well, that's natural, really, I suppose. You're only a green young chap after all. You're only seventeen.'

'I'm a man all the same!'

'Seventeen,' she said, busy putting things away. 'That's a good two years or more younger than me.'

'That don't matter, does it, Beth?'

'You tell me!'

'Well, married!' he said. 'We've always been friends, you and me, but I never thought of our getting married.'

'Then you'd better think now,' she said coolly. 'You might not get a better offer.'

A little smile moved across Jesse's face, followed at once by a wry grimace as the cut on his lip cracked open again.

'I don't understand it,' he said, wiping the blood away on his hand. 'A girl like you, taking a fancy to a chap like me . . .' He watched her setting aside the bowl of water, the iodine bottle, the packet of lint. 'Beth?' he said. 'Is that how it is? Have you took a special fancy to me?'

'Now is that likely?' she exclaimed. 'A much more clumsier article I never met in a month of Sundays! Nor a slower one neither. As if I was likely to fancy you!'

'Ah, just as if!' he said sadly. 'I reckon I knowed you was having me on.'

With a little cry, half impatience and half pain, Beth leant forward and drew his head against her breast. She held him close, rocking him roughly yet tenderly backwards and forwards, like a mother rocking a child. She let him go and leant against him, kissing him fully upon the mouth. She felt him tremble and heard him draw his breath in a sigh.

'Here,' he said, in a deep voice. 'You shouldn't ought to do things like that. It puts ideas in a chap's head.'

'I'm glad to hear it. I thought I was making up to a stone.'

'Oh, no! I'm a man sure enough. Make no mistake about that!'

He put out a hand and touched her hair, lightly, shyly, with the tips of his fingers. He looked at her with astonished eyes.

'Why, yes . . . I reckon it's all as plain as plain . . . And yet it's a big surprise just the same. Here, lumme, do you know what? – I shall have to speak to your grandpa!'

'Not just yet,' Beth said. 'Leave it to me to pave the way.'

Kate, looking up as Beth entered the kitchen, dropped her needlework into her lap.

'Goodness, girl, what *have* you been up to, getting yourself in such a mess? And what're them bruises on your neck?'

'Well, they're bruises, ent they?' Beth said.

Her grandfather laid his newspaper on the table and

turned himself round in his chair. He looked her over from head to foot.

'Seems like you've been having a tumble!'

'Seems I have,' Beth agreed.

'So brazen?' he said, looking at her with a gleam of satisfaction. 'Ah, well, so long as it ends the way it ought ... Have you fixed the day?'

'Not the day, no. Only the man.'

'Good! Good! I told Kit it was time he cut rough with you and your nonsense.'

'It's not Kit I'm going to marry – it's Jesse Izzard,' Beth said.

The old man's face became rigid, the fine nostrils stretched wide, the fine lips pressed together, bloodless and pale.

'Am I hearing you right?' he asked, dangerously.

'Yes, you are, and I mean what I say.'

'Then you'd better change your meaning quick sharp or I'll lay you flat on that there floor! D'you hear me, eh?'

'The man on the moon could hear you. There's no need to rant and rave like that.'

'You know what I was doing in Chepsworth this morning? I was seeing Baines about drawing up a deed of partnership for Kit and me. Yes, you can stare, girl! Tewke and Maddox! – A good pair of names! And all you've got to do is change from one to the other. God almighty! The business means almost as much to you as me. It's all a matter of family pride and you can't deny it.'

'I don't,' Beth said. 'But why not make it Tewke and Izzard?'

'Izzard!' he said, almost spitting the name in his contempt. 'Are you mad?'

'Jesse may not be a craftsman but he knows the trade and he's as honest as the day. As for the business side, I can always manage that.'

'Hah! You've got it all worked out, I can see! No doubt you're counting the days till I'm dead?'

'No,' Beth said. 'It was you that started on about the future, not me.'

'I'll be the one to finish too! Now get off to bed! Perhaps a night's sleep will clear your brain.'

'I'd sooner we talked it out now.'

'I've said my say. Get off to your bed.'

'I shan't change my mind. I shall marry Jesse whatever happens.'

'We'll see about that! We'll see what a bit of quiet reflection will do for you. Ah, reflection! – When you've thought about saying good-bye to the business, and this old house with its bit of land, and the comfort of having some money behind you. Now get out of my sight! I don't want to hear another word!'

And so Beth, exchanging a glance with her mother, went upstairs to bed.

At breakfast next day, and again at midday, grandfather Tewke refused to speak. He stumped in, stared through the window all the time he was eating, and stumped out again, grim-faced.

Beth kept away from the workshop all day, to avoid Kit Maddox. Jesse was still working at Anster and would come after work to see to his traps. He had said so. They had planned to meet. But that evening, although she waited for him in the fold, he did not appear, so she went indoors, where Kate and the old man were already eating, and sat down to tea.

'Is Jesse working late again this evening?'

The old man made no reply.

'He said he'd be here to see me at six.'

Again, the old man remained silent, pushing watercress into his mouth and chewing stolidly.

'Well,' Beth said. 'Seems I'll just have to go to Anster and see for myself.'

'Izzard ent there,' her grandfather said.

'Then where is he?'

'I went to Anster and paid him off. He'll have been busy today, looking for work.'

Beth rose from the table.

'Where d'you think you're off to?' he demanded.

'To the Pikehouse,' she said.

'Oh, no, you don't! You stop where you are!'

'I'll do as I choose,' Beth said.

'Go through that door, miss, and you go for ever!'

'So be it,' Beth said.

'Beth, you can't!' her mother pleaded. 'Please sit down and think things over.'

'Don't worry!' the old man said. 'She knows which side her bread is buttered. She ent leaving.'

'But I am,' Beth said. 'I've got no option so I'll get my things.'

'Things!' he shouted. 'You take no things from out of here! If you're going, you can go the same way you came in the first place, empty-handed and living on air!'

Beth stood for a moment in silence. Then she crossed the kitchen and laid a hand on her mother's shoulder.

'Oh, Beth, don't go!' Kate said, weeping. 'Not like this! It's all wrong. You must think things over.'

'I've done my thinking,' Beth said. 'Ages ago, when I first saw this coming.'

'At least say some sort of word to your grandpa!'

'No, no words!' the old man said, staring before him. 'Let her go to ruin the way she's chose. I don't want no words from her!'

So Beth, in silence, and without looking back, left the house that had been her home for eight years. She took the short-cut across the fields, crossed the Derrent by the stepping-stones, and climbed the steep slopes of Millery wood. She walked along the Norton road, turned on to the old turnpike, and so came to the little Pikehouse, lonely beside the edge of the wasteland, its white walls made pink by the level rays of the evening sun.

Jesse was hoeing in the garden. He waded out from among the beans and came to meet her.

'Glory! I've been thinking and thinking of you all day.'

'Is that why you fled without trying to see me?'

'I was stumped,' he said. 'The gaffer came to Anster and gave me the push. He said if I saw you he'd cut you off. I'd got to forget what you and me had fixed between us, 'cos you'd gone and changed your mind, he said.'

'Oh, ye of little faith!'

'You mean we *are* getting married then after all?'

'I'm sunk if we don't, 'cos I've been sent packing the same as you.'

'Glory!' he said. 'So you've left all that to come to me?' He leant on the handle of his hoe and looked at her with a radiant face. 'And all so quiet and simple, too, like rain coming down, or the sun shining, or the stars winking and twinking at night-time.'

'We must talk,' Beth said. 'You and me and Goody together.'

'Why, yes,' he said, and flung down his hoe. 'A parliament, that's what we want.'

Goody was busy gathering seed from the stocks and marigolds and love-in-a-mist that grew in the garden behind the house.

'Oh, it's you!' she said gruffly, straightening up in front of Beth. 'I thought I heard a durdle of voices.' Her queer little crooked face was hostile. Her eyes glimmered. Her voice was sharp. 'And what's the latest freak with you Tewkeses?'

'Did Jesse tell you we're getting married?'

'He told me something. In his cock and bull way.'

'You don't seem too pleased?' Beth said.

'It's a mix-up to me, a chap like Jesse, poor as a mouse, marrying into a family like yours. How's it going to sort itself out? Your grandpa ent exactly blessed the notion. Oh, no, not he! He's gone dead against it and Jesse here has got the push!'

'So have I,' Beth said.

'Eh?' Goody said. 'What's that you say?'

'I've got the push and all,' Beth said, 'with nothing more than the clothes I stand up in. I'm poorer than you've ever been in your life, Goody, for I'm out on the road.'

'That's different!' Goody said, and her dark little eyes searched Beth's face. 'You're one of us. Come indoors and eat some supper. This is your home from now on.'

In the kitchen, she lit a small lamp and placed it in the centre of the table. She set out a loaf, a wedge of cheese, and a jar of pickles. She set out three old horn beakers, much scratched and dulled, and a stone jug full of small beer.

'Sit up,' she said, attacking the loaf with a great curved knife, 'and don't be afraid to eat your fill.'

87

'I shan't,' Beth said, 'for I had no tea.'

'Lumme, you must be starved,' Jesse said.

They sat together, the three of them, in the circle of light from the lamp in their midst. The crusty bread and the crumbly cheese were the best Beth had ever eaten, and the beer, although its mildness teased her tongue, was the best beer she had ever drunk. She said so, and Goody was pleased.

'The only hunger we've known here is the hunger that gives a savour to plain food. We're a lot luckier than some in this world.'

She leant forward and refilled Beth's beaker.

'You'll sleep with me for the time being. Then when you're married, you two shall have the bed upstairs and I'll have the one down here.'

'I shouldn't like that, you giving up your bed for us.'

'That don't worry me,' Goody said. 'I'm lost in that bed since Walter's been gone. It's a good featherbed that we made ourselves when we was first married. It's a pity not to fill it as it's meant to be filled.'

'I'm bringing nothing to this marriage. Not so much as a packet of pins.'

'You've brought your health and strength, though, ent you? And as it's luckily harvest time, there's plenty of work for everybody. Jesse's already seen Mr Yarby. He starts at Checketts with me tomorrow. And you can go down with us first thing. You ent afraid of field work?'

'Not Beth!' Jesse said. 'She ent afraid of nothing on earth.'

'You might as well marry as soon as maybe. You can see Parson Chance tomorrow evening.'

'Just think,' Jesse said. 'Beth and me! – Mister and Missus! I can't hardly credit it even now. A chap like me, – no looks nor nothing – getting hisself a wife like Beth.'

'What d'you mean, a chap like you?' Goody said. 'You're a fine upstanding shape, ent you, with arms and legs and all the bits and pieces that make up a man? What more should a woman want?'

'Here we go!' Jesse said. 'I've started it now!'

'I've seen worse than you, boy,' Goody said, spearing a pickle in the jar. 'What's wrong with your looks, apart from them bruises? It's a good enough face as faces go. It's a good

88

strong man's face, with plenty of bone in it, and plenty of chin, and you've got your father's good clean blue eyes. And anyway! When the candle goes out last thing at night, it ent what you look like that matters then, boy!'

'Here!' Jesse said, growing red to the ears. 'What a thing to say! Right out like that! In front of Beth.'

'You're the one that's ruddling up, boy.'

'Ah, well . . .' Jesse said, looking everywhere but at Beth. 'You women've got us beat, I know, when it comes to having the last word.'

'We've got you beat altogether,' Goody said.

The vicar of Eastery-with-Scoate, the Reverend Peter Chance, was known for plain speaking. He stood on his hearth, a tall man with a big brown face and a shock of grey hair, and looked hard at Beth and Jesse, sitting before him.

'How long have you known each other?' he asked.

'Nearly all our lives,' Beth said.

'And this quarrel with your grandfather? Who's to blame, you or he?'

'Me, I suppose, for having the nerve to choose my own husband.'

'Jesse's made a wise choice,' the vicar said. 'A wife who's a fighter is worth her weight in gold to a labouring man.'

Jesse, sitting perched on the edge of his chair, convinced that its delicate carved legs could never support his full weight, gave a solemn nod.

'Just so long as she don't fight me!'

'You can't have it all ways, Jesse, my boy. Now tell me this. Shall you have children, do you think?'

'Indeed, I hope so,' Beth said.

'Why, yes,' said Jesse. 'Why, yes, indeed.'

'How many, d'you think?'

'As many as come,' Beth replied.

'Ah,' said Jesse, and was lost in thought.

'A wedding it is, then,' the vicar said. 'But one word of advice to you both. Hot heads and hot words should always be let to cool before bed-time, especially in marriage. Remember that.'

Afterwards, walking back down the fields to the Pike-house, Jesse laughed.

'Mr Chance should know about tempers if anyone does. Why, he got in such a paddy with the verger once, he said he would ring for matins hisself, and he pulled so hard he cracked the bell! He did! Honest John! You won't get melody for your wedding. You'll only get chanks.'

'We can always stop our ears.'

'He's a card, Mr Chance. Last winter, one time, at even-song it was, when folk was on the fidget with colds and such, he upped and said right out in the prayer, "Have pity, O Lord, on these thy afflicted gathered here, for a worse lot of snivelling, tissucking folk I have yet to meet in a Christian congregation." Right out like that, in his parson's voice, as though it was Scripture.'

'I'm sure he never said tissucking.'

'He did! Honest John! You ask Goody when we get home.'

Jesse fell silent, walking along with his hands in his pockets, watching Beth with a sidelong glance.

'What're we pelting along like this for?' he asked, stopping. 'We should be going nice and slowly, getting acquainted, as they say.'

'We'll soon be tied together for life. There'll be plenty of time for getting acquainted.'

'Well, what about something on account?'

Beth went forward into his arms and let him kiss her, and they stood for a while under a thorn tree, where the evening wind was riffling noisily through the leaves. They stood together enfolded in warmth, two beating hearts, two throbbing pulses, their blood moved by the same force. Then she drew away.

'We'd better get home. Goody'll be waiting supper for us.'

'We'd better, I reckon, before I get dangerous,' Jesse said.

'Three more weeks,' Beth said, 'and you can be as danger-ous as you please.'

It was harvest time, and they worked in the fields from first light, when the dew-drenched corn surrendered its strongest scent to the mowers; on through the long burning day; until after dark-fall, when the cooling dew descended again, and the big yellow moon came to light their last labours.

Burning sun was the order of every day that harvest. The fields were on fire with ripening oats and wheat and barley, and the hot brightness dazzled the eyes. Sometimes, bent double, binding the sheaves, Beth felt overwhelmed by the tide of the harvest, the tide of the corn with its waves of hot brightness going on and on. As she stooped and straightened, stooped and straightened, erecting the sheaves, the hot white gold land went tilting madly, the blue sky heaved, and the great tide of brightness threatened to drown her under its waves.

Day after day, her ears were filled with the rattle and whirr of the reaping-machines, the calls of the men, the harsh tseep-tsawp tseep-tsawp of somebody sharpening the blade of a scythe. Day after day, the sun swung round and the circles of light went spreading outwards, wheel upon wheel, radiating, it seemed to her, from the two very sheaves she held in her hands, as she built the corn-cocks up and down the fields of stubble, along the paths of sunlight and the paths of wind.

And when a lull came, and the waggons had creaked and rumbled away, and two or three fields were clean and empty, the women would be there, waiting to enter the stubble to glean. Sometimes, in the evening, the men would join them, and Jesse would work beside Beth and Goody. Then the jokes would fly, especially if the three Jimmys happened to be there.

'Does she never laugh, Jesse, this sweetheart of yours?' asked Jimmy Winger.

'Not to your face,' Jesse said. 'She wouldn't want to hurt your feelings.'

'She don't speak English, I don't suppose? Well, she wouldn't, would she, coming from Huntlip as I hear she do?'

'There's good pickings in this field,' said Jimmy Shodd. 'Some sheaves got forgot this afternoon, so I broke them up and tossed them about a bit all over. Ah, and Mr Yarby catched me at it, though he never said so much as a word. If he had, I'd have answered him straight – it's in the Scriptures, black and white, that if a few sheaves get forgot in the field they should not be gone back for but left for the sake of the widows and orphans and them that is strangers in the land.'

'Jimmy's a great man for the Scriptures,' said Hilda, his wife, working beside him. 'The Scriptures and dirty songs. – Jimmy can't be beat for them.'

'Was they really forgot, them sheaves you tossed about?' asked Jesse.

'Indeed they was! I was the one that did the forgetting!'

'Yes,' said Hilda. 'Jimmy's a great man for giving the Scriptures a chance to come true.'

Their jokes would fly, but after a while, being bone weary, they would fall silent, inching along, bent double, gathering up the spikes of corn, till the evening drew in, and, in twos and threes, they went from the fields.

Beth rarely spoke to Jesse during the day, but their work in the fields bound them together hour by hour, till a current of awareness ran in their blood. The work they did, bringing in the harvest, brought a feeling of richess: the money they earned together was wealth; the corn they gleaned was more than wealth; but the feeling of richness came from something beyond their little hoard of coins and grain: they were reaping their youth and their strength together; they were reaping their lives, and the harvest was a good one.

They were married on the third Sunday in September. Kate was there to give Beth away. There was no congregation, but a number of Eastery villagers, mostly women and children, hurried up on hearing the bell and were waiting in the churchyard when Beth and Jesse came out of the church.

As they stepped out into the sunshine, the bell's flat, dissonant clangour was abruptly stilled, and in the little shock of silence, Goody glared at the vicar.

'What's up with Jack Main? It's a poor bell, I know, but it ought to clank out longer than that for a wedding, surely?'

'Have patience, woman,' the vicar reproved her.

Goody, with new yellow daisies adorning her hat, stood scowling ferociously through her veil. Kate clutched her prayer-book and looked nervous, blinking short-sightedly all around. And Jesse, almost a stranger in Sunday blacks and stiff white collar, stood to attention at Beth's side.

'Ah,' said the vicar. 'Now listen to that!'

Heads cocked, they all listened, and over the fields, faintly but sweetly, came the ringing of Huntlip church bells.

'There, now,' said Jesse, in a hushed voice. 'They're ringing for us. Huntlip bells.'

'Yes,' Beth said. 'Yes, so they are.'

'And why not indeed?' Goody demanded. 'The bride's own parish! So they ought to ring!'

'Parson Wisdom and I are good friends, – when we're not falling out,' said Parson Chance. 'We arranged the ringing as a surprise. Now, if the wedding party will go ahead, I'll follow as soon as I've shed my surplice.'

'Right,' said Goody, 'we'll take it slow.'

Arm in arm, Beth and Jesse led the way, receiving a shower of rice and corn from the children ranged along the path. Kate and Goody walked behind. But now, as the little party turned towards the gate that opened on to the field-path, three figures stepped out from behind the yew trees. The first was Kit Maddox, the second Fred Lovage, and the third was the Huntlip simpleton, Jumper Lane, who carried a bulging sack on his shoulder.

.'What's this?' said Goody, pushing in front of Jesse and Beth and going up to Kit Maddox. 'Get out of our way. You don't look right for a wedding to me.'

'Well, we are,' Kit said. 'We couldn't find a sweep so we brought the next best thing instead. Here, Jumper! Let's have the sack!'

The soot, in handfuls, flew through the air. It hit first Jesse then Beth in the face, and spattered down all over their clothes. Goody, with a howl of rage, leapt forward and caught Jumper Lane a resounding smack on the side of his head. He staggered back against Fred Lovage, and the sack of soot fell and burst on the path.

'I'll learn you!' Goody cried. 'Coming and spoiling people's weddings! Take that! And that! And you, Jesse, get Beth and her mother out by the lychgate. I'll soon deal with this pack of whelps!'

Jesse took Beth and Kate by the arm. But Beth hung back and would not go.

'No! You know what Kit's like. He'll do Goody a serious mischief if he gets roused.'

Kit and his two companions were scooping the soot up from the path and pelting Goody in the face. She was almost blinded, and Jesse was going forward to help her, when out of the church, the skirts of his cassock flying behind him, burst the Reverend Peter Chance, wielding the heavy pastoral staff and shouting out in a great warlike voice as he rushed upon the trouble-makers.

'Out! Out!' he bellowed, and, using the oaken staff as a cudgel, he laid about him with all his strength. 'Out of my churchyard! Or we'll dig you a grave where you fall! Out, the lot of you, vicious scum!'

Again and again the sun glinted upon the cross as the staff rose and fell, belabouring shoulders and heads without mercy, driving the three young men down the path. The vicar pursued them, thud, thud, till they broke ranks and ran, out of the lychgate and headlong down the village street, followed by the jeers of the villagers in the churchyard.

'Good!' said the vicar, coming back across the graves. 'That's put them to rout, eh, Goody? We two together, like Horatius and Lars Porsena, eh?'

'Ah,' said Goody, peering at him with blackened face, through her blackened veil. 'Exactly so!'

'Vicar,' said the verger, standing by with a long face. 'The pastoral staff, sir! Of all things!'

'And what better purpose could the staff serve than driving the Vandal from a Christian precinct? Oh, here you are, man! You can take it. You're a sight too pious for me.'

And the vicar turned back to the wedding party.

The table, covered with a blue chequered cloth, was already laid with the wedding breakfast. There was farmhouse cheese, mature and strong, and soft summer cheese, flavoured with parsley, chervil, and chives. There were devilled eggs in nests of lettuce; chicken pasties garnished with cress; and plates piled high with the flat griddle scones, full of currants and raisins, that Goody always referred to as Welshcakes. There was bread of Goody's own making, and pale salty butter from Checketts farm. There was strong beer and elder wine.

'You,' said the vicar, pointing a finger in Beth's face, 'have not been in church these past three Sundays.'

'Of course not,' said Goody, before Beth could speak. 'It's bad luck for a girl to hear her own banns called.'

'That's rank superstition, Goody Izzard.'

'Is it?' said Goody. 'Let me fill your glass.'

'That Kit Maddox,' Kate said to Beth. 'He'll come to a bad end one of these days.'

'Now remember, don't let my grandfather put on you, milking the cows and things like that. See that he gets a girl to help.'

'Ladies and gentleman!' Jesse said. 'Goody here says I've got to speak. She's right, I suppose . . . but I dunno . . . well, it's like this here, and I'd better begin!' He stood very straight and stiff at the table, squeezing a Welshcake to crumbs in his fingers. 'Well!' he said, clearing his throat. 'I don't exactly know what to say. Unless it's thanks . . . from Beth and me . . . on behalf of us both, I mean to say . . . And God bless all here!'

'Bravo!' said the vicar. 'And I too will speak, pledging your health in this very good beer. May your pitcher never once be empty, and may you know a good old age!'

When Kate had gone, with the vicar to keep her company part of the way, Beth and Jesse changed their clothes and worked in the garden. Jesse dug the winter potatoes and stacked them away in straw in the shed. He dug the carrots and shallots and onions and laid them out to dry in the sun. Beth picked the last of the scarlet runners, setting a few aside for seed, and taking the rest in to Goody, who sliced them and laid them in salt in crocks.

The day was soft and warm and misty. The sun seemed reluctant to leave the sky. They worked on, Beth and Jesse, till even the twilight had faded away; till the little lamp was lit indoors and Goody called them in to supper.

On the kitchen table, the blue and white plates were set out ready; the old horn beakers and stoneware jug; and a baked ham with brown sugar glaze and pale pink meat that came curling off in delicate shreds as Goody carved with her big sharp knife. There was beetroot, sliced, in a little dish; crisp green watercress from the spring; jars of chutney and Chepsworth mustard.

'My stars,' said Jesse, coming to sit beside Beth at the table. 'A feast this morning and another tonight! It's worth getting married, to get food like this.'

'H'mm!' said Goody. 'If that's all you expect from marriage, I must take you aside for a little talk, boy.'

'That's enough!' said Jesse, reddening. 'You get on with cutting that ham!'

'Ent you mighty!' Goody said. 'There's nothing like marriage for making a man masterful all of a sudden.'

At nine o'clock she drove them to bed, and they climbed the steep stairs to the small bedroom under the roof. The featherbed, made ready by Goody, was plumped up high and covered over with a patchwork rug. Beth's nightdress lay on one pillow, Jesse's nightshirt on the other. The room, so small beneath its steeply pitched ceiling, held the day's warmth, and smelt of the day's sweetness and ripeness. It smelt, too, of warm thatch.

Beth went and leant at the open window, looking out at the starlit night, and Jesse came to lean beside her. The window was small. They were wedged together, shoulder and thigh, and Beth could smell the clean warmth of his body.

'It's a queer funny thing,' he said, 'feeling amazed and yet not amazed at the same time. D'you feel like that?'

They turned to each other, and she leant against him, within his arms.

'Jesse, put your hand on my breast,' she whispered.

Part Two

No, I'm a man, I'm full a man;
You beat my manhood, if you can.
You'll be a man if you can take
All states that household life do make:
The love-tossed child, a-croodlen loud,
The boy a-screamen wild in play,
The tall grown youth a-steppen proud,
The father staid, the house's stay.
   No; I can boast if others can,
     I'm full a man.

— *William Barnes*

CHAPTER ONE

To Jesse, the sight of his womenfolk working in the fields
was a thing that gave him a sense of wellbeing, and a sense
of pleasure, new every day. 'My Two,' he called them, when
mentioning them to the other workers. 'Have you seen My
Two this morning?' or, 'My Two are late coming up with the
oneses. – I must speak to them sharpish about that.'

In winter, they worked the chaff-cutter in the barn, or
chopped up swedes, or mended sacks. In spring, they picked
stones from the ploughed fields, thinned the turnips or sugar-
beet, or hoed the weeds from between the rows of drilled
corn. In summer, they dug potatoes and worked on the hay.
And he would come on them, sometimes unexpectedly,
sometimes knowing where they would be, but always with
the same little jolt of pleasure that made him laugh to himself, inside.

Beth, in the fields, stood out among all the other women as
a ringdove stands out in a flock of jackdaws. Her shining fair
hair was always smoothly coiled about her head, and she
carried herself with a certain dignity, free and easy and sure
of herself.

He would come upon her, about the farm, when she
looked so fine and carried herself with such an air: when her
glance was calm and the tone of her voice as cool as water;
and through his blood would run a quivering shock of
amazement, because she was his. He would come on her
with a sense of pride in her coolness and remoteness, but
always, underneath, there would be a darker, more secret
pride, because of all that lay between them; because he had
seen her with tumbled hair, with eyes closed and lips parted,
and had heard her voice crying out in need. Wherever he
went now, he carried the touch of her hands about him, and
the shape of her body imprinted on his. And because of what
there was between them; because she had made him aware
of himself and his power; now, when he walked about the

fields, stalking like a giant over the land, he carried with him a terrible strength and a terrible knowledge.

But there came a time when the sight of her at work in the fields filled him with horror. He wanted to rail at her and drive her out. But Goody said to leave her be, and the three Jimmys offered words of wisdom, each according to his kind.

'It's yourself you should watch,' said Jimmy Shodd. 'I've been through it and I know. Pain here! Pain there! It's the man that suffers every time.'

'You should've took my advice,' said Jimmy Winger, 'and stayed a bachelor like you begun.'

'Don't worry, Jesse,' said Jimmy Ling, who had once been a shepherd at Chepsworth Park. 'There's always more lambs lost than there is ewes.'

Every evening now, Goody drove him out of the house, into the garden to chop wood.

'Off you go!' she would say. 'Great solid ornament, lapsing about under my feet. There's plenty for you to do outside. We'll want good fires this coming winter. So off you go and work yourself out.'

'Shouldn't we ought to get Mrs Tewke?'

'No,' Beth said. 'My mother's no good at times like this. It's Goody I trust. She knows what to do.'

Jesse nodded, but doubtfully. He had always had faith in Goody in everything, but now, suddenly, he was unsure.

'Ah,' he said. 'I suppose she does.'

'No ah about it,' Goody said. 'Go swing your axe and work yourself out.'

And so he worked, every evening, till the firewood rose to the roof of the shelter and overflowed on either side.

The days were open and mild that autumn. The ground was moist but not wet, and ploughing was easy, especially on the stubble lands. So mild was the weather that one day in late October, he saw three swallows passing over, four or five weeks or more after the main flocks had gathered and gone. The date was Friday the twenty-fifth. He had reason to remember.

He was ploughing the field known as the Outmost, and whenever he reached the top of the rise, he would stop for a while to rest his team, and to take a good long look at the Pikehouse. He could see it plainly, small in the distance, with smoke rising from its chimney, with sunlight glinting on its windows, and with, it seemed to him, a great air of stillness upon it, alone there in its square of garden, between the lonely turnpike road and the lonely wasteland. He stood for a while, watching the house with screwed-up eyes, then turned again and ploughed down the slope.

It was wheat-stubble land, with a thick growth of couch-grass and bindweed, and the plough went through with a loud ripping of roots and stems. The soil heeled and rippled over, and the pale stubble vanished beneath the dark wave. With each new furrow, a new breath of the earth's smell was released on the air, and the ground steamed in the warm sun. Going downhill, the two horses, Goldie and Jessamy, kicked up pebbles that rang on their shoes; they travelled swiftly, with a creaking of harness and a jingle of brass. Behind him, Jesse could hear the crying of peewits coming in to feed on the ploughland, and in the neighbouring field below, Jimmy Shodd was singing a favourite song.

> 'I'm only a poor young ploughman
> And I cannot afford to wed
> But I've got a girl who is willing
> To share my barley-straw bed.
>
> 'Oh, my sons will have to be working
> And my dear little daughter the same
> Before I can marry their mother
> And give her an honest name.'

When Jesse got to the bottom, Jimmy was looking over the hedge.

'Any sign at the Pikehouse?'

'No, nothing,' Jesse said.

'You feeling all right? No cramps nor nothing?'

'No, nothing,' Jesse said. 'How much longer d'you think it'll be?'

'As long as your missus can spin it out,' said Jimmy. 'They're deadly wonderful people, women, for spinning things out.'

Jesse turned and ploughed up the slope, and this time, when he reached the summit, something was fluttering in the Pikehouse garden. It was Goody's signal. She had hung a table-cloth out on the line.

For a moment he stared, and then, scarcely knowing what he was doing, he pushed through the hedge and began to run.

When he burst into the kitchen, Goody was bending over the fire, and she turned on him in a passion of anger.

'What're you doing? D'you want Mr Yarby down on your tail?'

'Can't I see her? Just for a minute?'

'No!' Goody said, pushing him back towards the door. 'You just wait till you've finished work.'

'How is she, then? Is she all right?'

'You saw my signal, you great noop! That means she's dandy and the same applies to your baby daughter. So get back to work or I'll give you what-for!'

When Jesse went back to ploughing the Outmost, Jimmy Shodd was no longer singing, but plodding along woodenly, intent on his furrow. Jesse looked round and soon saw the reason: Mr Yarby was watching from the gate of the Uptops.

Betony lay in the cot on rockers that Jesse had made during the summer. Her face, just visible under the blankets, was red and wrinkled. Her mouth was open; her eyes tight shut.

'Shouldn't she ought to have a pillow?'

'No. Goody says not.'

'She's a nice little baby, ent she?' he said. 'All puckered and pink ... She's a tidy size, too, considering.' With a nervous finger, he drew back the blanket an inch or two. 'What's up with her hands? They're all tied up in little cosies! There ent nothing wrong with her hands, is there?'

'It's to stop her scratching herself with her nails, that's all.'

'Nails,' he said, with a little laugh. 'There, now. Just fancy that.'

He put the candle back in its place and sat down on the

stool by the bed. Beth was brushing and combing her hair, twisting it into a smooth golden hank where it lay on her shoulder. While he watched, she pinned it up at the back of her head, then dropped her arms with a tired sigh. Her face was pale. There was sweat like a dew on her lip and forehead.

'Are you all right?' Jesse asked. 'Ah, that's all very well for you to nod so serenely, but you've had a time of it, I know.'

'It's often hard work with the first, Goody says. But it won't be so bad next time.'

'Laws, there ent going to be no next time, surely? Oh dear me no! We ent going all through that again!'

Watching her anxiously, he saw her smile.

'We've done all right, ent we?' he said. 'We've got a nice little baby there, and I reckon we'll call it a day now.'

Goody came up into the bedroom and went to the cot. She spoke to Jesse over her shoulder.

'Are you going to eat your supper tonight, boy?'

'I ent all that hungry to tell you the truth.'

'Great fool!' she said. 'Great dromedary!'

'I saw three swallows today when I was ploughing the Outmost,' he said. 'Swallows, mind, on the twenty-fifth of October! Does that mean anything, I wonder?'

'It means they'll be late getting wherever it is they're going to,' Goody said. 'Africa, ent it? Some place like that?'

'I thought it might be an omen,' he said.

'Omens indeed! Great gobbermoocher!'

'Well, what d'you think of my daughter, then, eh? Gawping into the cradle like that! That's given you something to think about, being a grannie, ent it? So what d'you think of her? You tell me that.'

'She'll do,' Goody said, 'to be going on with.'

He was carting muck in the ten acre piece just above the farm. The weather was still open and mild, although it was almost the end of November, and he sweated even in his shirt-sleeves.

Goldie, the mare, did not care for strangers, and when a rider appeared in the next field, she put back her ears and began to fidget between the shafts. Jesse jumped down and went to soothe her. He held her head against his chest.

The next field was a narrow strip of three acres, and was newly planted with spring cabbage. Jesse did not at first recognize the rider, but when she walked her big black mare straight across the cabbages, carelessly treading them into the ground, he knew it was Mrs Lannam of Scoate.

She drew rein a little way off, and sat in silence, waiting for Jesse to meet her glance. She was long-faced and pale, with strange-coloured eyes, almost yellow, set wide apart under pencilled brows.

'What's the matter with that mare? Is she fractious?'

'No, ma'am. She just don't like strangers.'

'You're a stranger, yourself. To me, at least.'

'Not a stranger, ma'am. I've lived at the Pikehouse all my life.'

'Oh! You're Goody Izzard's son Jesse. Yes, I can see it now, though you've changed a lot since I last saw you. Indeed, you've grown into quite a personable man.' And she looked him over, with pale-shining gaze. 'I heard you had married. Is that so?'

'These fourteen months,' Jesse said. 'And got a baby daughter too.'

'Good God!' she exclaimed. 'You make it sound like a miracle, man!'

Jesse blinked and looked away. Her tone of voice, and the mocking way she looked at him, made him feel awkward and ill-at-ease.

'I must call on your wife some time,' she said, and rode off past him.

On leaving the field he met Jimmy Shodd, also returning with an empty cart, and they drove down side by side.

'I see you've had company, Jesse, boy. You want to look out or you'll land in a pickle.'

'Eh?' Jesse said. 'And how's that?'

'Her! Mrs Lannam! She's a bit of a plum. She spells trouble so just you watch out!'

'Get away! You're having me on.'

'No, not me. She's after your body. You mark my words.'

'I ent listening,' Jesse said, growing hot in the face and neck. 'Mrs Lannam! A lady like her!'

'D'you like her, then, Jesse boy?'

'Why, no. I can't say I do. I don't care for people riding anyhow over the crops like that. And if I was Mr Yarby I'd speak to her plain.'

'He would if he dared. But she's his landlord.'

'I'm glad she ent mine,' Jesse said.

When they got to the farmyard, Mr Yarby stood on the muck-bury wall, watching the comings and goings of the men.

'Izzard!' he said. 'You went ten minutes in front of Shodd so how's it happen you come back together?'

'I dunno,' Jesse said, worried.

'It was Mrs Lannam,' Jimmy said. 'She kept him talking and that set him back.'

'Mrs Lannam!' said Mr Yarby, sneering. 'So you hob with the high and mighty, do you, Izzard?'

Jesse backed his cart to the bury and began forking in the muck. Jimmy, beside him, spoke in a murmur.

'He's a stinker today. Got up the wrong side. Or else his missus's been on at him again about buying that Turkey carpet.'

'Turkey carpet?' Jesse repeated, and his voice, too loud, reached the ears of Mr Yarby, who turned and gave him a hard look.

When his load was complete, Jesse stuck his muckfork into the heap and climbed up on to the cart. He flicked the reins, and Goldie pulled off with a sharp jolt. But the cart only slewed, its axle screeching, its wheels sliddering in the slime-filled gutter.

'Whoa!' Jesse called. 'Easy does it, Goldie girl! Let's try again.'

Goldie relaxed, stepping sideways in search of dry ground, and the cart slipped further back. The near side wheel caught the bury wall, and Jesse, looking back over his shoulder, saw Mr Yarby go plunging headlong into the muck.

'Deuce!' Jimmy muttered. 'You've done it now!'

'By God!' Mr Yarby shouted, stumbling about, up to the tops of his gaiters in muck. 'You did that on purpose, you young swine!'

'No!' Jesse said. 'I never did!'

'Great useless clod! I've had about enough of you! You think I'm daft but I saw you leaving the horses up there in the Outmost a few weeks ago!'

'That was the day my daughter was born. I was only gone two ticks.'

'You were gone twelve minutes. I timed it myself. I gave you a chance for Goody's sake, but this is the finish! You can damn well clear out right this minute!'

'You surely don't mean that, Mr Yarby?'

'Clear out, I said!'

'Here!' said Jimmy. 'That ent hardly fair, master—'

'You hold your tongue or you'll follow!'

'You surely don't mean it,' Jesse said. 'Not leave my job! Where'd I get another at this time of year?'

'Don't ask me! Just get off my farm! Perhaps Mrs Lannam will look after you, seeing she's such a friend of yours!'

'What about my pay?'

'I'll give it to Goody on Saturday.'

Numbly, Jesse climbed down from the cart. He stood for a moment in a daze, resting his hand on Goldie's neck. Then he turned away and reached for his jacket.

'Go to Awner at Noak,' Jimmy murmured. 'He'll give you a job.'

'Thanks, I'll try him,' Jesse said.

He took a cut across the fields and followed the turnpike till he came to Noak Hall. He found the farmer clearing a ditch in the home pasture.

'Yarby in one of his puffs, is he? Ah, well, he's a worried man. Aping your betters costs a pretty penny. You know what they say about his kind?—

'Son learning latin-o,
Daughters dressed in satin-o,
Wife at the pian-o,
All to ruination go.'

'Ah,' Jesse said. 'You may be right. I wouldn't know.'

Awner, a sharp-eyed man with a jolly manner hiding a nature hard as nails, was willing to take Jesse on.

'But I can't promise more than the odd bit of ditching. A lot depends what I have to pay you. Will a shilling a day be all right?'

'I reckon so.'

'Then when can you start?'

'Now, this instant. Just give me the spades.'

That day saw the last of the open weather. The night brought a change, and the wind went round to the coldest quarter. There were a few people, and Goody was one, who awoke some time in the small hours, felt the change in their old bones, and had an inkling of what it portended. The long, mild autumn was gone, and the long bitter winter had come hard behind it, nipping its heels with the first frost.

Every night, on his way through the woods, Jesse picked up dead branches and carried them home, for Goody was right; they needed good fires that winter, and half their firewood was gone already. They needed all the food they could get, too, for their pig that year had died of lung fever.

One night, when he was pulling a dead branch of oak from the tangled thicket, a cock pheasant leapt into flight before him, and instinct sent him sprawling forward, arms outstretched and hands clutching. In one move, he had the pheasant against his chest. In another, he had wrung its neck. The feel of its warm body, limp yet twitching between his hands, filled him with horror, but once the bird was perfectly still, his horror passed. Death was a terrible, terrible thing, but death was nothing compared with dying.

He carried the bird home inside his jacket. Goody plucked it and cooked it that evening, taking care to burn every feather in the fire.

'I'd have liked one or two for my hat,' she said, 'but a pheasant's feathers tell too good a tale.' And then she said: 'Poaching is bad, boy, especially here, where the keepers are devils.'

'My dad used to say that a bird or a rabbit belonged to nobody until it was catched.'

'Well,' Goody said, patting her stomach, 'there's a part of that bird that's truly mine now.'

Jesse worked six days a week at Noak and earned five

shillings and sixpence. Goody worked five long mornings at Checketts and earned half-a-crown. But they were lucky, Goody said, for they had their full health and strength, an acre of garden that yielded well, and no rent to pay for the Pikehouse. And Jesse, coming home through the cold and the dark of those winter evenings, to a welcoming light shining out of the window; to a good fire burning inside; to his two women and tiny daughter, felt that he was lucky indeed.

There was comfort and warmth in that small kitchen. And there would be the day's stew: thickened with oatmeal; flavoured with thyme; swimming with onions, carrots, and parsnips; with potatoes still in their tasty skins; and with little dumplings, each containing some surprise, such as a spoonful of mushroom ketchup or a small cube of brawn. And later, just for an hour or so before bed-time, they would gather round close to the fire: he and Beth side by side on the settle; Goody creaking backwards and forwards in her rocking-chair opposite; and Betony in her cot between them. They would sit with the firelight hot and red on their faces, while outside the circle, the shadows flickered up to the ceiling and the cold wind crept at the walls. Then, if Jesse could get her started, Goody would talk of the old days.

'Go on,' he would say. 'Tell us the things you used to get up to when you was a girl living at Springs. You and all them brothers and sisters.'

And Goody would talk of Bob, who had gone to Australia; of William and Perce, who had gone to New Zealand; of Gret, who had married a prince's coachman and gone to live in a palace in Russia; of Lennard, who had a couple of wives too many and got into trouble with the law; and of Thomas, her favourite, who had died in the first quarry disaster in 1851.

'You'd have liked Thomas,' Jesse said, turning to Beth. 'He was the best of the whole bunch.'

'But you never knew him. He died before you was born.'

'Why, yes,' he said. 'But I reckon I know him just the same. I know them all, as if they was sitting with us this minute.' Looking at Beth, he saw her smile. 'You're laughing at me again, ent you? Oh yes you are! I saw it plain.'

'You do make me laugh sometimes.'

'Ah, I reckon that's why you married me, because I'm always good for a laugh.'

He liked to see her smiling and laughing. It made him feel very warm and happy, and brought his own laughter bubbling up inside him. Her smile was special, somehow, perhaps because it came so rarely. The sight of it always took him by surprise, and he would watch her until it faded.

Sometimes, however, he was anxious; because he had no regular work; because the worst of the winter was yet to come. Now that the ground was hard with frost, Awner was paying him by the piece, but he dared not grumble, for soon even ditching would come to a halt. Goody told him not to worry. 'We shan't starve! Not while we've got our health and strength. We'll have to look lively, that's all, picking up bits and bobs all round.'

The weather worsened. There was bitter frost every day and night. The morning Awner paid him off, Jesse tramped twenty miles, looking for work on every farm, but returned without so much as a promise. The next day, he called on a friend, Charley Bailey, who lived in a shanty on Norton common. He left with a ferret and ten nets.

Just about dusk, he went to an oak in the older part of Scoate woods, and netted seven holes that ran down between the roots and rudges. He put the ferret into the eighth hole and stopped the opening with a clod of earth. He sat on his haunches and prepared to wait.

Outside the woods, the light was only now fading, the first stars coming up in the sky. But inside the woods, it was already as dark as night, especially here in the oak and beech woods. Jesse never once looked upwards, for the light of the stars would impair his night-sight: he kept his gaze upon the ground, eyes sharp yet relaxed, like a badger's, and from where he crouched, he could see six of the netted holes at a glance.

Beneath him, a slight thrill ran through the ground. He felt it in one of the roots at his feet. He leant forward, ready to spring, and the rabbit hurtled into the net, rolling over and over, pulling the draw-strings tight behind him and wrenching the pegs clean out of the ground. Jesse chopped at its neck with the edge of his hand, and it was dead, with the one blow. He took it from the net and put it into his coat pocket.

The ferret appeared at the mouth of the hole, nose in the air, whiskers twitching. But when Jesse tried to take it, it turned and vanished again down the hole. So he replaced the net and sat on his heels for another wait.

Another rabbit bounded out and he killed it quickly. He put it into his other pocket. He had two does and was well pleased. They were not only bigger but sweeter to eat than the johnny bucks.

This time the ferret was gone so long that he feared it might be lying in. He got down on his hands and knees, put his mouth to the nearest hole, and gave a few little tight-lipped squeaks. The ferret emerged, nosing inquiringly into the net. Jesse caught it behind the shoulders and put it quickly into its bag. He put the nets and pegs in his pockets. Then he stood up and started for home.

The keeper, MacNab, was crossing the clearing, his twin-barrel gun in the crook of his arm, and his dog, a springer spaniel, close at his heels. Jesse stood perfectly still, his back to a tree, while man and dog walked past him. He waited as long as it took to count fifty and then he moved, slowly and cautiously, planting each foot as though walking on eggs.

'Right!' said MacNab, somewhere behind him. 'Step out to the clearing where I can see you and don't try any tricks!'

Jesse turned and ran full pelt, away from the sound of the keeper's voice, into the thickest part of the wood. The keeper shouted. The dog barked. The place became full of the trampling of feet and the smashing of old dead timber. Jesse dived at a clump of brambles, just as the keeper fired his first barrel. He received the skitter of shot in his legs, from his feet and ankles all the way up to his thighs and buttocks. He crawled forward, further and further into the thicket, and lay still, resting his face on a bed of dry dead leaves and prickles.

'Right, you!' the keeper shouted. 'I can see you fine so don't move!'

He fired again, but away off into the trees, and Jesse, knowing the man was only bluffing, trusted to luck and lay still. He heard MacNab reloading his gun, and heard him beginning to walk away, calling the dog to come to heel. But the dog was pushing into the thicket that gave Jesse shelter. He felt its cold body go brushing past him, then its warm tongue licking his face.

'Floss?' called MacNab. 'Floss, where are you? Damn and blast! Can't you come when I call?'

MacNab was returning. Jesse heard him. He knew the dog would give him away. She was wagging her tail and rustling the dry dead leaves on the brambles. He tried to push her away from him but now she was eagerly nuzzling the ferret that squirmed in its bag on the ground at his side.

'Floss?' the keeper called again. 'Got a scent of him, have you? Where are you, then, Floss?'

The keeper's voice came very close. His feet trod the brash at the edge of the thicket. His twinbarrel probed the bramble canes. But he dared not shoot because of his dog.

'Damn you!' he said, in his thick Scots voice. 'Are you after rabbits, you damned useless bitch?'

Jesse put his arm round the dog and held her against him. With his other hand he released the ferret. Surprised at its freedom, it remained still, sitting up on its little haunches, sniffing the air with quivering nose. It remained so close that its whiskers tickled Jesse's face, and its smoky smell was strong in his nostrils. Then, swiftly, it darted away. The spaniel wriggled and strained to be free, whining and crying in her throat, and after a moment, Jesse let her go.

She broke away from the thicket immediately under the keeper's feet, and the man swore, hurrying off in pursuit. Jesse heard her scrabbling the hard frozen earth of a rabbit burrow, where the ferret had gone to ground, and heard her yelp as the keeper swung at her with his boot.

'Come out of that, you useless bitch!'

Jesse waited, and when keeper and dog had gone off through the wood, he crawled from the thicket and stood up. His legs were very stiff and numb, but when he moved, they came to life again all too quickly. The pellets in his flesh were lumps of fire, pulsing and throbbing, and a few that had penetrated his left instep were scraping like gravel against the bone.

Once he was out of the old oak and beech wood, into the new plantation of pines, he was able to run quickly, making straight for the old turnpike. The moon was up now, white and bright, in its third quarter, and because of it, when he reached the road, he was able to see that a keeper stood guard there, patrolling the boundary of the woods.

Jesse got down flat on his stomach and crawled into the roadside ditch. Its bottom was ice, and he lay upon it full length, with the frosted grasses arching above him. The ice was soothing. Its coldness struck up through his clothes, slowing the pumping of hot blood, quenching the fires that throbbed in his flesh, sending his whole body to sleep. And as his body went to sleep, so did his brain, numbly and coldly, in a dead faint.

When he awoke, the moon was shining fully upon him. He struggled up on deadened arms and peered through the grasses fringing the ditch. The road was empty. The keeper had gone.

Inch by inch, he got on his knees. He struck at himself to bring the blood alive in his veins. He tried to stand up but only rolled over, slowly and daintily, head over heels, unaware of falling until he found himself on his back, staring up at the staring moon. He got on all fours and crawled to the road, and there he tried again to rise.

Something was badly wrong with his legs. He couldn't feel them. They had gone dead. Something was wrong with his head too. It was full of echoing, empty space. He went down again, and this time he lay there, going back into the cold deep sleep. But now there were footsteps coming along the frozen road. Now there were voices calling his name. And now there were arms about his body. Lifting him up. Bearing him on. He was wondering who, and what, and where, when suddenly his head fell back and the white moon put out its light.

He was burning hot. He was burning cold. His body was heavy, a dead weight upon his soul. His body was light and floated on air. It was gone altogether, like melted ice, and his soul was a flame, or two little flames, burning in darkness. He was rather worried about the moon going out like that, because Goody liked to hang her washing out in the moonlight, to make it white, and what would she do if there was no moon?

He could hear voices ... Beth's and Goody's ... quietly talking a long way away, but coming nearer all the time; cool words like hands, touching him coolly; drawing the blankets away from his mouth.

'Goody?' he heard Beth say, and her voice was suddenly very close. 'He ent going to die, is he, Goody?'

He wanted to speak. To offer some comfort. But his tongue was locked. He had no voice. And, anyway, what could he say when he himself did not know the answer? He could only lie still, waiting for Goody to answer instead.

'Laws! It'll take more than a handful of shot and a bite of cold to kill that boy! Of course he tarnal well ent going to die!'

'Why, no,' he said, deep inside himself, down in the burning cold and dark. 'I ent going to die. Oh, lumme, no. No lections of that!'

And just before he slipped into sleep, he heard Beth's voice again, close by.

'Goody,' she said, '*I saw him smile.*'

When he was better and allowed to get up, and he saw the deep snow lying all about, he stared in amazement. He felt he'd been gone from the world for ages. He could not believe it was only ten days.

'Snow,' he kept saying. 'That was all hard frost when I saw it last. I feel I've lost a whole chunk of my life.'

'You're lucky,' said Goody. 'You could've lost the whole lot!'

And when, growing stronger, he wanted to venture out of doors, she went to the mantelpiece, took down a tin that had once held tobacco, and rattled its contents under his nose.

'That's the shot that came out of your body! And a rare old job we had picking it out! So come home here with another load like that, and there'll be ructions, you mark my words!'

'Don't worry. I shan't go down further than the Uptops.'

'Bits of nuts and bolts and all sorts we twizzed out of you, boy!'

'And don't I know it!' he said, feeling himself tenderly.

'If that there keeper comes snooping round here, I'll throw all that shot in his nasty red face!' Goody said. 'Ho, yes! I'll give him MacNab!'

Jesse walked with a limp now, for two bits of shot had entered his foot, and although Goody had taken them out and the place had healed well enough, there remained some weakness in the instep, as though the bone had been displaced.

'You should give it time,' Beth told him. 'Don't be in such a hurry to walk about on it. You've got plenty to do indoors.'

'Why, yes, I'm busy as wheels. Look here, what I've made for my daughter, out of these little scraps of wood. That's a cow. That's a horse. And this one here will be a pig when I've finished carving a proper snout.'

'I'm glad you told me,' Beth said. 'Potatoes on legs, they look like to me.'

'Well, Betony knows what they are, anyway. She's been lying there, watching me make them. She knows that's a pig. She grunted at it.'

As soon as he could walk any distance, he went to Noak to ask for work. Awner had a wheat-stack he wanted threshed. He offered Jesse tenpence a day.

'Tenpence!' Jesse said. 'I call that mean, seeing it should be one and six by rights.'

He was rather surprised at himself for speaking out so boldly. He had never used such strong words before. But a great many things were coming more easily to him these days.

'Take it or leave it,' Awner said.

'I can't afford to leave it, as you well know, Mr Awner. That's exactly what makes it mean.'

When the threshing was finished he was idle again. There was more snow and he went with Goody every morning to help her dig a way through the drifts.

He was gathering sticks at the edge of the woods one day when Mrs Lannam rode up on her big black mare.

'You're guilty of trespass. Did you know that?'

'With respect, ma'am, we've had the chatting rights in these here woods since the year dot-and-carry-one.'

'Well, provided you don't damage the trees . . . or go after game . . .'

'Game? Why, that'd be poaching!'

'Yes, my fine fellow! You may open your eyes as wide as you please, but my keepers are very suspicious of you young men around these farms.'

'Keepers is always suspicious. It's what they're paid for. It's their nature, too, especially if they happen to be Scotch.'

'I never mentioned MacNab by name.'

'No more didn't I,' Jesse said.

He stooped and put a few pine-cones into his sack, and a few bits of stick. When he straightened again, she was still watching him with pale, shining eyes.

'I see you're limping. Why is that?'

'I trod on a nail,' Jesse said.

'You're not very civil, are you. Don't you take off your cap when you speak to your betters?'

'Not in a cold wind like this, ma'am.'

'I think you're a dog!' she said, laughing. 'I ought to give you a taste of my crop, but it would be a pity to mark that fine complexion.'

Jesse stooped to pick up more sticks. He snatched up dead branches, broke them against his bent knee, and put the pieces into his sack. He found it hard to look at the woman directly. Her eyes were too bright and her glance too inquisitive, flickering over him constantly. And her laugh, too, was very strange. It was not, he thought, a womanly laugh. It was husky and rough and rather hard.

'My word, you *are* strong,' she said, pretending to admire the way he broke the little branches. 'It's disgraceful that a strong young man should be idling about the place like this. I suppose you've been laid off because of the snow?'

'Yes. That's about it.'

'Come to Scoate in the morning,' she said. 'You might be able to help MacNab.'

Jesse slung his sack on his shoulder and stood upright, forcing himself to meet her glance.

'I reckon I'd sooner wait,' he said, 'and take my chance on the farms.'

'You mean you refuse?' she said, surprised.

'No, not refuse exactly, ma'am. Just thank you kindly all the same.'

She sat for a moment, straight-backed, still watching him with the same bright glance, though her smile had altered.

'I wonder what you're thinking, looking at me so straight and stolid and blue-eyed?'

'I'm thinking, ma'am, that you shouldn't be standing that mare in the cold.'

'I don't believe you. I think you're sly. Men of your sort! — I'd give a fortune to read your strange minds.'

She brought her horse round sharply and rode away over the snow, staring in at the Pikehouse window as she passed.

In the kitchen, when he went in, Beth was busy making bread, and Betony, lacking attention, lay grizzling quietly to herself. Jesse, without waiting to shed his coat, went at once to bend over the cot.

'What's the matter with my blossom? Is she all wet by any chance?'

'No,' Beth said. 'She's just having a grouse like we all do sometimes.'

'Maybe she wants feeding, then?'

'No. I fed her twenty minutes ago.'

'Well, I dunno! The way she's pursing up her lips, I reckon she wants another helpin.'

'Then you'll have to give it to her yourself.'

'Ah, you've got me there, ent you?'

He took Betony in his arms and held her up against his shoulder. The grizzling stopped. She was all smiles. He put his lips against her cheek and blew a raspberry, and she laughed and gurgled, nuzzling her face against his, her skin soft and warm and smelling milky.

'You're a sprucer,' he said. 'You ent hungry nor you ent wet. You're perfectly come-for-double all the way round.'

'I saw you talking to Mrs Lannam,' Beth said. 'What'd she have to say to you?'

'Eh? What, her? Why, nothing, really.'

'She took some time, saying nothing.'

'Well, about the bad weather, that's all. The snow and that. And about being laid off at the farm.'

'It's a pity she couldn't do something useful, like putting you in the way of some work.'

'Ah well,' Jesse said. 'She did in a way, in a manner of speaking as you might say. Only I said no.'

'You said what!' Beth exclaimed.

'She talked about helping MacNab, you see. But lumme! That's not my kind of work. Not keepering.'

'Since when've you been so fussy what you do?'

'That ent fussy. That's common sense.'

'Keepering brings in wages, surely? It's better than having nothing at all.'

'Maybe. Maybe not.' He laid Betony in her cot and went to look out of the window. 'But I ent going just the same.'

'Oh, you ent? 'Cos it don't just suit you! It ent quite exactly what you wanted?'

'That's right.'

'Well, that's a pity, that is, I'm sure! I'm sorry for you! I am, that's a fact. I suppose you prefer going poaching and getting yourself riddled with shot.'

'I'd sooner get shot than work with them that does the shooting. And besides—'

'Besides what?'

'Nothing,' he said. 'Just besides, that's all.'

'I suppose it's growing on you, this loafing about, doing nothing? Doubtless it suits you, stalking about with your hands in your pockets, coming and going just as you please?'

'Ah,' he said, staring out at the blinding snow. 'That suits me humpty-dinker.'

'Then take yourself off!' Beth said. 'Before I fetch you a clout by the ear! It makes me boil to think of Goody traipsing to Checketts every day while you stroll about like a little lord. I'd be ashamed if I was you! So get out of here before I turn nasty and say something sharp!'

'Ah, I'm going!' Jesse said, and stumped to the door. 'Now this instant! No delay!'

The world was very still and quiet in the snow. What few sounds there were travelled strangely, like the smack of axes cutting timber, a sound that bounced in its own echo: chacker . . . chacker . . . all around.

Jesse tracked it down at last, and came to a wood of ash and chestnut. There, at work with their axes, felling an ash tree, were two men: twin brothers, it seemed, for both were black-bearded and hook-nosed and both were equal in size, strength and temper.

'Is there work here?' Jesse asked.

'No,' they answered, speaking together.

'I've done some felling. Not much, but a bit. I worked for William Tewke of Huntlip.'

'The answer's still no,' one man said, 'so sling your hook.'

'If I was you I'd have lopped a few branches before I started felling that tree. She's going a terrible lumper when she goes.'

The two men stopped work and looked at each other. Then one of them turned, swinging his axe up between his hands, till the blade lay flat on his hairy palm.

'Get out,' he said, 'or I'll split you through from head to foot.'

Jesse turned and trudged away, and the smack of the axes started again. Chacker. Chacker. All around.

The world was very quiet and bare in the snow. The uplands were empty. Nothing moved. He went from Strutts to Deery Hill, from Palmer's Cross to the Big Man Stone, from Plug Lane to Litchett and Wadhill, without meeting a single soul.

At Wadhill, some gipsies were camping under the marl-bank. Their tent was pitched on a piece of ground scraped clean of snow and spread with matting, and a baby lay in a basket inside. The mother was cleaning a flannel shirt by rubbing it on her knuckles in the snow. The father sat on a log by the fire and smoked a clay pipe. And three children, a girl and two boys, sat on their hunkers, toasting their naked knees at the fire, where a round black pot hung steaming on a tripod.

Jesse stood, saluting them with open hand, the way his father had always saluted gipsies. But the dark shining eyes in the dark bony faces only stared and stared, without a flicker, until he turned and trudged away.

From the round hill at Checketts, known as the Hump, he could see the farm buildings among the elms; could see when someone moved about the yards; and could see where the cattle, eating the hay put out in the pasture, had trampled the snow till it looked like brown demerara sugar. He could see the whole of the Vale of Scarne, where the Naff ran, a winding ribbon black as ink, between the flat white meadows of snow. He could see to the outermost rim of the earth.

As the day wore on, it grew misty, and at three o'clock more snow began to fall; quickly, excitably at first; then softly and slowly, big feathery flakes that filled the sky and hastened the coming of darkness.

Jesse, trudging along the Checketts track, passed within inches of Mr Yarby, who stopped dead, a dark shape in the flying snow, and called out to him by name.

'Izzard? Is that you? Hang it, man! Can't you stop when you're spoken to? I've got something to say to you.'

But Jesse was in no mood to answer, and tramped on, his fists in his pockets, his shoulders hunched, while the snow fell and buried the earth.

That she should turn and speak to him so! And look at him with such glittering eyes! She, who knew him and understood him – that she should turn and rend him like that! He could never entrust himself to her again. The bond was broken between them forever.

He was going home because there was nowhere else to go; because his baby daughter was there, claiming him, heart and soul; but he would have to live inside himself in future, where Beth could not reach him.

Somewhere along the old turnpike he fell in with Goody, and they entered the Pikehouse kitchen together. The warmth of the place gave him gooseflesh. It made him shudder throughout his frame. He stood by the fire, utterly blind and indifferent to Beth, but watching Goody, who was fumbling underneath her skirts, drawing out the string bag which she wore hidden, tied round her waist, and in which she brought home the 'bits and bobs' picked up on the farm.

'One turmot, a few bits of tops, and some sprigs of corn I pulled from the stack. And how did you get on today, boy?'

'Well, I brought in a sack of kindling this morning.'

'So you did!' said Beth, much struck, standing, hands on hips, before him. 'You must be properly fagged, doing that!'

'What's up with you?' Goody demanded.

'He wants to watch out for hisself,' Beth said. 'I shouldn't like him to overdo things.'

Goody gave a little sniff, turning from Beth, who was now busy stirring the stewpot, to Jesse, who stood like a stock on the hearth.

'Mr Yarby sent a message. He says he'll take you back again. Soon as the weather's cleared up.'

'Did he?' said Jesse. 'Ah. There now.'

'You don't seem all that bucked about it.'

'Maybe it don't quite suit him!' said Beth, throwing the words over her shoulder.

'Here!' Goody said. 'What's up with you, girl, all curds and whey?'

'Ask your precious Jesse there! Seems work and him ent all that good friends. Mrs Lannam offered to help him and he was so grand he cocked his nose!'

'What sort of work?' Goody asked.

'Keepering,' Jesse muttered.

'Well,' Goody said, and sat on the settle, her hands in her lap. 'You must be a fool, Jesse Izzard. You could be in clover down there at Scoate, with nothing much to do but keep Mrs Lannam warm in bed.'

'Eh?' said Beth. 'What's that you say?'

'Aw, be quiet,' Jesse said. 'The pair of you! Just hold your tongues!'

'Mrs Lannam?' Beth said. 'Gone and taken a shine to Jesse? I don't believe it!'

'Why not? You went and took a shine on him your own self.'

'But she's gentry. Or supposed to be.'

'The gentry's no different. They're maybe more so if anything.'

'She's married, too.'

'Mr Lannam's over seventy, and frail as a lath. He keeps to his room in winter, they say, and only comes out in summer time to catch a few butterflies in his net.'

'I don't believe it,' Beth said. 'A woman like her! Running after a man like Jesse.'

'Oh, yes! There's many a promising lad has been set up for life after working at Scoate, and it wasn't keepering with MacNab that done it, I can tell you. Ask that husband of yours standing there. He'll have heard a few tales around the farm.'

'Don't talk to *me*,' Jesse said. 'I ent listening. I've closed my ears.'

'Then mind out of my way,' Beth said. 'How can I cook while you stand straddled across the hearth?'

Jesse went and sat at the table. He waited in silence for Beth to serve him, and he ate in silence from beginning to end. There was no savour in the food. He ate only to quell the shivers that racked his inside. He would not look at Beth, who came and went as if nothing had happened. He would not meet her glance when she sat opposite, eating her supper. But he could not close his ears when she spoke, and the sound of her voice, so brisk and cheerful, giving Goody the day's news, made him shrink inside himself, dreadfully. It made him harden against her. It turned him to stone.

And when he lay in bed that night, in the little room under the roof, lit only by the glare of snow outside, he would not watch even her shadow as she undressed, but lay on his back, cold and stiff, and made no move to welcome her when she slid, shivering, between the sheets.

'Still sulking?' she said, lying beside him.

'Ah. That's right.'

'What a waxy great fool you are, ent you?'

'If you say so. You ought to know.'

'You just want to punish me, sulking like this,' she said, 'You hate me, and want to pay me out.'

Not knowing how to answer, he remained silent. No, he didn't hate her, but hatred was there, certainly, because she had plucked down his bright shining pride, and because the good thing that had been between them now lay in ruins, and trust was gone.

'Jesse, I'm cold,' she said, with a shiver.

'Ah,' he said. 'It's a cold night.'

'Jesse, I'm sorry!' And the words came as though from a child.

'Ah, well, and so you should be!' he said roughly.

'I've always had a quick tongue. You know that. And you'd try the patience of Job sometimes ... But there! I've said I'm sorry and I mean it too.'

He turned towards her, a tremendous warmth moving throughout him, melting his bones and turning his blood to tears in his veins. He got on one elbow and leant towards her. His hand moved over her body and came to rest in the warmth of her armpit, and she drew him down to her, pressing his head against her breast.

'Ah, and so you should be sorry!' he said.

CHAPTER TWO

To Jesse, a ploughed field was the loveliest sight in the world, and if he himself had done the ploughing, his joy in the sight was manifold.

The moment he walked his horses on to an old grass ley or a stretch of stubble, he was lord of a little kingdom of acres, and nothing could ever pull him down. From the moment the ploughshare made its first cut, on to the time when the whole field lay brown and bare, he would not change places with any man in the three counties. He walked tall, and his shadow, falling across the sunlit earth, was something to see.

There was something neat and clean and perfect about a field newly ploughed. The sight of it was its own reward, for there a man could see his work made manifest indeed, when nothing came between it and the sky. The soil on these uplands was good loam, overlying clay and marl and gravel. In a drying wind, its surface was tawny. Under sunlight, it looked red. And after rain it became a rich dark brown, like strong tobacco. Jesse liked to see the ploughed fields looking clean and neat and empty. He almost resented the advance of the green corn across his kingdom of brown acres.

He never wanted to be a champion and win the ploughing matches at Chepsworth Park as Jimmy Shodd so often did.

His pride lay in the work itself. It lay in the feel of the stilts in his hands, and the motion of the plough as it ran the furrow. It was enough that he did a man's work; had charge of a team of good horses; and was left alone in the quiet fields in the two best seasons of the year.

'I ent clever,' he said to Beth, 'but ploughing is something I *can* do and not too badly, neither, it seems.'

As Betony grew from a baby into a child, he would take her on his shoulders and carry her around the fields in the evening, pointing out the birds on the ploughed land, the charlock yellow among the corn, the pollen blowing from a field of flowering grasses, or the tracks of a hare under the hedgerow. And Betony, fat little legs astride his shoulders, fat little hands entwined in his hair, would sit like a graven image above him, looking on the world with solemn eyes, as though understanding every word.

Beth often laughed at the way he talked to Betony. 'You'd think her a hundred, the way you go on.' But once, instead of laughing, she accused him of favouring Betony too much and leaving their new daughter out in the cold.

'Why!' he said, feeling very guilty. 'It's only that Janie is still such a morsel, that's all. But if she wants to come along with me, then come she may, for I've got two shoulders and Betony'll have to make do with one so's little Janie can sit on the other.'

He lifted them up, first one, then the other, and there they sat on high together, each held secure by a great square hand.

'There! Your dad's a regular beast of burden now, ent he? And what'll happen when your little brother or sister arrives, eh? I can't manage three. I shall have to make a little cart!'

From up on the ladder, where he was at work, white-washing the Pikehouse walls, Jesse could see a puff of dust moving along the Norton road. He stopped work to watch it: a pony and trap; wheeling round on to the turnpike; drawing up at the Pikehouse gate. With his paint-brush swimming about in the bucket, he climbed down the ladder and hurried to his womenfolk, who were planting potatoes.

'Company!' he said. 'Seems your grandpa is coming to call.'

Beth, who was big with their third child, straightened slowly, one hand pressing against her side, and looked towards the gate.

'So he is,' she said calmly.

'My stars,' said Goody, coming forward with her apron full of potato seed. 'Lord Sawdust hisself!'

The old man came clumping along the path, his shoulders held stiffly, his head erect, his hat well forward over his brow. He came to a halt in front of them, crossing his hands on the knob of his stick, and looked at each of them in turn, stubbornly resolved to face them out.

'Hah! I've struck you all of a heap, I can see! You didn't expect a visit from me, did you?'

He turned and looked at the two little girls: Betony, watching from among the currant bushes, and Janie, crawling about the path.

'I always said you'd quicken easy. But why does it have to be girls, girls? Still, by the look of you, there's another due directly, so maybe you'll have a son this time.'

'Maybe I shall,' Beth agreed.

'I suppose you're wondering why I've come? Well, it's because I've got a proposition. No, I shan't step indoors. I'd sooner stand and get it done.'

'Just as you please.'

'I want you to come back to Cobbs,' he said. 'You and your husband Jesse here. I'll make him my partner, all drawn up by Baines the lawyer, and his name can go on the gate and waggons, – Tewke and Izzard, the way you wanted it in the first place.'

'What's made you change all of a sudden?'

'That ent sudden. I'm getting old, and there's no one to follow me in the business, so I've got no choice but to humble myself to you, have I? I borrowed a leaf out of your book and done like you did when you was a youngster and came to me for help that time. You remember that?'

'I remember.'

'Well, there you are, – the mountain has come to the mommet,' he said.

'What about Kit Maddox?' Beth asked. 'Ent he in favour no more?'

Her grandfather gave her a shrewd glance.

'Don't you get all the news from your mother? She comes to see you often enough.'

'She said Kit was drinking, if that's what you mean.'

'Drinking! Hah! He soaks like a sponge, that boy, and he's tarnal well ruined hisself as a craftsman. Such hands as he had! And such an eye! – All lost now with drinking and fooling about all round. He's took up with some slut he brought home from Chepsworth, and they're living together bold as brass, and got a child, though nobody ever seems to see it. Ah, he's gone to the bad, that boy, and it's all your fault for letting him down the way you did.'

'He always was bad,' Beth said, 'like an apple with the maggot in it.'

'Ah, well! It's history now. So what d'you say to my proposition?'

'I can't answer straight out like that. I'll have to talk to Goody and Jesse.'

'What! What! Yes, maybe so. Well, there's no hurry. No hurry at all! You talk it out and let me have your answer directly.' The old man turned and looked at Jesse. 'You seem pretty fit, young man, and my granddaughter, too. She don't seem to've suffered nothing from marrying you. So let me shake you by the hand to show what's past is past beween us.'

Jesse wiped his hand on his trousers and gave it to the old man to shake. He tried to speak, but was given no chance.

'As for you, Goody Izzard! You needn't stay here in this little box of a house by yourself, you know. There's plenty of room for you at Cobbs. But I must be off and leave you to talk the matter over. I'll expect your answer as soon as maybe.'

'Old snake!' Goody muttered, as they watched him drive off.

'Laws,' Jesse said. 'We ent going to pull ourselves up by the roots like that, are we?'

'Not me!' Goody said. 'I ent leaving my little box of a

house for nobody. But that don't stop you two from going if you want to.'

'We shouldn't want to leave you by yourself, Goody,' Beth said.

'That's nothing. It's yourselves you must think of. Not me.'

'Then it rests with Jesse,' Beth said. 'But goodness, man, what's up with you? You look like you've swallowed a lump of camphor.'

'Yes, well,' Jesse said, staring into his pail of whitewash. 'You're asking me to give up going to plough, ent you?'

'When?' Beth demanded. 'When did I ask you? I don't recall asking you nothing!'

'But you think we should go, though, I dare say?'

'Not if you don't want to, boy. Oh dear me no! We'll put the matter out of our minds and let my grandfather know according.'

'I never said I didn't *want* to go, exactly.'

'My stars!' Beth said. 'It's hard to know what you do want, the way you durdle and get nothing said! Suppose you get on with whitening the house and try unpicking the knots in your brain while you're at it? Then perhaps we'll know where we stand.'

'Ah,' Jesse said, and went back to his ladder.

When he had finished, and the walls were a dazzling new white again, and he had washed himself under the pump, Goody called him in to supper. He sat at the table and watched Beth cutting the bread.

'I've thought,' he said, having waited in vain for her to ask him. 'I've thought about it and I reckon we'll go. I've been counting all the different points.'

'That's a marvel, that is. Let's hear what they are.'

'Well, a carpenter gets nearly twice what a farm labourer gets, for a start.'

'That's true. We'd be rich, very nearly.'

'Then, again, I shouldn't be laid off at Cobbs as I am often-times at Checketts when things is bad in winter.'

'Another point, true as the first. You've sorted your thoughts out pretty nicely.'

'Then, again, if our third child should chance to be a son,

126

well, that's a wonderful start for my boy, to be born into a trade like that.'

'True again,' Beth said. 'Any more points to come?'

'Well, not exactly,' he said, fidgeting with a knife on the table, 'except that your grandpa shook me by the hand.'

'So he did, to be sure! I saw it myself, large as life.'

'It's all very well, laughing at me so solemn and all, but just you think! – A partner in a proper business! Tewke and Izzard, your grandfather said. Just think of that! I reckon they go pretty well together, don't you?'

'Like stew and dumplings!' Goody said, setting the teapot down with a thump beside him. 'Like liver and lights! Or fleas and hedgehogs! They go together humpty-dinker. Now move your elbows, Tewke and Izzard, and make room for me.'

'Goody,' Beth said. 'Are you sure you don't mind our leaving you?'

'Not me!' Goody said. 'Why should I indeed? With my own featherbed to sleep in again and no crying babies to wake me up? I'll be in clover and no mistake.'

She rattled a spoon on to the table and whisked the cosy from the pot. She looked first at Beth and then at Jesse, treating each to a sharp little frown.

'You mean to visit me sometimes, I suppose, and bring the children to see me in my little box of a house? Right you are, then! You get on and fashion your lives and never mind about studying me. Why, I can hardly wait to see you go!'

Jesse had never been inside the house at Cobbs before, and secretly he found it daunting. There were too many rooms and too many passages; too many staircases everywhere; he lost his way often at first, and Kate, hustling him out of the stillroom or pantry, or out of the passage that led to the cellar, seemed to think he was queer in the head.

'But there!' she said, talking to Beth in front of him. 'It's not what he's used to, a great house like this. We must make allowances, I suppose.'

He was rather frightened of Kate: she used so many unfamiliar words. Furniture at the Pikehouse had always been simple, with simple names such as dresser or cupboard or shelf or stool. But here at Cobbs, according to Kate, he must say 'chiffonier' and 'whatnot' and 'pouffe'.

'Your mother is desperate grand,' he whispered, alone with Beth in the parlour, before tea the Sunday they arrived. 'She's rather a lady, ent she, the way she talks?'

'It's the house,' Beth said. 'She got grand ideas when she came here and they've grown worse while I've been away.'

'What was it she called that there chest when she was talking just now?'

'A commode,' Beth said.

'A commode. That's right. I heard it plain.' He looked at the polished mahogany chest, with its three big drawers and its shiny brass handles, and shook his head in perplexity. 'I always thought a commode was something else entirely,' he said.

Kate's greatest joy on their arrival was in the two children, Betony and Janie, and she kept swooping upon them to give them biscuits or knobs of sugar. Grandfather Tewke also paid them a lot of attention and had them up to sit on his lap. He let them examine his silver watch-chain; his coins with the head of King William IV; and the watch itself, with its two little doors and pretty engraving.

'I'm told you can talk,' he said to Betony, 'so you ought to be able to call me granddad.'

'Say granddad,' urged Jesse, whispering into Betony's ear.

'Dad-dad,' she said.

'D'you call that talking?' the old man demanded. 'Oh, you do, do you? Then we'll have to take your word and your nod, shan't we?' He let them slide down from his knees and watched them as they went to Beth. 'I've got nothing against girls. They've got their uses like anything else. But it's that there boy I've set my sights on. Oh, yes, I'm counting on him!'

'Supposing it's another girl?'

'Get away!' he said. 'Nobody don't have girls forever. It ent on the cards. No, this third one coming will be a boy. I can feel it in my bones.'

Jesse's worst moment was on Monday morning, when he walked into the workshop yard and saw by the men's faces that they had not been warned of his coming.

'My grandson-in-law,' said grandfather Tewke, and allowed his words to fall with full weight: 'my grandson-in-law's come back, as you see, and from now on he'll be my partner and right-hand-man.'

There was a silence, and a few of the men exchanged glances. Steve Hewish was leaning against the workshop wall. He took his pipe from his mouth and looked thoughtfully into the bowl.

'I suppose, in that case, we'd better call him Mister Izzard?'

'Laws no!' Jesse said. 'I've never been nothing but Jesse here, nor never will be, I shouldn't think.'

'You've always been Jesse Slowsides to us,' said Sam Lovage. 'But now you're Jesse Sideways, I reckon, if we call you by your limp. What happened to you? Was you trod by a heifer?'

'Ah, we heard you'd gone back to the farm,' Steve said. 'What made you give it up? Too much brain work for you, was it?'

'Enough of that!' grandfather Tewke said sharply. 'Jesse here has got to be treated with proper respect. Is that understood?'

'Proper respect, – yes, surely,' said Sam. 'After all, he married Beth.'

'Christ!' said Kit Maddox. 'We all know why she chose him! She likes her own way, that's why, and wanted a mud-scrape to wipe her feet on whenever she felt inclined that way. She wanted a man who'd always be putty in her hands.'

In looks, Kit had changed. With his drooping moustache and thick streaks of grey in his black hair, he seemed middle-aged, although not yet thirty. He had grown lantern-jawed, and his skin was furrowed from eyes to mouth. He still dressed in a showy way, and wore a thick green leather belt, much adorned with shiny clips and badges, but his clothes were not smart as in days gone by: they were ragged and dirty and ill-fitting.

'Well?' he said. 'I'm speaking the truth, ent I? We may as well have it out in the open. What say you, Jesse Sideways?'

'I don't much mind *why* she married me,' Jesse said. 'She just did and that's all-about-it.'

'It's certainly shot you up in the world. Partner! Hah! Don't make me laugh! You wouldn't be nothing if it wasn't for Beth.'

'Maddox!' said grandfather Tewke, in a warning voice. 'I won't have none of you talking to Jesse in that way, so mark it, man, or you'll get the push!'

Kit shrugged. He said no more, but walked away to the side of the yard, there to open his trousers and make water against the hedge.

That first day in the workshop was the longest Jesse had ever known, and there were many more such days to follow. After so long away from carpentering, his work was poorer than ever, and grandfather Tewke was constantly at him for wasting his time and timber and nails.

'Laws, gaffer,' Steve Hewish would say at these times, 'your right-hand-man is only a left-handed sinner after all, I'm sorry to say.'

The men had always been quick to make game of Jesse, but now that his name had gone up on the sign-board, jealousy made them extra spiteful. They withheld advice, letting him finish a piece of bad work before they pointed out the errors, and then, when they did speak out, it was always in front of the old man, and always with a false politeness.

'Mister Izzard, – or Jesse if I might presume to call you that – did you honestly mean to put that there fingle on upside down?'

Once, when he was shaving a bar for a sheep-crib, he leant clumsily on his draw-knife and broke the blade with a loud crack. He caught a few smiles on the faces around him and heard Bob Green make some remark. But no one spoke to him directly. They were waiting, as always, for grandfather Tewke to bawl him out. And then, as he was bending over his toolbag, with a great bitterness rising in him, a shadow fell across the ground and a new draw-knife was laid on the stool beside him. He glanced up, and there was George Hopson, the gloomiest, most taciturn man in the workshop, already walking away, without waiting for a word of thanks.

Kit was an open enemy from the start and was always

trying to provoke a quarrel; by elbowing Jesse out of the way, allowing timbers to fall on his foot, or making remarks about Beth.

'I saw Madam in the orchard this morning. She looked through me as if I was glass. That made me laugh, I can tell you, 'cos she was sweet on me at one time.'

Jesse said nothing, but went on working.

'D'you hear me?' Kit said, 'Or are you dunny as well as daft?'

'No,' Jesse said. 'And if you're wanting to use the lathe, there's no need to jostle 'cos I'm just finished.'

Early in May, they were all out at Middening, felling timber in Sudge woods. The days were cool, with short sharp showers that made the air smell fresh and sweet, and a brisk wind that kept the white clouds moving swiftly high up in the spring-blue sky.

The timber was oak, all well-grown trees, tall and straight and thick in the stem. Work started at seven in the morning and stopped when the light had gone from the woods, and all day the passing time was told and measured, not by a clock as at the workshop, but by the smack of the axe, the whanging of the two-handled saw, the ring of the hammer hitting a wedge, and the crash of a tree as it fell to the ground.

Every day, a fire was lit in the middle of the clearing, to burn the brash and the worthless loppings, and the smell of the wood smoke would drift strong and sharp on the rain-washed air. Jesse carried the smell of the wood-smoke home with him, in his clothes and hair, and the stain of the oak-bark brown on his hands. 'I smell like a rasher of bacon,' he said once to Beth. 'Or a kippered herring – I ent sure which.'

He had more joy in those days in the woods than he had known since returning to Cobbs. They were good days, and he worked well. He came to know the balance and swing of his axe, and the feel of the smooth hickory handle, fitting exactly into his hands, as though it were but a part of himself. He learnt to let the weight of the axe be master of the weight of the stroke, and he came to judge the bite of the blade to a shaving. The work was good, and its strong rhythm got into his blood, leaving him somehow free and clear-eyed.

The men, too, enjoying the change of surroundings and the change of work, were all in good humour, and Timothy Rolls, who was often Jesse's partner in stripping the bark from a fallen tree, now talked to him in a friendly way.

'The smell of the woods is a proper tonic. And that ent just a manner of speaking. — I mean it like gospel. It's snuffing the smell of the juices that does it. Cleans your lungs out all the way through!'

Every morning now, it was Jesse's job to fetch the two horses from Anster and follow grandfather Tewke to Sudge woods. But one morning, a Wednesday in May, Kate ran after him across the fields.

'It's Beth!' she said. 'She's fell on her back on the bedroom floor.'

'Laws!' he said. 'Is she hurt bad?'

'No, no, but it's started her pains and she's asking for Goody to come and tend her.'

Jesse left the horses and ran with Kate towards the house.

'I'll take the trap. I'll be quicker that way. You go in and look after Beth.'

He drove straight to Checketts and brought Goody back at a rattling speed.

'Should I ought to fetch the doctor?'

'I'll tell you that when I've seen your Beth.'

At half past ten he was allowed upstairs to the bedroom, and as he went in, Goody came to him with his child in her arms.

'You've got a son and I'm told his name is William Walter.'

He took the child and moved to the bed. His head spun: he was trying to look at his wife and son at once. Beth lay very still and watched him, her eyes very pale, as if shock and pain had washed out their colour. Yet her gaze was as clear and calm as ever, and just as steady: it always astonished him, the calm steady look of her clear eyes.

'Are you all right, then?' he asked gently.

'Right as ninepence,' she said in a whisper.

'Goody?' he said. 'Is she telling the truth, this wife of mine?'

'She's as right as she can expect to be after turning somersaults on that mat,' Goody said. 'She should take things easy for a while, however.'

'And my son? Is he in good order too?'

'He's all there, if that's what you mean. A bit quiet, maybe, but so he might be, with his mother shaking him out so rudely, before he'd sent word he was ready to come. But he'll be all right. We'll see to that.'

'Wife, you gave me a turn,' Jesse said.

'You ought to go. My grandpa'll be wondering where you've got to.'

'I ought, I suppose. I've left the horses out there somewhere. Here, who'll take my son?'

When he arrived at Sudge, the men had stopped for their elevenses. Timothy Rolls sat on a log, toasting a piece of cheese at the fire, and Fred Lovage was warming his tea in a tin mug.

'Where the hell have you been?' asked grandfather Tewke, as Jesse arrived with the horses. 'We can't hardly move here for want of carting these butts away.'

'It's Beth,' Jesse said. 'She had a fall and it's brought the baby double quick.'

'God almighty! Why didn't you say so? Is she all right? Eh? Is she? And what about him?'

'A boy sure enough, and doing all right, Goody says. And he's going to be called William Walter, after you and my own dad.'

'D'you hear that, Lovage? D'you hear that, Rolls? I've got a great-grandson, – William Walter he's going to be called – to inherit the business when I'm gone.' And grandfather Tewke went striding about from one to another, striking each of them on the back. 'By God! It's a change to have something the way I want it for once. A great-grandson! Just think of that!'

'Well, I congratulate you, gaffer,' said Steve Hewish. 'Though come to think of it, Jesse here done all the work.'

'Ah, I'd never've thought he had it in him,' said Sam Lovage.

'Jesse,' said Fred. 'You can share my tea!'

'And my Welsh rabbit,' said Timothy Rolls.

'Did you get Dr Wells?' asked grandfather Tewke.

'Goody said there wasn't no need.'

'Well! All's well that ends well! And Goody shall have a whole drum of snuff from me for this.'

'I'd say this calls for a celebration,' said Timothy. 'What're you going to do to mark the occasion for us, gaffer?'

'You can mark the occasion by getting a move on to do some work! Grandson or no, we've idled enough for one day, so eat them elevenses and get off your backsides, quick sharp! I'm taking the horses to pick up the crab.'

All except Kit Maddox had come to shake Jesse by the hand. He now drew near for the first time.

'Funny, ent it, the way we're so different? I never went to hold my wife's hand when my son was born.'

The men fell silent. Most of them drifted slowly away.

'Jesse Sideways?' Kit said. 'I'm talking to you!'

'You're spitting a bit, too,' Jesse said, wiping his hand across his eyes.

'So what? Is that something?'

'Look,' Jesse said. 'I know you're jealous of me but it's no use trying to start a quarrel 'cos I shan't play my proper part.'

'Jealous! I've got no cause to be jealous of you!'

'Fine. That's humpty-dinker, then, ent it? We can get back to work.'

'Don't tell *me* when to get back to work!'

'I've told you, – I ent a fighting man, so it's no use your crowding me up like this.'

'If I was to hit you, would that make you fight?'

'It might,' Jesse said. 'Or it might not. I can't be sure. But I ent scared of you if that's what you mean, 'cos I'm about twice your weight and build, and my hands don't shake so bad as yours, neither. So you hold your tongue and leave me be and I'll do the same for you exactly.'

He turned and went to the lock-up chest where the tools were kept overnight for safety. He took out his knee-pads; his two small axes and rubbing-stone; and his big American axe with the curved handle. He bent over to put on his pads.

The quarrel was almost gone from his mind. He was thinking of Beth and his baby son. But now there came a shout of warning, from two or three of the men at once, and when he looked round, still stooping, fastening a strap, he saw that Kit had taken a burning branch from the fire and was bearing it, smoking fiercely, across the clearing. Jesse was too slow in moving. The burning branch was laid across the back of his neck and held there an instant before he was able to squirm away. The men came running and gathered round, keeping a safe distance from Kit, who threatened them with the burning branch. But grandfather Tewke, descending on them in a passion of rage, snatched the branch from Kit's hand and threw it back on to the fire.

'You're sacked!' he said. 'Get out of these woods before I whip you out as you deserve!'

'Sacked?' Kit repeated. 'You can't do that, without proper warning nor nothing. I ent going to take it. You've got no right!'

'If you don't get out, I'll send for the law and you'll go to gaol for assault, boy!'

'What about my pay? You owe me three days!'

'Get out of my sight,' the old man said, 'and don't let me see you at Cobbs again.'

Jesse, in pain, was on his knees on the ground, fighting a heaving wave of sickness. He saw, dimly, that Kit was collecting his tools to go.

'Jesse?' said grandfather Tewke, just above him. 'Can you hear me, Jesse? Timmy's going to put plantain leaves on that there burn for the moment. Then we're getting you home. D'you hear that?'

'Ah,' Jesse said. 'I hear all right.'

He felt Timmy's fingers like tongs of hot iron upon his neck, and braced himself as his collar was peeled from his burnt flesh. He sucked in his breath between his teeth, and fell forward in a dead faint.

They carried him home unconscious to Cobbs, where Goody roused him and gave him a drink of weak tea. She cleaned the burn with soap and water, put on a dressing and bandaged him up, and made him lie down for a while in the parlour, with the curtains drawn to shut out the light. Only then would she let him go upstairs to Beth.

'How d'you like my smart new stock?' he asked, as he sat, stiff-necked in his bandages, on the side of the bed.

'You should have known better than turn your back on Kit Maddox.'

'What'll become of him, now your grandpa's gave him the push?'

'Don't grieve for that,' Beth said fiercely.

During the next few days, the men were full of gossip concerning Kit Maddox, and Liney the pitman, who lived near Collow Ford, had something to report every morning.

'He ent paid his rent, and when old Trigg called down on Monday, Kit ran him up on to the footbridge and pitched him over into the brook.'

'Kit's still got no work,' said Bert Minchin. 'He plays his squeezebox in the public every night and passes his cap round after. But he don't get much in it 'cos folk is turning against him on all sides.'

'I hear his wife's just as bad,' said Sam Lovage. 'Well, I say wife for decency's sake, 'cos I hardly know what else to call her ... But she's a Tartar, too, so I've heard, and there's terrible rows in that cottage sometimes.'

Kate hearing these stories, would shake her head and say what a mercy it was that old grannie Maddox was not alive to see how Kit went on. And Goody, who was staying at Cobbs to look after Beth and the new baby, would just as surely say: 'It's Kit's baby son I think of mostly. What a life he's got compared with our young William Walter!'

A week later, Jesse began carting the oak-bark from Sudge woods to the tannery at Chepsworth Bridge. He made three journeys the first day, and was driving home through Hunt-lip that evening when he heard a commotion at Collow Ford. He jumped from the cart and hurried down Withy Lane, and several boys rushed past in the dark, whirling clappers and cans of stones.

Outside Kit's cottage, a crowd of twenty or thirty people were gathered, hammering on the door and on the shutters locked across the window, beating saucepans and dustbin lids, and shouting to Kit to come out. A few carried lanterns hung on sticks, and by their light, Jesse saw that foremost among the crowd was Emery Preston, the young landlord of The Rose and Crown. Jesse turned to question the smith, Will Pentland, who stood at his door, watching with set-faced approval.

'What's he done!' Will repeated. 'What *ent* he done would be more like it! He went into The Rose and Crown and knocked old Mrs Preston against the wall because she denied him drink on credit. That's what he done. And her nearly eighty-three years old! Why, I'd leather him silly if I was to catch him, but it's Emery's privilege to do that and he means to have it sure enough.'

Someone had brought a baulk of timber and given it into Emery's hands. He was telling the crowd to stand back while he rammed the door. Immediately after the first blow, the crowd grew silent, watching Emery at work. The second blow broke through the door, and the baulk became lodged in the jagged hole, and then, as Emery struggled to pull it away, the casement above was thrown open and Kit leant out over the sill.

'I ent coming out! Nor you ent coming in neither! I'll see to that!'

He turned back into the bedroom, but reappeared at once, to lean out over the window-sill, holding his twelve-month-old son in his hands, high above the heads of the crowd.

'One more try at that door and I'll toss the boy on to them cobbles! I shall! I mean it as sure as hell is hell! And you'll be to blame, Emery Preston, so just you mark it!'

The people were utterly silent now, and their upturned faces, perfectly still, had a strange likeness one to another, horror casting them all in the same mould. The child, in short cotton frock and muslin napkin, kicked his naked feet on the air and flailed about with his thin arms. In the light of the lanterns, his face seemed all eyes, very dark and deep and round, gazing upon the crowd below. His mouth was drawn down at the corners, and as his father gave him a jerk, raising him up even higher, he gave a long and drawn out cry, in a thin voice almost too small to hear, so frail was it, and so tired.

'Well?' Kit shouted. 'Are you lot going and leaving me in peace or must I toss him down like I said?'

'Rubbish!' a voice called from the back of the crowd. 'He won't do it! Not his own child! Take no notice, Emery Preston! Bost down that door!'

'No, not I!' Emery said, and cast the baulk of timber aside. 'I've had enough! I'm going home,'

'Me too,' said Martin Coyle.

'And me,' said Oliver Rye.

'We're going now!' Billy Ratchet shouted. 'So take that babby inside where he's safe, and may the Lord inflict you for treating him so!'

'Get moving, you sanctimonious old swine, you! You and all your party there! Get off my doorstop or I'll drop him yet, by God I will!'

The people began to move away, and Jesse with them, but, looking back at the cottage window as Kit was withdrawing inside, he saw, in the dark room behind, a shadowy figure waiting and a woman's white arms reaching out for the child. Then Kit reappeared again.

'Hey, you! Jesse Sideways! Tell old Tewke he owes me my wages. Three days' work, the damned skinflint, and I want it quick sharp, so tell him from me!'

'Yes, I'll tell him,' Jesse said.

On Saturday, when Jesse knocked at Kit's cottage, the window was still shuttered and barred, and the hole in the door was stuffed with sacking. After a while, there came the sound of furniture being dragged back inside; then the sacking was plucked away and a woman's face appeared at the hole. Jesse, bending to speak to her, could see only a pale-lipped mouth and a sharply pointed chin.

'I've brought Kit's wages. Is he in?'

'He's in, yes. Upstairs on the bed. But he won't come down to see anybody.'

'Then give him this,' Jesse said, and handed the money through the hole. 'How's your baby? Is he all right?'

'He's right enough.'

'Have you been shut up like this since Monday? Laws, it ent good for you nor your baby to stay shut up in the dark like that. Nor Kit neither.'

'I know that!' she said. 'I keep telling him so but he won't let me open the door or the window, not even to get a breath of air. I'm near going mad, shut up like this. I'm near as mad as Kit himself!'

'But he's got to come out sooner or later. He can't stay locked in there forever.'

'He's scared to come out because of the people. Will Pentland says he'll be safe enough now, but Kit won't believe it. He knocks on the wall for Hesper Tarpin to bring bread and milk to the door.'

'Ent there nothing I can do?'

'No, nothing. Only—'

'Only what?'

'Pray for me and the boy,' she said, and withdrew from the door, replacing the sacking in the hole.

By the following Monday, the woman was dead, and Kit had vanished with the baby. Liney Carr was the first to bring the news to the workshop, and each of the others, on arriving, had something to add. The smith, Will Pentland, had tried Kit's door at five that morning, and it had opened. Inside, the woman lay stretched on the floor with her head against the bars of the grate, and with terrible marks on her throat and forehead. Kit must have stolen out in the night, taking the baby with him, but although many people had searched the district, not a trace could be found, and now a policeman from Chepsworth was in charge.

The carpenters talked of it all day, but quietly, soberly, all very subdued. And in the house that evening, the women talked in the same quiet way.

'I always said I'd be sorry for any girl that tied up with Kit,' Beth said, 'but I never thought to have such cause as this.'

Jesse awoke from a deep sleep to find Beth sitting up in bed beside him.

'What is it?' he said.

'I heard a noise outside in the yard.'

'It's the rain, that's all. It's coming down like bows and arrows. Just hark at it against that pane.'

'No,' she said. 'It sounded like somebody shifting timber. There! Did you hear it then?'

Jesse listened, but heard only the sound of the rain.

'Your ears is sharper than mine,' he said, getting out of bed, 'so I'd better go down and see what's what.'

He put on his trousers and went downstairs to the kitchen. He lit a lantern and took it with him, through the office and out to the yard. The rain was a cold and steady downpour, in straight white shafts, bouncing off the ground. He took a few steps and was soaked to the skin.

'Who's there?' he called, in a loud voice.

He went on, between the big square stacks of planking, out to the space in front of the workshop. He held his lantern down low, moving forward, slightly stooping, looking for footmarks in the mud. He heard sounds behind him and swung round, but it was only grandfather Tewke, clad in oilskin and sou'wester, squelching across the mud in his gumboots, with his old-fashioned shotgun under one arm.

'Beth roused me up. She says we've got burglars. By God! They'll get what-for if I catch them stealing my goods and timber! D'you see any sign?'

'Somebody's been here,' Jesse said. 'The mud's all poached up along here.'

He turned again, taking another few steps forward, still searching the ground for marks. He stood upright to peer about through the rainy darkness, and as he raised the lantern higher, a pair of booted feet swung slowly round in front of his eyes. His nerves gave a twitch along his arm, and the flame of the lantern flickered and leapt. He felt the old man come up behind him, and he raised the lantern as high as he could, to show how Kit had hanged himself in the big oak tree.

There was a ladder against the bough, and Jesse went up and cut the rope, and brought the body down to the ground. He knew by the awful lolling of the head that the neck was broken, and when he felt the dead hands flopping against him, his own live flesh coldly shrank on his bones.

Grandfather Tewke had gone ahead with the lantern, to

open the workshop and light the way. Jesse carried the body in and laid it on a trestle table. He forced himself to remove the noose from the neck, to push the wet hair back from the forehead, to wipe the rain from the dead face, and to fold the hands together on the breast.

Grandfather Tewke held the light, looking down at Kit in frowning anger. He watched as Jesse covered the body over with canvas, and then, as though released from the fascination of Kit's dead face, began to move about the workshop.

'The lock on the door was broke,' he said. 'Kit's been in here. Now I wonder why? Ah, I thought as much! Come here and look.'

It was Kit's old place at the workbench, and there Kit had laid his baby son, wrapped round in a shawl that was pinned close with a pewter brooch. The child lay unnaturally still, eyes closed, lips parted, seeming scarcely to breathe at all.

'He's alive, just about,' the old man said, and bent over to sniff the child's mouth. 'He's been put to sleep with a sup of brandy. Let's take him indoors.'

Jesse picked up the child and carried him quickly into the house. All three women were in the kitchen, and Kate was reviving the fire with the bellows.

'Kit's gone and hanged hisself in the oak tree,' the old man said. 'We've just been laying him out in the workshop.'

'Is he dead?' Kate gasped.

'Of course he's dead! It's what you'd expect after hanging, ent it?'

'Laws,' said Goody, seeing the child. 'Is he dead, too, the poor mite?'

'Dead drunk!' the old man answered. 'Set on early by his father.'

'Give him to me,' Goody said. 'What a poor little nottomy scrap of a babe! He's hardly more than skin and bone. Who knows what he's been through these past few days?'

She sat down with the child in her lap, close to the stove, where a handful of sticks were now burning. She undid the brooch and opened the shawl, and as she did so, a piece of paper flew to the floor.

'A note,' she said. 'Pick it up and read what it says.' And, holding the child in the curve of her body, she began rubbing his arms and legs. 'Well, Jesse? What's Kit Maddox had to say in his last will and testament there wrote down?'

Jesse frowned at the scribbled note but could not understand it. He gave it to Beth, who took it under the lamp to read.

'It's about the child. It says, "My son is not to go in the Institution." '

'No more he shan't!' exclaimed Goody. 'Institutions indeed! He's fell in with us and with us he stays or my name ent Goody Izzard. Here, Jesse! – Warm me that milk. I think the babe is waking up.'

The child was certainly opening his eyes, slowly and stickily, because the eyelids were rimmed with scurf. The light at first made him recoil, and he hid his face against Goody's bosom, but then he rolled over and lay against her arm, gazing around with filmy eyes that rolled and swivelled in their sockets.

'Drunk, sure enough,' Goody said, and, taking the cup of warm milk, held it for the child to drink. 'There, that'll soon quench the poison inside you.'

She took off his frock and vest and the three-cornered napkin that was tied in a knot about his loins: all were filthy and specked with blood from the many flea-bites that mottled his skin, and Goody, having screwed them up in disgust, threw them into the fire to burn. Jesse brought her a bowl of warm water, a tablet of soap, and some soft lint. Beth brought a bundle of baby clothes, and Kate brought a jar of elderflower ointment.

Tenderly, Goody washed the child's face, his hair, his body, his thin-fleshed limbs. Then she dried him, anointed his sores, and dressed him in the clean warm clothes. And all the time, he was perfectly quiet, perfectly still, his body slack within her grasp. But at least there was some touch of colour in his cheeks now, as he sat on her lap in the glow of the fire. And his eyes were losing their filmy look, growing steadier, with intelligence in them; beginning to follow Goody's movements.

They were so very deep and dark, these eyes, that they

resembled the eyes of a sad-faced snowman: looking on the world in a hollow fashion; blank as coal-knobs; expecting nothing, yet very watchful in a still, deep way, as though they were keepers of unfathomed knowledge.

'Shall we be keeping him, then?' asked Jesse. 'Bringing him up with our own?'

'No,' said Goody. 'You've got three children already. You don't need no more. This little nottomy's going to be mine, to keep me company out at the Pikehouse.'

'Gracious,' said Kate, 'can you manage a baby at your time of life, Goody?'

'Will you be allowed to keep him?' asked Jesse.

'I'll get Parson Chance to speak for me. He'll soon sort it out.'

'That's good,' said Beth, smiling at Goody, nursing the child.

'What's his name?' Goody asked.

'Laws,' Jesse said. 'I've never heard it, I don't believe.'

'Nor me, neither,' said grandfather Tewke. 'The blasted kid! – that's all Maddox ever called him And I know when Parson Wisdom went down in March to chivvy Kit and the woman about the boy's baptism, they laughed in his face and said they weren't yet decided what name to give him.'

Goody was shocked. She drew the child close and rocked him gently, her brown wrinkled face full of rage and pity. That a child past twelve months should still be nameless! – Why, even a cat or a dog fared better than that. She had never heard of such a thing in her life before. Such an unchristian thing. No, never! Never! And then at last she calmed down.

'I'll see Mr Chance first thing in the morning and we'll have a christening as soon as maybe.' She set the child on his feet on her lap and held him upright, looking into his deep dark eyes. 'I shall call him Thomas, after my brother that died,' she said. 'He couldn't be named after a better man. It'll maybe make up for all he's been through.'

CHAPTER THREE

There came a day when Betony, aged four and a half, could not be found in the house or garden; the orchard, the fields, or the workshop yard. Beth said she must have wandered out to the road, and Jesse, thinking how easy it would be for a small girl to stumble into the Derrent, ran along the bank as far as the village, searching the waters as he went. But Betony was perfectly safe. She was with a crowd of people that had gathered to watch a platoon of soldiers drilling on the green.

That was the first summer of the war in South Africa. The platoon, belonging to the Three Counties Infantry, based at Capleton Wick, was marching southward, collecting recruits as it went, and Betony, hearing the beating of the drum, had followed them all the way to the green. She could scarcely be bothered to glance at Jesse as he arrived and joined the crowd. She had eyes and ears only for the tall sergeant and the marching soldiers and the little drummer in red-flashed helmet and red sash. And Jesse, swinging her up into his arms, was also happy to stay and watch.

A last command rang out, the drumbeats stopped, and the soldiers, drawn up in a block of fours, stood at ease on the green. The sergeant turned towards the crowd and his glance happened to light on Jesse.

'Ah! Now you're the kind of man we want exactly!'

'What, me?' said Jesse, with a burning face. 'Laws, I shouldn't be no sort of use as a soldier!'

'You surely have some care for your queen and country, haven't you, young fellow?'

'Why, yes, I suppose, but—'

'You can't have Jesse,' said Oliver Rye. 'He's lame in one foot.'

'Oh! That's different! That's no use to us. And no one expects a lame man to volunteer as a soldier.'

The sergeant was casting about again, looking for more likely material, when old Dr Mellow, who had once been a great scholar at Oxford, but who now lived like a tramp on Huntlip common, pushed to the very front of the crowd and spoke out in his splendid voice.

'Why should any man, lame or not, fight in a war that doesn't concern him and which shouldn't have been begun in the first place?'

'Why?' said the sergeant. 'Surely every man in England must want to protect his interests from the thieving Boer?'

'What interests are those?' the doctor asked, and turned to Mattie Makepiece, standing beside him. 'Have you got a gold-mine in Cape Province?'

'Not unless my uncle Albert's gone and left me one in his will,' said Mattie. 'And that ent likely, 'cos that was the Arge-and-nines he went to, I believe.'

'And you?' said the doctor, turning to old Mark Jervers, the road-mender, on his other side. 'Have you got a diamond-mine in Kimberley?'

'Not now,' Mark said sadly. 'I had to sell it to pay for me boots.'

'Then, sergeant, what interests are these you're asking the men of this village to fight for?'

'England's interests are yours and mine, sir!' the sergeant said angrily. 'They're what make us rich.'

'Rich?' cried Billy Ratchet. 'There's nobody here richer than fourpence! It's them that own the gold-mines and such that should go and fight for them if they've got a mind to! Not our boys here!'

A wave of approval ran through the crowd, and one or two women began to shout abuse at the sergeant, who turned abruptly and faced his platoon. At the first command, they stood to attention. At the second, they turned to the right in fours, towards the road. The drummer stood ready, drumsticks up, touching his nose, and the sergeant paused for one last remark to the crowd.

'I never thought to find a village in England that wasn't willing to do its bit!'

'Get away!' said Annie Wilkes. 'My eldest boy's been gone from the start.'

'And my boy Dave,' said Queenie Lovage.

'And two of mine,' said old Jim Minchin. 'And others besides.'

'Then I hope they don't die for want of support from home,' said the sergeant, and in the silence that followed his words, he turned and signalled to his dummer. The drumbeats rang out, and the soldiers marched smartly away.

Jesse withdrew from the crowd and set Betony down on the ground. He took her hand and started for home. But she, hanging back, was still watching the soldiers, and as they vanished along the road, she suddenly burst into storms of tears.

'Gone!' she said, sobbing. 'Soldiers all gone!'

'Why, yes,' Jesse said, getting down on his haunches and drawing her against his knees. 'They couldn't stop on the green forever, could they?'

'I want to go too!'

'What, and leave your poor dad all alone by hisself?'

'No!' she said, choking, and her sobs became more anguished than ever.

'Laws,' Jesse said, 'you mustn't cry like that, my blossom. Just look at that starling watching you from Mrs Merry's garden.'

'Don't want to look!'

'That's a pity, that is, 'cos it ent often you see a pink starling just sitting like that as bold as brass.'

'Pink?' she said, forgetting to cry. 'Where is he, pink?'

'Why, there, on that laylock. Ah dang it! Now it's flied away!'

'Was it really pink?'

'Pink as piglets,' he said, drying her eyes with a corner of her apron. 'And with little spectacles on his nose, to see you all the plainer with.'

'He wasn't!' she said, striking his chest with her small fists. 'It's not true!'

'How d'you know if you never saw him? Why, I bet that pink starling has flied off to Cobbs. He was heading that way right enough. And when we get back he'll be sitting perched on the workshop roof. You mark my words!'

A few days later, Betony was missing again, and this time

146

he found her in the school classroom, a slate on her lap, a chalk in her fingers, and a look of rapture on her face as she squeakily traced a large pothook, helped by eight-year-old Agatha Mance. At sight of Jesse, the storm-clouds gathered at once on her brow, and her legs entwined themselves round the bench. Miss Likeness suggested that she should stay, and Jesse, with some misgiving, gave in.

Betony was four and a half. There were many younger than she in the class. But it grieved Jesse to see her going to school, so small, such a baby, yet already growing away from him, making a separate life of her own. He felt he had lost her. He felt she would never be the same again. And he used to slip away to meet her coming across the fields, expecting to find a little stranger. But Betony, although enjoying her new life, was just as close to him as ever. Her day was not complete until it had been unfolded to him. Her joys shone all the more brightly, and her troubles dwindled, the moment he shared them.

'Glory be!' he used to say. 'You make school sound like a picnic. I could almost wish myself back on the bench.'

The habit he formed, of going to meet her after school, went on a long time, even when he had ceased to be anxious. It went on because they both liked it, – it was their special time together, out of the day – and the path across the fields of Anster became woven with certain events, some small, some large, that occurred in their lives.

Here, at the stile by Tommy Trennam's cottage, he met her with the news of Roger's birth. Here, beside the copse of birch and rowan, he pulled her from a snowdrift during the blizzard that came so suddenly one day in April 1911. Here, in the field called Big Piece, they came on the mare, Flounce, giving birth to the foal, Jingle, and watched from a distance, through the hedge, so as not to disturb her.

'If I was to walk and walk and walk ... where should I come to at the end?'

'Well, now,' he said, 'a lot'd depend which way you was going.'

'South, of course! – Nobody ever goes north!' she said.

'Then you'd come into Gloucestershire,' he said.

'And after that?'

'You'd come into Wiltshire.'

'And after that?'

'What, still walking and walking and walking?'

'That's right. Where would I come to?'

'You should ask these questions at school.'

'But this is the holidays,' she said. 'And anyway, I'm asking *you*.'

'Ah, I know, and I've got my thinking-cap on, too.'

'Don't you know, then?' she asked, surprised, with just a little touch of scorn. 'Don't you know what comes after Wiltshire?'

'Dorset!' he said, with a grunt of triumph. 'That's where you'd come to, sure enough! And you'll have to watch out now, my blossom, or the rate you're going you'll walk right over into the sea.'

'The sea? But we ent come to London yet.'

'Why, no, that's right. No more we ent.'

'Then where is it?' she asked, frowning.

'I dunno. It's down there somewhere. You must ask your mother.'

'Is the sea very big?' she asked him.

'Fairish,' he said. 'Yes, pretty big, really, all told.'

'Is it bigger than Slings Pool?'

'Why, that's only a puddle compared with the sea!'

'Have you ever been in a shop?' she asked.

'No, nor never want to, either,' he said.

'Have you seen the sea?'

'Seen it?' he said. 'What, seen the sea? Why, not in so many words, exactly.'

'Have you or haven't you?'

'No,' he said. 'But your mother's seen it, I believe. You must ask her. – She'll tell you all about the sea.'

But Betony rarely talked to her mother. She preferred him, even when his answers failed to satisfy her.

When the other children began to go to school, he went less and less often to meet them coming across the fields. They had one another. He was not needed. So he went only on special occasions, or when an old impulse moved him.

Janie, a year younger than Betony, was at first her devoted slave. She had no life of her own, – no thought, no wish – except by reflection. She was the moon to Betony's sun. But later on, when Betony grew dictatorial, Janie withdrew from her and moved closer to William instead, and Jesse, who saw it happening, feared that Betony would be hurt. She was different from all the rest. She took things to heart so passionately. But he need not have worried, for the younger children, though clinging together, forming a separate group of four, still looked to Betony as their head. They were the little sheaves of corn, bowing to the big sheaf of corn in their midst.

They formed a group for the sake of the strength the union gave them, and because they were all of one kind, while Betony was different. But they depended on her to guide them, to protect them, to help with their lessons, and even, sometimes, to direct their games. It was only when she grew too fierce and demanding that they withdrew from her. It was only when she was unkind that they closed their ranks against her completely. They were rarely unkind to her.

One wet Saturday in winter, when he was all alone in the workshop, making a coffin, he looked up to find Betony watching him with a stiff white face.

'I don't like you making coffins!'

'Somebody's got to make them,' he said.

'Not you! Not you! Promise you'll never make coffins again.'

'I can't promise that,' he said, smiling.

'You must!' she said, and her terrible passion made her voice very rough in her throat. 'You must ! You must!'

'Well, I shan't,' he said. 'That ent for you to must at me, my blossom.'

Betony turned and ran out, but a little while later, as he was tidying up the workbench, she came back with the four other children and marched them straight to the finished coffin that stood on end against the wall.

'There, look at that!' she said to them. 'That's for poor old Mrs Sharpey, lying dead in her house at Blagg. They'll nail it down tight and put her into a hole in the ground for the worms and beetles to eat her up.'

Janie and William turned away. Roger went white, and Dicky, the youngest, began to cry.

'That's nothing yet!' Betony said. 'Wait and see what else I'll show you!'

She took Dicky's arm and began pulling him away, prodding the other three before her.

'Where're you off to?' Jesse asked, stepping directly in her path.

'To see the hole they've digged for Mrs Sharpey.'

'Oh no you don't!' Jesse said, and made her release little Dicky's arm.

He sent the younger ones back to the house. Then he took hold of Betony by the waist and lifted her up to sit on the workbench.

'Ent you ashamed of yourself, my blossom, frightening your sister and brothers like that?'

'No! I'm not!'

'Nor sorry for making Dicky cry?'

'No! I'm not!'

'Well, I'm ashamed *for* you, even if you ent ashamed for yourself. I am! That's a fact! A big girl of nine, frightening a poor little chap like Dicky ... I'm more ashamed than I know how to say.'

'I don't care if you are or not!'

'Don't you?' he said. 'Then you'd better run along, I reckon, 'cos I don't love you when you're like this. No, not a morsel! So you'd better be Miss Sally Forth.'

He began to be busy, taking a hand-brush and sweeping the shavings off the bench, but he could see Betony, sitting just where he had put her, her hands in her lap, her head and shoulders beginning to droop, her chin sinking against her chest. He could see the last of her stubborn defiance lingering on in tight-closed lips and flaring nostrils.

'What, not gone yet?' he said, as though in surprise. 'It's no use sitting there like that, you know, 'cos I meant what I said. – I don't love you when you're naughty. What is it, then? D'you need help in getting down?'

He put out his hands, but without touching her, merely waiting for her to move. And now, as she looked towards his waiting hands, her little face went to pieces. Her lips quivered, her eyes crumpled and closed tight, and she became unbelievably small, her face and body melting against him, her hands groping upwards about his neck.

'There, there, don't cry,' he murmured, and rocked her gently within his arms. 'Of course your dad loves you! He loves you as dearly as dearly can be!'

He took her up and bore her about, holding her close, trying to draw the throbbing heartache out of her and into himself. For he was the guilty one. He was the one that ought to suffer. He was the one whose heart should break.

'There, there! It's all over now . . . Shall we be sensible people again, you and me, before someone sees us in all this mess? Eh? Shall we?'

The cause of the trouble was almost forgotten. His only concern was to comfort the child and bring the blue light back into her eyes, where the grey tears had quenched it. And that was how it always was, whenever there had been trouble between them.

He knew he sinned by denying his love, and each time he paid for it in dark guilty shame. Yet whenever she was haughty with him, flouting him and tossing her head, he was lured into the same dark sin all over again. He had to bend her; to break her defiance; to keep her bound to him in small-ness, as she had been bound to him from the first. The words would be said: – 'I don't love you' – and only when he had brought her to him, creeping, small, into his arms, did the guilt follow.

Once or twice every month, on a Sunday, Jesse drove out to visit Goody, bearing gifts of honey and jam from Beth, and taking his tools to do odd jobs about the Pikehouse. And sometimes Betony went with him.

When she was young Betony loved the Pikehouse because it was so amazingly small. She liked the steep stairs, almost a ladder, and she liked the tiny window under the eaves, where, in the springtime, you could watch the sparrows pulling the straws from the thatch, and the martins building their nests underneath. She also liked the strange shape of the house, with its two flat corners at the road end, and the funny recess where once a board had announced the toll fees.

'Why did people have to pay?'

' 'Cos the road belonged to Mr Lannam and he had to keep it in repair,' Jesse told her.

'Why don't they pay now?'

'A new road was made, going round by Hallows, and nobody hardly uses this road now.'

'How much did it cost for a pony and trap?'

'Sixpence,' he said.

'Then we shall pay . . . just like the people long ago.'

So Goody had to come to the gate, while Betony stayed stitting up in the trap, pretending to search her drawstring purse, and at last dropping a clammy sixpence into Goody's waiting hand.

'Good day, Mrs Izzard,' she said primly. 'What fine weather for the time of year. I hope your floppydocks is doing well?'

Betony liked the Pikehouse garden because of all its different scents. Lavender, rosemary, sage, thyme, all grew in amongst the peas and beans and carrots and marrows. There were sharp-smelling marigolds, sweet-smelling pinks, and a bush of lad's love, as Goody called it, which, when you rubbed the feathery leaves in your fingers, smelt sharp and sweet at the same time.

At first, whenever Jesse and Betony went on these visits, the boy Tom would not be there. He had only to see them driving up and he would be off, across the turnpike and into the woods. It was always the same, Goody said. – Whoever called, Tom would never stay to see them. His only friend was Charley Bailey, living in his shanty on Norton common: he had plenty to say to Charley, it seemed, but nothing to say to anyone else.

Betony was full of curiosity concerning Tom. She asked Goody endless questions.

'He's not your grandson, 'cos his name is Maddox and not Izzard, so why d'you let him call you grannie?'

'Tom's adopted,' Goody said. 'What else would he call me if not grannie?'

'Does he go to school?'

'Yes, he goes to Norton. When he goes at all.'

'Here!' Jesse said. 'You ought to make him go to school, Goody.'

'You're one to talk! My goodness me!'

'Ah, and look at me now. Biggest dunce this side of Ennen.'

'Tom's all right,' Goody said. 'He likes to work on the farm with me, and he's learning plenty, even if it don't come out of books.'

One Sunday in winter, as Jesse and Betony drove to the Pikehouse, they were caught in a cold downpour of rain. Jesse drew up the cape and they kept dry enough, but he was worried, on arriving, to see Tom go running into the woods as usual, clad only in trousers and shirt.

'The boy'll catch his death,' he said to Goody. 'Keep Betony here while I go and fetch him.'

It was cold and wet even in the shelter of the big pine trees, for the rain was heavy and drove through the branches, rattling down on the matting of needles that covered the ground. Jesse went quietly through the wood, and found the boy sitting under a tree, his back to the trunk, where the rain streamed darkly down, his knees drawn up under his chin, and his arms folded about his shins. He seemed not to care that he was soaked from head to foot, that his hair dripped into his eyes, that his shirt clung like a rag to his shoulders. He seemed scarcely to feel the cold, but kept himself knotted hard against it, sitting still, without a shiver, looking into the wood.

When Jesse spoke to him, he started up at once like a deer, and would have run off but that Jesse caught him by the arm.

'You've no reason to run from me. Why, I've known you since you was a little tucker dressed in frocks. You wasn't scared then. Nor you ent now, surely, are you?'

'No,' Tom muttered, but his arm was rigid in Jesse's grasp.

'You come home and get dried out before you catch your death of cold.'

'No. I don't want to. I'm fine as I am.'

'There! And I was hoping for news of Charley Bailey. He's a friend of yours, from what I hear, and so he was mine when I lived at the Pikehouse.'

'I know,' Tom said. 'He mentions you sometimes.'

The boy fell in beside Jesse and together they returned to the Pikehouse. At sight of Betony, sitting perched on the settle, he was ready for flight again, but Goody sent him upstairs to change, and when, in answer to her call, he came reluctantly down again, she flung a towel over his head, pressed him on to the stool by the fire, and held him there while she dried his hair.

Beth had sent Goody a parcel. It contained a fruit-cake, a bottle of brandy, a screw of snuff, and a large tin of drinking-chocolate. Goody now took the chocolate and made them each a beaker full. Tom sat hunched on his stool, the towel still over his head, his steaming beaker between his hands. In the firelight, his newly dried face was a smooth dusky brown, shiny about the nose and cheekbones, but shadowy at the jaws and temples, where the thin flesh went hollowly in. His eyes, with the flickering flames reflected in them, seemed almost black.

Betony, sipping her chocolate, studied him for a long time.

'Are you a gipsy?' she asked suddenly.

Tom merely stared into the fire.

'Can't he speak?' she asked Jesse.

'Why, yes. But he's shy, you see, and you've got to give him a bit of time.'

'Is he a gipsy? He looks like one.'

'Of course he ent. He's just dark, that's all.'

'How old is he?'

'Well, try him again,' Jesse said, 'and see if he answers you this time.'

Betony leant a little forward, as though she thought the boy might be deaf.

'How old are you?' she asked loudly, and, when he stayed silent. 'Don't you *know* how old you are?'

'Tom,' said Goody, in a quiet voice. 'Betony's speaking.'

Tom's glance flickered to Betony's face.

'Nine,' he muttered, and looked back at the fire.

'Can you read and write?' Betony asked him.

'Anyone can,' Tom muttered.

'How much can you read?'

'Solomon Grundy. Reynard the Fox.'

'Is that all?' Betony said, and, as he fell silent again: 'D'you know your tables? D'you know your sums? Do you know how to do division?'

Jesse put his hand on her arm.

'You're going too fast. Try talking to Tom without putting him through the hoop. Ask if he'll take you and show you the badger's earth when you come next time.'

'Will you?' said Betony, again leaning forward towards the boy.

'If you like,' he said.

'Will the badgers be there?'

'You wouldn't see them. Not in the daytime.'

'Then why go?' she said, staring. 'Where's the point if there's nothing to see? I call that silly. I do indeed!'

The boy looked at her for an instant, and then away, and she could get nothing more out of him for the rest of the visit.

Driving home afterwards, Jesse took her gently to task.

'Tom's younger than you. You should go more slowly and try to bring him out of his shell.'

'I don't think he's right in the head.'

'Oh yes he is! He's just wild and shy and unused to strangers. He ent got a family like you, remember. He's only got his grannie Izzard. But you could help him if you had a mind to. You could teach him things and be his friend.'

'Yes,' said Betony, much struck. 'I shall teach him things and be his friend.'

Thereafter, when she went with Jesse to the Pikehouse, she made an effort to be friends with Tom. She persuaded him to take her exploring in the woods, and she gave him small presents, such as a tracing of a map of Great Britain, a blue-whorled pebble out of the Derrent, and a piece of candy from Capleton Mop. Tom, in turn, gave her a sheep's horn picked up on Norton common, a man-shaped potato dug from the garden, and a lark's egg, beautifully shaded and speckled in brown. Betony received these presents with grave appreciation, but threw them away on the journey home, and on the third occasion, Jesse, having seen from the boy's face what it cost him to part with the lark's egg, was very much grieved.

'What d'you do that for? Poor Tom would be sad to see his lark's egg thrown away like that.'

'But he didn't see! And what do I want with a smelly egg?'

Jesse was silent a short while, staring thoughtfully at the pony's ears.

'Ah, well,' he said at length. 'I dare say Tom does the same with the things you give him.'

Betony stared. Such a thing had never occurred to her.

The friendship lasted perhaps a year, and then came to a sudden end. Betony, playing schools with Tom, became angry because he could not recite the poem she had set him to learn on a previous visit. She rapped his knuckles with a little cane and ordered him to stand in the corner. He refused and there was a quarrel.

'You're hopeless!' she said. 'You never want to learn anything!'

'What was it she wanted to learn you, Tom?' Jesse asked.

'Poultry,' Tom said. 'Bloody dancing daffodils.'

'There!' said Betony. 'That's fine expressions, I must say! And it's not the first time he's used them neither!'

She looked at Jesse, and then at Goody, who was sitting opposite, darning a sock.

'He don't only swear. He poaches too. And he goes to see a smelly old man who lives in a hovel and keeps ferrets. His name's Charles Bailey and it's him that teaches Tom to swear. Well? Ent you going to give him what-for?'

'Laws,' Jesse said. 'Poaching! Lumme!' And he winked at Tom.

'Poaching is stealing!' Betony said. 'Little thieving toad!'

'You be careful who you're miscalling,' Goody said. 'Keep a civil tongue in your head, young miss, or else a still one.'

'I shall speak if I want to. It's only the truth. Tom is a poacher. I've seen his snares.'

'So are others I could mention, and I needn't look further than your own dad.'

'My dad is no poacher!' Betony said.

'He was, though, at one time of day.' Goody got up and went to the fire-place. She took down the tobacco-tin full of shot and rattled it under Betony's nose. 'Ask your dad where them pellets come from! You ask him. Go on!' She put the tin back and returned to her chair. 'Ah, and ask how he got that wonky foot!'

Betony came to Jesse and stood leaning against his knees.

'Shall we go home now?' she said.

'Why, no. I aim to stop another hour or two yet.'

'I don't want to stop any longer. Not in this little tiddly house. I don't like it. I think it's queer. Tiddly little house it is!'

'Hah!' Goody said. 'Tiddly it may be, but you was glad enough to be born in it, however.'

'I wasn't born here! You're telling lies!'

'I should know, seeing I brought you into the world.'

'You didn't! You didn't! It's all lies!' Betony tugged at Jesse's jacket. 'I want to go home. Now. This minute!'

'Then you'd better start to walk, my blossom, 'cos I ent coming. Not until I'm good and ready.'

'I'm not walking! It's too far!'

'Then you'll have to wait for me, that's all. And no more tantrums, mind, or I shall get cross and then there'll be ructions!'

He took hold of her and lifted her on to the settle beside him, and there she remained, in silence, for the rest of the visit. She would not have tea when they had it. Nor would she say her farewells when she left. And Jesse, glancing at her pale, tight-clenched face as they drove home, feared she would not easily forgive Goody for humbling her pride.

Sure enough, a fortnight later, when he was setting out for the Pikehouse, Betony did not want to go. And the next time the same. And the next after that. He went alone, or with Beth, or with one of the younger children. Betony went on other journeys, but never to the Pikehouse.

At about this time, she became even more devoted to learning. She was top of the school in all things and could do no wrong, either in the eyes of the vicar, who taught her the Scriptures, or in the eyes of Miss Likeness, who invited her home for special coaching.

'Miss Likeness wants me to sit for exams, to go to the Grammar School, Lock's, in Chepsworth.'

'The Grammar School! Lumme! And how long will you be there, then?'

'Until I'm sixteen. Or seventeen, perhaps.'

'Fancy all them years at school! That'd never've suited me. I'd have bost a blood-vessel at the thought.'

'Bost!' she said. 'What a word to use!'

'Why, what's wrong with bost, you odd little article, you?' he demanded.

'Liddle aarticle!' she said. 'Zackly so! Sure nuff!'

'Ah, you're getting too grand for me,' he said, turning back to work. 'Seems I can't never say the right thing these days. Or else I say it all countryfied. I reckon us two shall soon be strangers.'

But at sight of the sadness coming into her face, he knew she was no stranger after all. She was still his favourite, and he was still all in all to her.

He had the pony and trap standing ready in the fold, and was dropping his tool-bag in, when Betony hurried out of the house, putting on her hat and coat.

'Great-grumpa says there's a barge gone aground on Sidley Ait. Can we go and see them hauling it off?'

'I was going to see your grannie Izzard.'

'Oh, but the barge'll be gone by this evening,' she said, 'and I wanted to write about it in school tomorrow.'

'All right,' he said. 'I can go to the Pikehouse next Sunday instead.'

But the next Sunday, Betony wanted to attend the dedication service in the newly restored church of St John's in Dingham, and they had to start out soon after dinner. The next Sunday again, she and he were invited to tea with Miss Likeness, to talk about the Grammar School. And the Sunday after that, when the bad rains had come, and the Idden had burst its banks at Uphams, Betony wanted to see the floods.

'Here!' he said, as they stood together on Woolman Bridge. 'Are you keeping me away from the Pikehouse on purpose?'

'On purpose?' she said. 'Why should I do that?'

'I dunno. I just wondered, that's all.'

Looking at her, he could not be sure if she lied or not. Her stare was so straight, so surprised, so puzzled. And, even if she lied, he could not be angry because in his heart there was always a pleasant warmth that undid him. It was his weakness, that he liked to be all in all to her; that he liked her clinging, possessive ways.

There were other people on the bridge, and he saw how often their eyes came to rest on Betony's face, how often they smiled at the things she said. It was not that she was wonderfully pretty. But she was so very harvest-fair. Her hair was so bright, her skin so golden, her eyes such a wonderful shade of blue. And then, too, there was her smile, – her mother's smile, but more frequent – that came unexpectedly, springing into being out of nothing at all, casting its warmth and brightness all about, so that other people broke into smiles as well.

She seemed not to notice the glances that came her way, and Jesse was glad, for she was brightest and best when she could forget herself like this: watching the swans swimming along the streets of Upham; the boys with rods and lines, fishing pots and pans from the flood-water; watching farmers in boats, rescuing cattle.

When they got home, and were talking of all the things they had seen, Beth interrupted with a sudden attack.

'Ent it time you went to see Goody instead of gadding about the country?'

'Yes, I reckon it is, and I shall be going just as soon as maybe.'

'Why not next Sunday?'

'Ah, well, me and Betony planned taking some clothes and toys and such to Upham next Sunday, for the poor little mites that are flooded out of their homes down there.'

'Then when will you go and see Goody?'

'I shall go, don't you worry, just as soon as there's time.'

But somehow another three weeks went by, and Beth drove out to the Pikehouse herself, taking the younger children with her.

'Well?' Jesse said, when they came back. 'Any message from Goody?'

'No, nothing,' Beth replied.

'What, nothing at all?'

'Why should Goody send you a message? She's probably forgot you even exist.'

'Did you tell her how busy I am just now?'

'I told as good a tale as I could make it.'

'And didn't she have nothing to say to that?'

'Just nodded, that's all.'

'Well, dammit!' he said. 'What's the news at the Pike-house, then, or must I squeeze you like squeezing a cow?'

'The news is all right,' Beth said, busy bringing food to the table, 'except for the rain coming in through the roof.'

'What's that you say?'

'There's two or three holes in the thatch,' Beth said. 'You said so yourself some months back.'

'But are they got bad, then, since I was there last?'

'Goody ent complaining. She's got it all worked out to a tee. If the rain's in the west, she puts her bed under the window. If the rain's in the north, as it has been lately, she puts her bed alongside the stairs. The drips ent too bad there, so long as she covers the bed with canvas.'

'Dear Lord!' Jesse said. 'I'd no idea things'd worsened that much!'

'Are you interested, then?' Beth asked, surprised. 'I thought you was too busy gallivanting to worry yourself about your mother.'

'Aw!' Jesse said, and shifted uncomfortably in his chair. 'I didn't know things'd got so bad with that there roof-thatch. I'll take the day off and go first thing.'

'Oh no you won't!' said grandfather Tewke, looking up from his supper. 'You've got that threshing-floor to finish at Outlands.'

'Then I'll go on Sunday,' Jesse said. 'But by golly! Fancy that roof gone as bad as that! Somebody should've said something sooner.'

'There's plenty been said,' Beth retorted. 'It's the doing that's in such short supply.'

'Ah!' he said. 'That's right, surely.'

And, looking at Betony, who sat as though deaf to what was passing, he knew he had been too weak with her, letting her rule him as she pleased.

On Sunday morning, he loaded the cart with spelks,

twine, and trusses of straw, and hoisted the cover to keep things dry. It was raining hard, as it had done endlessly all that autumn, and he wore his mackintosh coat and cap, prepared for a wet day's work on the roof of the Pikehouse. Betony watched him from the dairy.

'Must you go on a day like this? So wet? So cold?'

'Yes, my blossom, indeed I must. Won't you change your mind and come with me?'

'No,' she said, and turned indoors as he drove off.

The Pikehouse garden was a puddle of mud. Seedling cabbages, flooded out of the ground, lay in the gutter along the path. Sodden potato-haulms lay in a heap, and the potato-ground was all churned about, where Goody had laboured to salvage the crop. The beans on their sticks were laid low in the mud and sodden onions floated on scummy water in the hollows.

Looking up at the roof, he saw how rotten the thatch had become since his last visit; how the holes had widened, especially round the chimney. He saw, too, how sooty the smoke was that rose from Goody's fire.

In the little porch, there stood a box of windfallen apples, very green and wet, and a box of carrots covered in slime. Goody's old overcoat hung from the nail and her boots, plastered thick with yellow clay, were on the mat with their toes turned in, as though she had just that moment stepped out of them to go indoors.

When he entered the kitchen, she was sitting in her rocking-chair, fast asleep, her chin on her chest, her hands tucked inside a fold of her apron. He touched the back of the chair as he passed and set it rocking gently. It creaked a little, as always, but Goody did not awake to the sound as she always had done in the past. She remained asleep, with her head bowed, rocking gently to and fro. Jesse went round and stooped to look into her face. He touched her hands, and they were cold, like the leaves of a lily. He touched her forehead, and knew she was dead.

When he checked the rocking of the chair, the whole room became very hushed, for the clock on the mantelpiece had stopped, and the fire in the hearth was only a heap of wet, smoking sticks. Jesse drew up the three-legged stool and sat by Goody, looking at her, with his elbows resting on his knees. He sat for some time, in the hushed stillness, because he wanted to look at her and keep her company, to think about her, and talk to her, quietly, in his head.

Then he went out to look for Tom.

Part Three

Within the woodlands, flow'ry gladed,
By the oak tree's mossy root,
The sheenèn grass-blades, timber-shaded,
Now do quiver under foot;
An' birds do whissle auver head,
An' water's bubblèn in its bed,
An' there for me the apple tree
Do lean down low in Linden Lea.

– *William Barnes*

CHAPTER ONE

The scarecrow, in sacking skirts and shawl, with a turnip face and with yellow daisies in its hat, stood up in the hedge in the fields at Anster, and Betony often went to see it. She made it her friend, telling it things that would otherwise have remained untold and it always listened, its head a little on one side, the daisies nodding on their wire stalks.

She could no longer talk to her father, because of the change in him. Whenever she sought to draw him apart, he would look at her in a strange way, with a strange and sad shake of his head. Often he seemed not to hear her at all. So she talked to the scarecrow.

It stood high in the hedgerow, guarding two big fields at once, the eighteen acre on one side, the twenty-six acre on the other. All the land about was still as sodden as could be, the flood-water lying in great pools wherever you went. The eighteen acre field had been sown with barley, the twenty-six acre with wheat. The wheat came struggling up bravely, small blades of brightest green, standing up from the puddled soil. But the barley rotted away in the ground.

'The farmers reckon they're likely ruined, and my great-grumpa says he's never known such everlasting weeks of rain. Some folk in Upham have got a foot of water in their kitchens again, and there's a baby been drowned, too, so I hear this morning.'

The scarecrow listened. Its stillness was friendly and sympathetic. It knew she wasn't to blame for the floods; for the people made homeless; for the baby drowned in that Upham cellar.

After a time, however, the scarecrow invaded her dreams at night, and instead of being her only friend, it turned against her. She dreamt she was walking in a narrow lane, and the scarecrow was with her, always a little way in front, up in the hedge, against the sky. She could not escape.

She could only go faster, – walking and walking – until her legs felt ready to break.

And when at last, weeping with weariness and anger, she stopped and stamped her foot, the scarecrow would turn very slowly round and would look at her under the brim of its hat. And now its eyes were live, human eyes, looking down, full of human thought, at Betony standing there below.

'Looking! Looking!' Betony shouted. 'Why are you always looking at me?'

She stopped going to visit the scarecrow. She tried talking to her mother instead.

'Are you sorry Tom has come to live with us?'

'No,' said her mother, busy ironing. 'Why should I be?'

'Are you glad, then?'

'You should be helping Janie clean your bedroom.'

'I've done my half,' Betony said. 'D'you think Tom is right in the head?'

'Right as ninepence! Maybe righter.'

'I'm not so sure. I think he's queer. He never looks me straight in the eye.'

'Perhaps he don't care for what he sees there.'

'I think he steals,' Betony said.

'So do you,' her mother answered. 'You stole fourpence from your granna's purse a week or two back and ten sheets of paper from your great-grumpa's office on Tuesday.'

Betony stared at the steam rising from Roger's shirt as the iron travelled to and fro. Then she looked at her mother's face, which was calm and unclouded, with no trace of anger in it; no trace of threat.

'That wasn't stealing. Not *proper* stealing. Besides, I never spent the fourpence nor used the paper 'cos someone went and stole them from *me*.'

'There now, just fancy,' her mother said, going to the stove to change the irons. 'That someone was me.'

Betony sat, aware of the temper stirring her blood.

'If I'm so bad as everyone says, why don't you tan me?' she demanded.

'I might if you was to get any worser. But you've got sense if only you'd use it, and sensible folk give over stealing once they know they've been catched out.'

'Sensible! Sensible!' Betony said, and slid from her stool. 'I'm going out of this stupid house and I'm staying away for ever and ever!'

'Very well, don't slam the door,' her mother said.

Outside, in the workshop yard, Betony watched her brothers at work, filling the big basket with sticks. William was doing the chopping as always, being proud of his skill with the little chopper, and as he went chop-chop-chop very quickly, the sticks flew about on all sides. Roger and Tom picked them up, and Dicky made them tidy in the basket.

'Tom Maddox!' Betony said, as he stooped to pick up sticks at her feet. 'Take care how you lumber into folk, you clumsy thing!'

'Then stand clear,' William commanded. 'You're in our way.'

'Tom Maddox, my mother don't like you,' Betony said. 'She thinks you're tenpence short of a shilling!'

Tom paid no heed. He went on gathering up the sticks and dropping them into the basket. But William stopped work and stared at her.

'Did mother say she didn't like Tom?'

'Nobody likes him,' Betony said. 'He's too black by half. Just look at him there, sticking out from all us fair ones as though he'd been dipped in a bag of soot. He don't belong here. He's not one of us!'

Glancing behind her, towards the workshop, she saw that her father had come to the door.

'Betony!' he said, in a warning voice.

'Go back where you came from!' she said to Tom. 'With the gipsies and tinkers. We don't want you here! You're too black for us!'

Her father's hand struck hard across her buttocks, and the shock and pain were a kind of lightning, that burnt through her flesh and melted her bones. He had never so chastised her before. He was changed completely. And she fled from him in shame and outrage; in terrible hatred; in terrible, unforgiving wrath; and ran headlong from the workshop yard. She ran without pause, along the road and over the bridge, down on to the bank of the Derrent and along to the place where the flood was at its worst.

Under the willows, downstream, two men in a punt were spearing eels. One was the idiot, Jumper Lane; the other Dr Mellow, the Oxford scholar who lived like a tramp. They looked at Betony on the bank, and Jumper, grinning from ear to ear, held up an eel for her to see. She sat on a log and pretended to fasten her buttoned boots. Then she took out her prayer-book and pretended to read.

The punt was moored by a long rope tied to a stake among the rushes. The two men allowed it to drift to the limits, then hauled themselves back and drifted again. Betony watched, growing colder and colder, for the air was thick with wet weeping mist, and the willows dripped on her from above. She told herself the cold was nothing. Soon, very soon, she'd be past it for ever. Past cark, past care.

The punt went backwards and forwards again and again. The two men showed no sign of growing tired of their sport. And now Tommy Trennam had come to the sluice with his rod and line and was settling there for the afternoon.

Betony leapt to her feet with a shiver and turned towards home. She would not be able to drown herself today. There were too many people at the brook.

'Come to the table,' her mother said, 'or aren't you hungry for your supper?'

'No. I'm not hungry. Not a bit.'

'Maybe you're sickening for some sort of chill?'

'She's sulking,' said William. 'Our dad gave her a smack.'

'Betony's very well able to speak for herself. Are you ill, girl? If so, you'd be better in bed.'

'I'm all right,' Betony said.

'Then come to the table as you're told.'

Betony sat between William and Janie and looked at the food set out on the table. She saw sticks of celery standing up clean and white in the beaker; she saw a big wedge of pale Welsh cheese; and she saw her favourite spiced liver sausage, already sliced at one end.

'Cheese or sausage?' her mother asked her, standing with knife and fork poised.

'Sausage, please,' Betony said.

In bed that night, when her mother had been to say good

night, Betony relit the candle and sat up to write in the blank leaves at the back of her prayer-book.

'What're you writing? Janie asked. 'Is it a diary, like before?'

'Mind your own business,' Betony said.

'Mother will notice the candle burnt down. She always notices, you know that.'

'Dear, dear! What a terrible thing!'

'I suppose you're practising a tidy hand?'

'Oh, be quiet, and go to sleep.'

'Fancy!' said Janie. 'The best scholar in the school, yet she can't write a tidy hand!'

'If you don't be quiet, I'll singe your hair.' Betony threatened, and held the candle above Janie's head. 'That's right, Miss Poke-and-Pry, hide yourself under the bedclothes and shut your noise or you'll be sorry!'

She had not looked at her father all through supper. She would never look at him ever again. It was her resolution, recorded now in the back of the prayer-book, and nothing would ever make her change her mind. She had set it down in her best hand.

It was all too true that her writing was untidy. Miss Likeness said so every day.

'You write good sense, Betony Izzard, and your spelling and punctuation are fair. But your handwriting! How do you expect to win a scholarship to Lock's with handwriting like that?'

'I shall try to do better,' Betony said.

'Betony, you must give more attention to work,' said Miss Likeness, 'and less to playing games with your sister and brothers.'

'I never play games,' Betony said.

Janie, who heard her give this answer, took her to task about it at home.

'Just look at you now! What're you doing if not playing games?'

'This isn't a game. It's an expedition.'

'Where to?' William asked. 'What're you tying the toasting-fork on to that pole for?'

'You'll see when we get there,' Betony said, and turned to

Tom, who was standing nearby. 'Not you!' she said. 'We don't want you with us.'

'If Tom ent coming, neither am I,' said William.

'Nor me neither,' Janie said. 'Not if Tom ent concluded as well.'

'What, that little melancholy, casting a damper on all us others? He don't never talk nor laugh nor nothing.'

'He still misses his grannie Izzard.'

'What, that old witch? Why, she's not even dead, I don't believe!'

'She is,' Janie said, in a shocked whisper. 'She's been buried at Eastery these many weeks gone by.'

'Who says so? Who really knows? We're never there when all these things are said to be done, are we?'

'Mr Hemms went out to put the words on the stone,' said Wililam. 'I heard my father say so hisself.'

'A stone is nothing! Just words, what are they? Grannie Izzard is still alive. I've seen her myself so I ought to know!'

'Betony, don't be silly,' Janie said, and they all murmured against her like bees. But Tom said nothing, merely looking at her with his deep dark gaze.

'I'll show you,' she said. 'If you don't believe it, just come with me.'

She laid the toasting-fork on the bench and crossed the fold to the gate of the paddock.

'Well?' she said, looking over her shoulder. 'Are you coming or not?'

She pushed through the gate, and they followed slowly. She crossed the paddock, the pasture, and the hazel copse, and turned along the hedge that formed the boundary with Anster. When she reached the stile, the children were coming more closely behind her.

She crossed the footbridge over the Derrent, plodded up the meadow bank, into the swamp of the eighteen acre, and led the children straight to the scarecrow.

'There! – What did I tell you?' she demanded, giving Tom a little push. 'There's your grannie, like I said!'

Seeing his face, she was suddenly frightened. His eyes were such unfathomed hollows. His stillness was almost more than she could bear. But then he turned and darted away and went running down the steep field and meadow, with the flood-water flying from under his heels.

'Betony, you're wicked!' Janie said. 'A nasty, horrible, wicked thing!'

'Leave her alone,' William said. 'Let's get home and talk to Tom.'

'Don't you want to go spearing eels, then?'

'Eels!' said William. 'So that's what the toasting-fork was for! And where do we borrow a boat, eh?'

'I know where,' Betony said.

William and Janie exchanged a look.

'No,' William said, decisively. 'We've had enough of you today. We're going home to look for Tom.'

She could take them with her just so far, these three brothers and one sister, but once they rebelled against her tyranny, they stood like stones and she could not move them.

'Oh, very well!' she said, some days later. 'It's no odds to me if Maddox comes too. But don't blame me if he scares off the eels!'

They went to the Derrent after school. Betony pointed out the mooring, almost hidden among the reeds, and William hauled the punt to the bank. But as they eagerly scrambled in, Tom hung back, his hands in his pockets.

'I ent coming, I ent too keen. Nor I don't think you should go neither.'

'Laws,' William said. 'After all that swither!'

'I don't trust that water. Not after the floods. And the sluices is open, higher up.'

'A punt is as safe as the Bank of England. It couldn't capsize if it tried till domesday.'

'I ent coming all the same. I'll stay here and watch.'

'Suit yourself,' William said. 'Seems five is enough in this little punt, anyway.'

He dropped the rope into the water and pushed away from the muddy bank. The punt drifted, slowly at first because of the reeds; then faster as it gained the middle stream. William reached for the brass fork, tied with string to a five-foot pole, but Betony refused to yield it.

'It's my turn first. It was my idea.'

'Hah!' said William. 'You ent likely to spear an eel! You've got no muscles, being a girl.'

'Mind yourself,' Betony said, 'and give me room.'

The three younger children sat together on one thwart, little Dicky safely wedged between Roger and Janie, while William and Betony stood erect.

'Well, get a move on!' William said. 'We're nearly run to the end of the rope.'

'You've got to look for the likely places,' Betony said, with a little sniff.

Standing at the very edge of the punt, she gazed over into the brook, which was brown and soupy, marbled by swirling yellow mud. There was a greater depth of water than she had thought, and its power thrilled in the boards at her feet. Watching the dimples in the surface, she was held enraptured by their speed, and felt a dizzying pull towards the water, just as the waters and tides of the earth were said to pull to the changing moon.

There came a jerk as the punt reached the end of its mooring. She threw out her arms to keep her balance, and sat down heavily in the bows.

'Laws!' William said. 'We shall do marvels at this rate, shan't we?' He took up the rope and began to haul the way back to the bank. 'Let me try this time. We'll be here till dark if we wait for you.'

'Very well!' Betony said. 'Since you're so clever, let's see you try.'

They drifted again, William now standing with feet wide apart, leaning out over the water, the fork held aloft in his right hand. Janie and Dicky were beginning to splutter. The sight of William so fierce and warlike, with his round sturdy rump stuck out so boldly and his stockings going to sleep in his boots, was too much for them. They broke into giggles, and Roger and Betony followed suit.

'Shut your noise!' William whispered. 'You'll scare every eel from here to Middening.'

He plunged the fork into the water, letting the pole slide through his fingers but grasping it firmly again at its end. Then he leant back and drew the fork clear.

'Bost it!' he said. 'The fuddy thing don't touch the bottom! You should've got a longer pole.'

'I told you, you've got to look for the likely places,' Betony said. 'Dr Mellow worked closer in.'

He tried again, and the fork touched the bottom, stirring up a cloud of mud. He leant back, withdrew the fork in great triumph, and swore to himself as he saw that the prongs were still bare. The punt jerked to the end of the painter, and they returned again to the beginning. William made try after try, but all he speared was an old leather bottle.

'Some people,' Betony said, 'aren't so clever as they seem to think.'

'D'you want to try?' William challenged, without taking his gaze from the water. 'You're welcome enough if you think you'll do better.'

'You say that now! After bending the fork like you have!'

'Lumme, I saw one! I did! Honest John! I must've just missed him and stirred him up!'

Desperate with excitement, he thrust the fork with all his might into the water. The prongs speared the bottom and stuck fast, and William, stretching too far to tug at the handle, toppled over into the brook.

Betony fell on her knees and reached out to clutch at his hair. But her fingers only scrabbled water. William had sunk to the muddy bed.

The three younger children sat huddled together, whimpering and moaning, and Betony sprawled, wriggling out further and further, her thighs on the gunwale, her feet hooked under the thwart. Her chest and her chin were touching the water. Her arms reached out ... reached out ... to save. But when William came to the surface, he was already several yards away. The Derrent had never before seemed so wide, nor its drift so rapid.

The punt reached the end of its painter and jerked to a stop among the reeds. William swept past, his fair hair showing like a handful of straw in the water. Betony wriggled back into the punt and tried to unfasten the rope. The wet knots defied her. So she stood up and began to shout.

'Tom!' she shouted. 'Tom! Where are you?'

Tom was running along the bank, making downstream towards the sluice. She saw him go wading into the water; saw him leaning over the sluice-gate, facing upstream, with arms hanging; and saw him clasping her brother by the collar, holding him up against the hatch. Tom had no strength to lift William bodily over: he could only hold on, keeping William's face above water.

As Betony hauled the way back to the bank, she saw that help was coming quickly, for Bert Tupper, working at Luckett's, had heard their noise and was racing to the sluice-gate. When she and the other children got there, William lay face down on the bank, and Bert, astride him, was squeezing the water out of his lungs.

'Is he going to die?' Betony whispered, frightened by William's closed eyes, by the queer look of his pallid skin, by the mud trickling forth between his lips.

'He'll be all right. But we've got to see he don't take a chill.' Bert took off his jacket and wrapped William round in it, close and tight. He stood up with the boy in his arms. 'Can you run?' he said to Roger. 'Then race off home and tell your mother to warm a bed for this young tucker and a sup of something to scald out his guts.'

Roger ran off, and Bert followed, hugging William close to his chest, with the other children trotting beside him. But when they reached home, and their mother came to meet them, Betony withdrew from the bustle and stole unnoticed into the barn. She mounted the ladder into the hayloft.

There, she climbed on the stacked hay, into a space between two trusses. It was warm and dry in there, and smelt of summer. It smelt of clover dried in the sun. With her legs drawn up, her arms clasped round them, and her chin resting upon her knees, she filled the little space completely. She fitted it, like a nut in a shell. She merged into the warmth and darkness.

She did not go to sleep, and yet she had dreams, of spring and sunlight. She dreamt she was being carried on her father's shoulders, riding along between the apple trees, her head among the blossoming branches, the pink and white blossoms reaching into the blue sky. She saw them and touched them, and the pollen was yellow on her brown fingers.

Then she was slipping from her father's shoulders, slipping and sliding down his back, and as she slid down, she saw the scar on the nape of his neck, where the flesh had once been badly burnt and had healed in terrible mottled puckers. No, it no longer hurt him, he always told her. He scarcely knew it was there now. He no longer felt it. But Betony felt it, a silent screech through her head and body, whenever she happened to see the scar.

Down below, Janie was calling from the fold.

'Betonee ... Are you up there in the hayloft again? Betony? Mother wants you.'

Betony stayed perfectly still, hearing only the blood in her ears, and the silence that fell when Janie had gone.

Then her father's voice came calling, and this time her heart went up in flames. She moved and nudged a truss of hay till it teetered over and flumped on the floor. Her father heard it. He called out at once.

'Betony! I know you're up there, so come on down! You're acting like a silly mommet.'

A pail rattled. The pump-handle creaked six times.

'Suit yourself!' he shouted to her. 'If you want to starve, that's up to you!'

She heard him limping across the cobbles; heard the house door close with a slam; and knew, truly, that he no longer cared if she lived or died, for he had left her alone in the darkness, cold and hungry, at the mercy of the rats.

Once again she heard the silence; endlessly, endlessly; until a step rattled the ladder, and someone came up into the hayloft, straight to the little place in the hay.

'Come along,' said her mother's cool and quiet voice. 'It's past eight o'clock and you've eaten nothing for seven hours.'

Betony gave herself up, a prisoner, and her mother's hands led her home.

'You can hide!' granna said. 'Going off on such missums and nearly getting your brother drowned!'

'Ent you ashamed?' asked great-grandpa. 'Suppose young William had catched a fever? I think you should ponder on that, girl, I do indeed!'

'She's pondered enough,' her mother said.

'Is William bad, mother?' Betony asked.

'Ha, he's just about beside hisself with consequence, that young man, – sitting up in bed, with everyone running round after him, including your father. You needn't worry about William. He's making the most of today's mishap.'

'Well, cheer up, Betony,' granna said. 'It's all over now. You needn't look so full of woe.'

But Betony, though relieved that brother William was unharmed, could not be cheerful. She was to blame for what had happened. She was always to blame, and the world was against her. She knew she would never smile again.

William, having been kept in bed three days, was allowed up for supper on the third day. He looked very pink and clean in the face – like a choirboy, Janie said – and his hair shone, smooth and yellow, brushed close to his head.

By supper-time, he was crimson with excitement, for everyone, on coming into the kitchen, made a great fuss of him, asking tenderly after his health and bringing him presents.

'Come on, mother!' he shouted, rapping his knife and fork on the table. 'Where's this special supper granna says we're having? Is it haddock with parsley sauce?'

'Be patient,' Beth said. 'I'm waiting for your father to settle down.'

'What, me?' said Jesse, taking his place. 'Why, I'm as ready as ready, I am! I'm just about fammelled for that there good smell.'

'Then I shall dish up,' Beth said.

She opened the oven and removed a deep earthenware basin that steamed and sizzled and smelt of fish. She brought it to the table and set it down in their midst, and when they leant forward, peering into the steaming basin, they saw it was filled with stewed eels.

William's face was a picture. His jaw had fallen. His mouth was ajar.

'Well, my son?' Jesse said gravely. 'Ent that exactly what you desired?'

'Laws! Shall I like them?' William said, and when they all laughed: 'Yes, I shall! I shall! I shall!'

'Of course you'll like 'em. It's a dish for a king.'

'They give you brains,' granna said, ladling a helping on to a plate.

Betony, catching her father's eye, felt a ripple inside her. His glance, for her, had not been so merry and warm for a long time. And she felt herself growing in stature again; felt she could do many wonderful things and be wise and clever and good and kind. And then, suddenly, Janie had to open her mouth and speak about something that didn't concern her, and the moment was spoilt, the warm good feeling was all undone.

'Fancy,' said Janie. 'Look at Betony, actually smiling! She said she'd never smile again.'

'I didn't! I didn't!' Betony cried.

'Oh yes you did. You wrote it in your prayer-book. I saw it myself and so did Roger.'

'Sneaky little toad!' Betony shouted, and, leaning across in front of William, she slapped Janie's face.

'Betony, go to bed at once!' her father said in an awful voice.

'Here, she ent had her supper,' Beth said. 'Betony, say you're sorry for hurting Janie, then eat up like a sensible girl.'

'I shan't say I'm sorry nor I shan't eat up!' Betony shouted, and bounced from her chair. 'I'd just as soon go to bed and starve!'

She ran out, slamming the door, and went stumbling upstairs without any candle to light the way, pulling off the chaplet her father had given her on her birthday and hurling it at the clock on the landing.

'Eels!' she said, groping her way into the bedroom. 'Horrible, stinking, slimy things!'

She took her prayer-book from under the mattress and tore out the pages, letting them flutter in shreds to the floor, where they lay glimmering in the darkness.

'There now!' she said, as she stripped off her clothes. 'Verily now I shall go to hell!'

She crept into bed and lay, stiff and cold, with her nightdress wound tight round her legs like a shroud. Tonight, when at last she should go to sleep, it would be forever. Her spirit willed it. She would die peacefully, and be taken from her bed, and be laid in the waterlogged earth in the churchyard, in a small coffin made by her father. And a silence would fall over all the land.

But although she slept, even before her sister had crept into bed beside her, it was not for ever. She awoke, as always, to the misty flare of the candle-flame in the morning darkness, the splash of water from jug to bowl, and Janie's little whimpering cry as she braced herself for the cold wash. The morning had come. The day must be lived through.

Life knew best, after all, for time put sorrow further and further behind, until, looking back, you saw it growing small in the distance; and there were other things – little healing things – to set beside it. There were even times of merriment, like the day her father took to smoking a pipe, when everything was again as it should be.

It was after supper one wet cold evening, the time of day when great-grumpa turned his chair to the hearth and took up his paper, and the children were allowed to gather round the fire, to toast themselves before going to bed. At these times, while granna made the kitchen tidy, and their mother searched the dresser drawers for stockings that wanted mending, their father would sit and talk to them, asking about their day's lessons. But this evening, having settled himself comfortably into his chair, he suddenly produced a pipe and tobacco and, without a word, began smoking.

They were dumbfounded. They stared and stared. Plenty of other men might smoke tobacco, including most of those in the workshop, but never their father! The thing was undreamt of. It made them all cry out at once, and granna, emptying sugar into a basin, whirled around with her hands at her breast.

'Whatever's the matter, screeching out, little devils, like that?'

'I dunno, I'm sure,' Jesse said, blowing smoke at the ceiling, 'unless it's my pipe that's causing the uproar.'

'Pipe?' said great-grumpa, looking at him over the paper. 'Since when've you took to smoking a pipe?'

'Since today, at one o'clock.'

'Where did you get it?'

'It was presented to me by Owner Jackson when I was at Upham, fetching a load of deal off his barge.'

'Do you like it?' Roger asked.

'Why, yes, I do. It's a nice little pipe and I took to it like a dog to a bone. It was made in Seay Forest, carved out of birchwood, and still got the bark on the bowl, d'you see? Ah, bost it! The damn thing's gone out.'

'Let's see you light it again,' said Janie.

'Ah, that's something to see, ent it, eh? There's a lot of skill goes to lighting a pipe. It ent just a question of puff and blow.'

'Why d'you hold the match-box over the bowl like that?' asked William.

'That's the proper way. It acts like a damper and gives me a good strong mighty draw. Ah, and I get a nice little tune on it, too, don't I? Can you hear it, Dicky, piping away?'

'Is that why it's called a pipe, dad?'

'It might be. I hadn't thought of that before. But here! You're making fun of me, ent you? You're playing me up the garden wall!'

'Why, no,' said William, who could mimic his father exactly. 'Not us! Not likely! Oh dear me no!'

Jesse was working furiously at his pipe, looking around the circle of faces, with a great show of not watching what he was doing, when the box of matches fizzed into flames. He jumped up and forward in one move, shooting the match-box into the stove, and the children gaped as it burnt up prettily in the fire, while great-grumpa, rustling his paper down again, glared fiercely at Jesse.

'Are you determined to burn the house down?'

'Why, no,' Jesse said. 'Not determined exactly. Oh dear me no!'

The look of surprise still remained on his face, as though he could not quite believe in such a calamity happening like that, a box of matches alight in his hand. And the look was so fixed in his round blue eyes that the children again broke into laughter.

'Here!' he said, turning to point his pipe at Tom. 'Are you gone against me like all the rest? Eh? Have you? I reckon you have. You're laughing at me the same as these others.'

Tom blinked, uneasy at finding himself the centre of attention. He looked away with his slow, shy smile. He was sitting perfectly still as always, hunched on his stool, with his arms folded upon his knees. He sat with the rest of them, a part of the family, listening to all they had to say, and yet he was still a stranger among them, the strangeness lying in what he was, in the way he was made, the way he kept so quiet and still.

His stillness vexed Betony. It made her feel, often, that she had been caught showing off, noisily, stupidly, like a child, and that was wrong, for she was the elder by eighteen months. She was wiser. She knew more things.

She would do her best, she thought, as she half listened to William and Janie arguing across her: she would try to be kind and helpful to Tom, if only because her father wished it. Her father was good. She wanted to please him. She wanted to be like him in every way.

'Well, Betony?' her father said, out of the noise all around her. 'Am I to be allowed another box of matches?'

'Yes,' she said. 'I'll go and get them.'

The long wet season ended at last. Christmas brought wind, giving the land a chance to dry, and the new year brought frosts, which lasted until the beginning of March. The children made a slide at Sitches Bottom, but Betony never went sliding now. She hurried home straight from school, having homework to do every day. The chimney-corner was given over to her use, a quiet place, out of the way, where she could sit with her writing-box on her knees and work.

'Betony's studying,' William would whisper, and would make much ado of going on tiptoe, leading the others back and forth, back and forth, until Betony called on her mother to drive them away.

Sometimes, the boys used to hide her satchel, or rub out

the notes she had made in her notebook, or sharpen her pencils at both ends. They sewed shirt-buttons on to her sampler and painted her pencil-box red, white and blue.

They teased granna, too, putting sticky burrs into her mittens, or tying knots in the sleeves of her nightdress. Once they hung a dead owl in place of a partridge in the larder, and granna, whose sight was poor, took it out and started to pluck it, when their giggles warned her that something was wrong. 'Ah, well, boys will be boys,' great-grumpa would say, laughing, and granna would retort angrily: 'That's exactly what I've got against them!'

Then, one day, Roger borrowed the old man's watch, which he found hanging from the knob of the corner cup-board. It was a Sunday, and great-grumpa was having his afternoon nap in the parlour. Roger sat down at the kitchen table and carefully took the watch apart. He studied the parts through granna's lens, cleaned every one with a tiny paint-brush, and carefully put them together again. Sadly, the watch no longer went. Nor would its casing quite close as it should. So Roger hung it back on the door-knob and hoped for the best.

Great-grumpa's fury was something to see. He seemed to the children to grow enormous, and looked as though he would smite them to the floor.

'Ah, well, boys will be boys!' their granna said.

On Monday, their mother took the watch in to old Mr Hines, in Chepsworth. She delivered it back in good order that evening.

'There's no damage done. And I'm the one that paid the bill.'

'I should damn well think so!' said great-grumpa.

'Mr Hines said Roger'd done well for a boy his age. He said we should put him to learn the trade.'

'Did he?' said Roger, bright-eyed.

'Why in God's name go to a clocksmith when you've got a trade on your own doorstep?' great-grumpa demanded.

'I dunno that I want to be a carpenter,' Roger said.

'Hell's bells! You're talking rubbish!'

'When the time comes, Roger shall choose for hisself,' Beth said.

'Glory!' said Jesse. 'That's different from me, then! You made me be a carpenter whether I liked the idea or not.' And he looked up, laughing, as Beth passed his chair. 'You did, wife, and don't you deny it!'

Betony, watching her father and mother together, saw the bright glance that flickered between them, and the hint of annoyance in her mother's face. And afterwards, when she had her father to herself, she talked to him about it.

'What would you have been if not a carpenter?'

'I'd have been a labourer on a farm.'

'Why d'you do as my mother tells you?'

'She generally knows what's best, that's why.'

'But you're a man. You shouldn't always be giving in. My mother's too fond of her own way.'

'So's somebody else I could mention.'

'Not me! Not me!'

'Yes, you, little peewit. You're just the same. It's the Tewke in you.'

'I wish I was all Izzard, then, that's all!'

'You wouldn't have much of a head-piece in that case,' he said. 'You'd be a dummel like me.'

And Betony, though she denied it, knew her father spoke the truth. She knew she had her mother's quickness, both of temper and of brain.

It was not easy to like Tom. He was too strange. He did such mysterious and meaningless things, such as stealing salt from the dinner-table.

Betony, in her chimney-corner, had the kitchen to herself, for her mother and granna were busy next door, sweeping up the ants that had invaded the store-room. The kitchen table was laid for dinner. A mutton stew steamed on the hob.

She was sitting there, biting her pencil, when Tom came in and stood looking intently at the table. He was quite unaware of her presence in the corner, perhaps because it was Saturday morning, when she was usually cleaning her bedroom. He looked at the table for some seconds, listening, head cocked, to the noises in the store-room; then he took a small pill-box out of his pocket, filled it with salt from the pewter salt-pot, and went out again, very quietly, although wearing hobnailed boots.

Betony followed. She stood in the dairy and watched through the window. Tom crossed the fold and went into the cartshed. He climbed on the cart-wheel and hid the pill-box up on the ledge of the shed wall, in the worm-eaten space at the end of the crossbeam. Then he left the shed and went off to the orchard, where the other boys were trimming the hedges. Betony went into the cartshed. She had to discover. She had to see. But there was nothing more to learn about Tom's secret. The pill-box was just a pill-box. The salt was just salt.

The following morning, before church, she saw him go again to the cartshed; saw him take down the pill-box, open it to look inside, and put it back again in its place. She stood waiting, and watched him grow pale as he turned and found her standing there.

'It's salt,' she said. 'I saw you take it.'

He said nothing, but stood still, hands in pockets, staring into space.

'Why salt?' she asked. 'Where's the point? What use is it?'

'Nothing,' he muttered, and walked off.

That evening, the pill-box was gone, and Betony never saw it again.

One frosty evening, when the younger children came in from sliding, they bore signs of having been fighting. Dicky's coat was torn at the seams, the other boys had bruised and dirty faces, and even Janie, so trim and correct, had lost the ribbon from her hair.

'I hate Prudie Green!' said little Dicky. 'She called me a pudding-face! Oh yes she did!'

'And how did it start, all this name-calling?' his mother asked. 'Was it you or Prudie Green?'

'It was Archie Slewton, saying things about our Tom,' said Janie, and, catching a quelling glance from William, would say no more.

'Well, all you children go outside and play for a while longer, 'cos I want a little talk with Tom. Yes, you too, Betony.'

'*I'm* not going outside!' Betony said. 'I'm doing my homework.'

'Do as you're told,' her mother said.

Betony went to the barn with the others, and they crouched in a circle, warming their hands at a lantern placed on the floor in their midst.

'Well? What's the mystery, then?'

'Don't tell her!' William said. 'She'll take it out on Tom.'

'No, I shan't! I swear it solemnly, Bible oath.'

'All right. You'll hear it from them lot at school, anyway, sooner or later.'

'Whatever is it, for goodness' sake?'

'Seems Tom is a bastard,' Jane said. 'That's what Archie Slewton said. So did Tibby Lovage.'

Betony gave a little shiver and reached further forward, spreading her hands very close to the lantern.

'Laws,' she said. 'Is that all?'

'There's worse than that,' William said. 'They say Tom's father was a murderer and murdered Tom's mother down in the cottage next to the smithy. People went down with pots and pans and treated him to the rough music and the policemen came and hanged him in a tree.'

'I don't believe it!' Betony said.

'No more don't I!' Janie agreed.

Tom came into the barn, and they all stood up.

'What did mother say?' asked William. 'Did she say it was true, about your father being a murderer?'

'Yes,' said Tom.

'I expect he had a brain-storm,' Janie whispered, 'like Maisie Morgan did that time.'

Tom said nothing, but seemed to shrug. Betony picked up the lantern and raised it so that she could see his face.

'Don't you care that your father murdered your mother and got hanged for it?'

'No,' Tom said. 'That's nothing to me.'

'Haven't you got any feelings, then?'

'No. I haven't.'

'That's what I thought. You're made of stone.'

'Betony! Remember your promise!' William said.

'I shan't torment him! I've wasted enough time already. I'm going indoors to get warm.'

In the following days, however, the new knowledge was almost constantly in her mind, and she watched every chance of catching Tom alone.

'What's it feel like, being a bastard?' she asked, waylaying him one day in the paddock. 'Does it make you feel bad inside? And being the son of a murderer? – Does it give you nightmares?'

Tom said nothing, but kept on the move, across the paddock, into the pasture.

'I shan't torment you,' she said. 'I just want to know what it feels like, that's all. I'll be sympathetic if only you'll let me.'

Again he said nothing.

'Does it hurt?' she asked. 'Do you blame God?'

But Tom just kept walking, faster now, feet crunching the frosty grass, making towards the open fields.

'I think you're silly!' she shouted after him. 'You can't go on like that forever. – Always stepping aside to get out of my way. Not forever, you can't! Forever is a long time!'

But it seemed she was wrong. Forever was nothing to Tom. It was no hardship to him to go off on his own for hours on end, if that was the only way to escape her. The order of things was set between them. Time made no change. He would talk to the others, but not to her, and when they were all gathered together in one circle, it was no hardship for him, as it would have been for Betony herself, to make himself nothing and take no part in the quick flying talk.

And if all else failed to protect him from Betony's probing, he would go to Beth and attach himself to her without a word. He would help her feed the hens and collect the eggs, or would sit in the cowshed and watch her milking the two cows. He knew he was utterly safe with Beth, like a blackbird sheltering under a thorn.

CHAPTER TWO

It was four miles to Chepsworth, even the short way, over the fields, and Betony, walking to and fro every day, always looked forward to crossing the railway at Stickington Halt, for it marked the half-way point in her journey. There, too, in the morning, Nancy Sposs would be waiting for her, and the rest of the walk would be nothing at all. It would simply fly. – There was so much to say. And in the evening, they often stood at the level crossing for as much as an hour, to resolve an argument or finish a story before parting.

Nancy was three years older than Betony. She had been one of the first ten pupils to enter the Grammar School, Lock's, with one of the new scholarships for poor children. She would speak in her blunt, matter-of-fact way of the early days in Miss Mussoe's form, when the scholarship girls were kept apart with a screen around them to prevent their smell, their germs, their lice, from spreading among the 'daughters of gentlemen'.

'It's different now,' Nancy would say. 'There are more of us . . . and not enough screens to go round.'

At first, Betony found Nancy Sposs repellent. She thought her too gruff, too hard and masculine in her ways. Nancy's body was thick and solid. Her face was coarse-skinned, and her hair grew very low on her forehead, giving her the brutish, scowling look that she herself called her 'donkey beauty'. But behind that low forehead there lay a keen and logical mind, perfectly disciplined, yet full of energy and imagination. She had warmth, too, and Betony found her a good friend.

Nancy was top of the school in all sciences and in English. At fifteen she founded the school debating society, and led her team against the boys' school, engaging pupils and masters alike in debating compulsory religious instruction, the Montessori experiments, and women's suffrage. She knew exactly what she wanted from life, and her sights were fixed on a Cambridge degree, a career in chemistry, and a vote. Yet in spite of her high-flown ambitions, Nancy's feet were on common earth. She came from a poor home, and her family was always her first consideration. Her father was a linesman on the railway. Her mother took in washing. If her father fell ill, which happened often, Nancy went gardening at Chepsworth Park, thus making up for his lost wages. If her mother fell ill, Nancy stayed at home to deal with the wash. And she always found time to help her schoolboy brothers, who hoped to become clerks on the railway.

Once or twice every summer holidays, Nancy would spend a day at Cobbs. She was interested in everything: in all the old buildings; in the work going on in the workshop; in the men themselves. But most of all she was interested in Tom.

'He's somehow alone . . . Even with your family, all such a crowd together, he still seems alone. And he never talks to *you* at all. Now why is that?'

'I wasn't very nice to him when he first came. I was cruel to him. – I realize that now. I feel guilty about it sometimes.'

'So you ought,' Nancy said.

'Oh, it's true I'm bad!' Betony cried. 'I'm all the things I least admire! D'you know that? I'm all the things I least want to be!'

'Poor little soul,' Nancy said tartly.

'Can people change?'

'If they want it enough, they can work marvels. But you don't really want to change. You don't really think about other people. You don't even see them except in relation to yourself.'

'Thanks very much! Sometimes I wonder why I'm friends with you.'

'I'm your conscience,' Nancy said.

When Nancy left Lock's to go to Cambridge, Betony was completely lost. Looking about her at school, she realized how little she had seen for herself, how little she had thought about her surroundings. She had been looking through Nancy's eyes and relying on Nancy's thinking for more than three years. She had worked well enough, but like a pony, between blinkers, content to nod sedately along, relying on extra mural contact with Nancy to stimulate her own ideas. Looking about her, she thought the other girls dull and insipid, and worst of all, feared that she herself must be like them. She made friends in time, but there was never anyone else like Nancy.

One summer day, at the level crossing, she met Geoffrey Danville, who had come to the Halt to collect a parcel of books for his father. A train went past, the Slow Train from Here to There, as Nancy had called it, and Geoffrey remarked that it was running late. They stayed talking a little while, and thereafter, every evening, he came on purpose to walk with her a little way along the old drove road.

Betony then was fifteen. Geoffrey was older by eighteen months. His father was rector of Woody Layton and a canon of the cathedral, and his mother was related to Mr Champley of Chepsworth Park. Betony thought Geoffrey the most handsome boy she had ever seen. He was so tall and graceful; his hair was a beautiful chestnut brown; his features sensitive and refined. Even his name was beautiful: an aristocratic name, she thought; and Geoffrey himself did not deny it.

Through Geoffrey's eyes, she caught many glimpses into a new and exotic world: a world of vast drawing-rooms, with Persian carpets on the floors, and Worcester china in use every day; where silk-vested clergy conferred in groups, grave-faced from the burden of sacred duties, while their ladies drifted serenely about from terraced garden to croquet lawn. And she heard many interesting things, such as how the young viscount could scarcely write his name, and why the dean's daughter had gone to live in Cheshire.

She wanted to share Geoffrey with her sister and brothers; to give them a chance of seeing into the larger world; but when Geoffrey came to Cobbs, the visit did not proceed as she had planned it.

The trouble began when they were showing him round the orchard, for he trod in a very wet cowpat. His distress, and the trouble he took in cleaning his shoe, brought them all to an astonished standstill. They were first baffled, and then enchanted, and, lastly, full of helpful ideas. William offered to ask for a loan of his granna's jemimas. Roger fetched the garden barrow and offered to wheel Geoffrey about in style. And Janie repeatedly rushed forward, making great play with her pinafore, flicking liquid manure from Geoffrey's face and person.

'I'm afraid you think me fastidious,' he said, retreating before her.

'Laws, no!' Janie assured him. 'You're a fusspot, that's all.'

'Don't the cows make muck at Woody Layton?' asked William.

'Not,' said Geoffrey, 'in the Rectory garden.'

'Then you don't grow much rhubarb, I don't suppose?'

'No rhubarb, I'm afraid.'

'What're you afraid for all the time?'

'That is merely a figure of speech.'

'Ah, a figure of speech,' William said, nodding solemnly all around. 'Merely. Yes. Quite so I'm afraid.'

'Stop it!' said Betony, pinching William's arm. 'Don't you know how to behave when we've got company?'

'Comp'ny?' said Roger, and, putting his hand inside his shirt, began scratching under his armpit. 'Lumme, no!' he said, wriggling. 'Comp'ny indeed! Whatever next? Jumper Lane's the one for that!'

'Let's go on the common,' Janie suggested, taking pity on Geoffrey for Betony's sake. 'We might find some mushrooms.'

Janie fell in on one side of Geoffrey and Betony on the other, both seeking to protect him from the boys.

'Betony says you come from a very old family. She was telling us, the other day.'

'Well,' said Geoffrey, 'my ancestors came over to England with the Conqueror.'

'Ours were already here,' said William, deliberately treading on Geoffrey's heels.

'And your dad's a parson?' Janie prompted.

'Rector, yes. As a matter of fact, he's very friendly with your man here, Mr Wisdom. They were up at Oxford together, you know. He's a nice fellow, isn't he? Wisdom, I mean?'

189

'He's all right,' Janie said. 'We like Mr Chance of Eastery best.'

'Ah, yes, Parson Chance. A good enough man, my father says, but rather indulgent with the common people.'

'I dunno about indulgent!' said William, angrily, from behind. 'We have a saying, that more gets done by Chance than Wisdom in these two parishes, and it's true, too!'

'Oh, tes frères colériques, Bétoine!' said Geoffrey. 'Qu'est-ce que je fais pour les fâcher? Parlons en français. Ainsi on pourrait peut-être éviter d'autres disputes.'

'Très bien,' Betony said. 'Ainsi soit-il!'

With only two terms of French behind her, however, she soon foundered, while Geoffrey swam on in full flood. She could but tut in the gallic manner, picked up from Mademoiselle Jones, and hazard a reckless affirmative when Geoffrey's tone seemed to demand it.

The boys were delighted, and pranced in front.

'Ooley mooley vooley voo!' William said to Roger.

'Kesker petty wetty bong!' replied Roger. 'Wee! Wee! Widdley wee!'

And they danced in front, capering, gesticulating, clapping one another on the shoulder, then pretending, by mime, to be onion-sellers pedalling along on their bicycles.

'Oker della looner! Monna me Peru!' sang William. 'Pray tomato bloomer! Poorer queerer moo!'

'Mong Jew! Mong ong-yongs!' shouted Dicky. 'Wolla cherry bee-cee-clett!'

'Ting-a-ling, ting-a-ling!' shouted Roger. 'Scoozer, scoozer! Silver play!'

'Oh, really!' Geoffrey exclaimed, stopping abruptly in his tracks. 'Betony, I beseech you! Can't you stop their silly behaviour?'

'Well, I think you'd better stick to English,' Betony said, rather snappishly.

'It may have escaped your notice but I *am* speaking English now.'

'Ting-a-ling, ting-a-ling!' shouted Roger. 'Scoozer! Scoozer! Silver play!'

'Take no notice,' Betony said. 'They'll soon get tired if you ignore them.'

But Geoffrey only grew more fractious, until he was on the brink of tears. He went home early, and Betony, going with him as far as Tupton, tried half-heartedly to make amends.

'I'm sorry about my brothers' behaviour. But it's only their fun, you know. They don't mean any harm.'

'I'm sorry, too,' Geoffrey said, sniffing, 'I'm not accustomed to that kind of thing.'

Betony pitied him, knowing he had suffered; yet she wanted to laugh at him, too, because he was such a Mary Ellen. When they said good-bye, she knew she would never see him again, but she felt no regret: only shame at having been so bedazzled by him, and guilt that her feelings had changed so quickly.

'Shall you go to university, Betony, and try for your cap and gown like Nancy Sposs?'

'No.'

'Why not? You're clever, ent you?'

'Not clever enough,' Betony said.

She had never faced the question squarely before, and now, in doing so, she knew she was accepting another hard and uncomfortable truth.

It was all a necessary part of growing up, this coming to terms with imperfection. She remembered how shocked she had been, years before, on hearing great-grumpa refer to George Hopson as the best carpenter in the workshop. Surely her father was best? It was quite unthinkable that he should only be second-rate. But as time went on, she was forced to see it. She was forced to find comfort in reminding herself that skill was not everything. – Other things mattered as much, if not more, and her father was a good man in a great many ways. But acceptance was difficult, always hard-won.

In scholastic achievement, Nancy Sposs had served as a buffer, for Betony, always top of the village school, might have expected a similar destiny at Lock's if she had not perceived at once that Nancy's powers and self-discipline towered far above her own. Here, acceptance had come almost unnoticed, eased by friendship. It was enough for

Betony that she had made friends with one of the cleverest girls at Lock's. It mattered nothing that she was not to be numbered among them. She hardly thought about it at all.

Now, in answering Roger's question, she had accepted another truth. She had taken another step forward.

It was her habit to note the progression, because it seemed so dreadfully slow. She felt herself somehow lagging behind, for her sister and brothers were all so certain, knowing exactly what they would do. Janie, fifteen, was courting Martin Holt: they planned to marry in three years' time. William and Tom were established in the workshop, and Roger, though still determined to be a watchmaker, had agreed to serve two years with great-grumpa so that he had 'something behind him'. And Dicky, at school, counted the days impatiently, eager to join his brothers at the workbench. They were all so clear-eyed and self-assured: beside them, Betony felt herself blind and muddled; felt herself falling slowly to bits.

She did well enough at school. She was average in maths, geography, biology, but shone in history, English, and art. She never behaved badly in class; was never a rebel; and never questioned any rule, tradition, or piece of information; all of which made her a favourite with her teachers. This gave her no pleasure. It only depressed her. Nancy Sposs had never been tame and predictable, and Betony wished she were like Nancy Sposs. But it was no use wishing. She must be herself, once she knew what that self might be. Meanwhile, she was just a sponge.

Miss Maiberry used to invite certain girls to breakfast or tea in her rooms in Chepsworth, for she believed in Small Improvements. She taught them the use of sugar-tongs during afternoon tea, and how wrong it was to cut toast with a knife at breakfast. She gave advice on pressing their clothes, and most important, on how to accomplish a creaseless sleeve.

Betony now wore the regulation dress of the senior pupils: long skirt of navy blue serge; black leather belt with silver buckle bearing the school insignia; white blouse with tight cuffs and high collar; dark red tie with fine pink striping. Her mother ironed her blouses to perfection, and Betony had always been proud of the straight sharp crease in each long sleeve. Now, however, perceiving how grave had been her error, she hurried home from Miss Maiberry's demonstration, heated the irons on the kitchen stove, and showed her mother how a sleeve ought to be, beautifully rounded, and innocent of creases.

Beth was impressed. She watched admiringly.

'My word! If I'd known you was such a dab at ironing I'd have let you take over long since. But there! It's never too late to make amends so finish them shirts of the boys' and then get on with this basketful here.'

'But I can't! I've got homework to do this evening.'

'First things first,' Beth said. 'There's plenty of time.'

Thereafter, the family ironing frequently came Betony's way, and thereafter, too, she was careful to keep any new accomplishments to herself.

Miss Maiberry was nice but it was Miss Neott, the headmistress, whom Betony most admired. Miss Neott, aged fifty, was handsome and hawklike, with peppery hair impeccably trained about her ears. Her voice was soft but rather compelling, and endowed the simplest words with richness. Betony often emerged from Miss Neott's lessons resolved to speak the most perfect English, though the resolution failed as soon as she was at home again.

When Betony was half-way through her seventeenth year, Miss Neott asked her if she had any ambitions.

'I suppose you're not obliged to seek employment? No doubt there's plenty to do at home?'

'Oh, but I don't want to stay at home! I want to see something of the world.'

'The world?' said Miss Neott, with a little gleam.

'Well, England, that is.'

'Ah, you don't mean to emulate Miss Gertrude Bell?'

'No, I'm not so ambitious as that,' Betony said.

Miss Neott said nothing more just then, but during that term she asked Betony to help some girls who had lost time during the influenza epidemic. In the end-of-term tests, the girls did well, and Miss Neott praised Betony's coaching.

'A teacher's work can be very rewarding.'

The word dropped delicately into Betony's mind, like a small pebble dropping into a pool.

'If I'm to teach, I suppose I'd better think about going to college.'

'Not necessarily,' Miss Neott said. 'I may be able to help you there. We both know you have teaching ability, and if we nurture it in the next twelve months, well, – at the end of that time I may be able to do something for you.'

From then on, Betony studied with set purpose, and when, at seventeen, she won her school diploma with honours, she was called to Miss Neott's room to discuss plans for the future.

'I remember, Betony, that you wished to see the wider world. If you still feel the same, I can write to a friend of mine, Miss Telerra, who is headmistress of a private school, the Oldbourne and Simsbury High School for Girls, in the suburbs of London.'

'Oh, thank you!' Betony said.

'Miss Telerra requires an assistant teacher and I think if I write to her she may accept you without a preliminary interview. You will write, too, of course, and I will help you compose your letter. Miss Telerra's school is similar to Lock's. Does it appeal to you?'

'Oh yes!' Betony said. 'London! My goodness!'

'The *suburbs* of London,' Miss Neott said.

'Yes, of course!' Betony said. 'The suburbs of London. Yes, indeed.'

At home, when she told her news, Janie and William seemed put out.

'D'you truly want to leave home?' asked Janie. 'Go to London? All alone?'

'Of course! Everyone wants to go to London!'

'I don't think you ought,' William said. 'Mother, she shouldn't ought to go to London, our Betony, should she?'

'Betony's old enough to suit herself. She's a sensible girl. She'll take good care, I'm sure of that.'

'Well, I wouldn't go to London,' said William. 'Would you, Tom?'

'No,' said Tom. 'I'm well enough here.'

Jesse said little or nothing throughout all this, but later, walking with Betony in the orchard, he looked at her with sad reproach.

'Don't look like that!' Betony said. 'I shan't go anywhere if you look like that.'

'Don't mind me, my blossom. You must do as the spirit moves you, even if it does mean going to London.'

'The *suburbs* of London,' Betony said.

'Seems you're going to be something special, what with letters coming and going by post and all.'

'I'll be a teacher, that's all.'

'That's special, ent it? Not like your dad, a dilladerry sort of chap, who's never been nowhere in all his days.'

Betony put her arm through his.

'Miss Neott's waiting to hear from Miss Telerra. It'll all take ages yet, I dare say.'

But Miss Neott received an answer within a matter of days, and Miss Telerra, it seemed, was pleased to offer Miss Izzard a post on her staff, to teach history and English throughout the school, at a salary of thirty-six pounds per annum. Because of the urgency of her need, and because she trusted Miss Neott's judgment, Miss Telerra would waive the customary personal interview, and would be glad if Miss Izzard could take up her appointment at the start of the summer term. Miss Neott helped Betony to compose her letter of acceptance, and confirmation arrived by return.

The kitchen at Cobbs seemed suddenly filled with bolts of cloth. Granna was never without her spectacles, never without needle and thread and some half-made garment between her hands, and the two flat-irons were never allowed to grow cold.

Jesse, busy making a travelling-box, said it would never hold all the clothes that were being made, and if he were to make a bigger one, no train would be able to carry it. The travelling-box was made of ashwood, covered in canvas, painted dark green, with Betony's initials in black on the lid. It had rope handles and leather straps, and a shiny brass lock that locked with a tiny figured key.

The time passed terribly slowly, yet when it was gone, she wished she were able to call it back. And at the last, saying good-bye to her family, she found herself wondering all sorts of things about them, thinking of questions she wanted to ask. She had left it too late, and felt she would never now have a chance to know them.

'There's three-pound-ten,' said great-grumpa, putting a purse into her hand. 'Not for wasting, mind, but for necessary needments.'

'Be sure and always air your clothes,' said granna.

'Write us a letter every week,' said Janie.

'And picture-postcards!' said the boys in chorus.

'Remember, Betony,' said her mother, 'if you don't like it there, don't delay in coming home.'

'Of course I shall like it!' Betony said.

'Good-bye, Betony,' said Tom.

'Good riddance, too?' she said gaily, and Tom shrugged.

Her father drove her to Chepsworth station, and saw her safely on to the train. He stood on the platform, filling his pipe, packing the tobacco much too hard, gazing at her as she leant from the window of the carriage door.

'Got your box?' he asked abruptly.

'Yes. You carried it aboard for me.'

'Got that address wrote down, have you, where there's a room bespoke for you?'

'I've got all Miss Telerra's directions written down, father.'

'What's her name, where you're going to lodge?'

'Mrs Bream.'

'Ah, I knowed it was something to do with fish. Here! Look at that! That guard has gone and got off the train!'

The whistle blew, and the train began very gently to move. Betony leant still further out of the window, and her father began to walk with the train.

'Lumme!' he said. 'Seems you're going any minute now. I seen that guard nipping on and off, the one with bright buttons and the little green flag. He's a caution, he is! But I dare say he knows what he's about.'

'We're moving now!' Betony cried. 'We're moving properly this time! Good-bye, father! Good-bye, our dad!'

'You take care up there in London!' he called out, walking

faster, dragging his foot. 'Take care, my blossom, and don't get trampled to death in them crowds!'

The train gathered speed, and he was left standing on the platform. Betony watched him and went on waving to the last. He looked very lonely, standing there.

That last glimpse almost spoilt her journey, saddening her, making her feel that she had done wrong in leaving him. But then resentment arose in her, and she cast off the guilty sadness, telling herself that she had a right to enjoy the new life now beginning.

As far as Long Stone, she had the compartment to herself, but there two middle-aged men got in, sat down in opposite corners, and put up their papers. Betony marvelled. She looked at them for signs of pretence. That people could actually board a train and be rattled along at high speed, yet show no more feeling than if they were taking a stroll down the road! It was amazing. The two must be seasoned travellers indeed. Some day, perhaps, she would be the same. But for the present she was content to be a new scholar and wonder at everything she saw.

Surely the primroses growing along the embankments were bigger than any at home? Surely the sky over Oxfordshire and Buckinghamshire was different from any sky seen over Huntlip? And surely the towns she passed through were peopled with being more real, more important, possessed of a higher cast of mind, than any she had left behind her? The towns were exciting. The towns were where great things got done. And London was the apogee, the capital city over them all. Surely the people who lived there shaped the world?

The journey ended all too soon, and when she saw the grey city smoking under the blue spring sky, she experienced a sighing, dying-away feeling inside her, for now the miracle of this first moment, could never, never come again. She stood up, face pressed against the window, and watched the railway lines opening out, wider and wider, more and more rails, running together and parting again, a zig-zag complex of glistening steel. The train ran in under shelter, and the daylight took on an underwater shade of green. Was this London? It was indeed. 'Paddington! H'all change!'

A porter carried the box to an exit, and Betony boarded a northbound bus. She paid a fare of fourpence, and, after travelling fifteen minutes, was set down outside The Panting Hart, at a five-road junction in Stanton Broadway. There, as she stood with her box at her feet, again consulting her written instructions, a man approached and touched his cap.

'Carry your trunk, miss? Anywhere!'

'Matlock Terrace,' Betony said.

'No distance at all. Just ten minutes across the park.' The man, although small, cheerfully took the box on his shoulder. 'Charge you a bob,' he said, tentatively.

'Thank you. That's very kind.'

'New to London?' he asked, as they walked. 'Up from the country? I thought as much. Come for a holiday, I suppose?'

'No, I'm going to teach at the Oldbourne and Simsbury High School for Girls.'

'Well, I'll go to Putney to see the boat race! My eldest girl's a pupil there. She got a scholarship three years ago. Florrie, her name is. Florrie Smith. What's your name, miss, so's I can tell her when I get home?'

'Miss Izzard.'

'I'll tell her I met you. She's a good girl, Florrie. You'll like her, I know.' He walked a little way in silence, glancing often into Betony's face. 'I expect you're wondering,' he said, 'at an out-of-work chap like me having a daughter at the High School?'

'I wasn't wondering anything,' Betony said.

'You won't say nothing about it, will you? At the school, I mean. — That you seen Florrie's father out tootling for coppers? Better not. They're a very superior class of girl at the High School, and I don't want them making things hard for Florrie.'

They were crossing the park, and he pointed towards the eastern boundary.

'The school's over there. See the white wall behind them aspens? You'll be nice and handy in Matlock Terrace.'

They passed between two tall iron gates, and crossed a curved road to the terrace of houses on the other side. Number fifty was at the centre. It had net curtains in loops across the windows, and stained-glass panels in the door.

The man carried the travelling-box up the steps and set it down inside the porch. He looked pained as Betony offered him his shilling, but took it from her and once again touched his cap.

'All the best, Miss Izzard, and if you should hear of anyone wanting a carpenter, you might remember Joe Smith.'

'A carpenter?' Betony said.

'That's my trade, – when I can get the work,' he said, and went off with a last salute.

Betony turned and pulled the bell, and the clangour of it echoed through the house. A curtain moved at one bay window, was held back by jewelled fingers, and, after several seconds, allowed to fall.

Mrs Bream, who came at last to open the door, was a stately woman with corkscrew curls at her temples, a large face, and large strong teeth, very white and square. She was stately and slow in all she did, and she stood in the hall, her hands folded upon her stomach, looking at Betony's travelling-box as if it presented a grave problem. It seemed the maid, Ruby, had chosen that moment to scald herself with a saucepan of milk, and was still busy in the basement, dressing her arm with bicarbonate paste. Mrs Bream, therefore, was obliged to call her daughter, Edna, to help Betony with the box. It was no trouble. The fault was the maid's. Ruby was rather a clumsy girl.

'Of course, Miss Izzard, I wouldn't ordinarily have taken a guest unseen, but for Miss Telerra's personal assurance.'

Betony, following with Edna, under a looped velvet curtain and up the stairs, was not sure how to answer. She made a polite noise in her throat. On the landing, where an oriel window gave good light, she and Edna inspected each other across the box. The girl was lively and fresh-faced, with rather prominent green eyes, and all the time her mother talked, she kept making faces and glancing skywards.

From the landing, they climbed another flight of stairs to the attic, where Mrs Bream opened a door and led the way into Betony's bedroom. The room, being high, was full of sunlight, and the casement window looked on the park.

'I've given you a front room, as you see. The view is a

large part of this house's charm, I think, and all my guests agree, I'm sure.'

She spoke as if her house alone enjoyed the view, instead of sharing it with ninety neighbours, and again the girl Edna sucked in her cheeks and rolled her eyes derisively.

'It's a very nice room,' Betony said, and, divining from Mrs Bream's silence that this was scarcely an adequate tribute, she added warmly: 'I shall like it here. I shall indeed!'

'Edna is at the High School,' Mrs Bream said. 'You are much of an age, so I'll leave it to her to make you feel at home here.'

The moment her mother had left the room, Edna collapsed on to Betony's bed.

'Poor mother! She's no idea how funny she is!'

'Funny? I didn't think her funny at all.'

'What *did* you think her, pray?'

'I thought her rather dignified.'

'That's her transformation! She dare not make a careless move for fear of upsetting those little curls. But let's talk about you! How old are you? Eighteen? I'll be seventeen on June the twelfth. But I'm old for my age, don't you think? I'm very mature, mother says, and Mr Thorsby thinks so, too.'

Betony herself was only seventeen, but thought it wiser not to say so.

'Mr Thorsby?' she said instead.

'One of our lodgers. Whoops! – I mean guests! And the only one worth troubling about. He's a surgeon, and rather fine. But what about you! Fancy you teaching at Old and Sims. You must be very clever.'

'Only ordinary,' Betony said.

'Have you got to see Telerra in the morning?'

'At nine o'clock.'

'Sooner you than me! But she's not so bad, considering. Now tell me – where would you like to go this afternoon? We've got plenty of time to wander round town, so what would you like to see?'

'Anything and everything!' Betony said.

For the residents of Stanton Rise, all journeys began and

ended at the Broadway, and so, from outside The Panting Hart, they took a bus to Marylebone. They went to the waxworks of Madam Tussaud; walked along Oxford Street, gazing into the shop windows; and went to Robini's for tea and gateaux. They then travelled by bus to Chelsea and walked along the embankment there.

'It's lucky you've got some money,' Edna said. 'I spent my allowance ages ago. Are you sure you don't mind paying for everything? I'll take my turn when I'm in the dibs.'

'Of course I don't mind,' Betony said.

'That young man was looking at you. The tall one with the dark moustache. They've got dreadful sauce, some of these men. Did you see him stare?'

'No. I'm still seeing the Kings and Queens of England.'

'What? Oh, the waxworks! Aren't they splendid? All so real! Now what did you want to see next? Oh, yes, I remember! Let's ask the way.'

Outside a tobacconist's shop, a woman in slippers was sweeping the pavement, and they asked her the way to Dr Johnson's house.

'Dr Johnson?' the woman said. 'There's nobody here of that name. If you want a doctor, you must go to Walker's Mews and see Dr Snell.'

They nodded primly and walked on, but once out of earshot, they clung to each other and spluttered with laughter. It was too delicious, Edna said. The old woman had made her day.

They returned home for dinner at seven, and Betony met her fellow lodgers: Miss Wilkings, who sold flowers from a stall outside The Panting Hart; Mr Lumbe, a plump young man of twenty-two, who worked in a bank in Oldbourne; and Mr Thorsby, a severe-looking man in his late thirties, who seemed to Betony to be cold and remote and absent-minded. She also met the head of the household, Mr Bream, who said she must not expect him to be clever, for he was only a businessman and only knew 'how to manage the works'. The works being a steam laundry in Simsbury Green.

Edna, describing the fruitless search for Dr Johnson, was scolded by Mrs Bream, the last to take her place at the table, for leaving a tureen of soup to grow cold on the dumb-waiter. Her father defended her. So did Mr Lumbe. Mr Thorsby said nothing, but sipped his glass of water and stared into space.

'What d'you think of London, Miss Izzard?' Mr Bream inquired. 'Dirty old place, eh? All smuts and smoke?'

'Oh, no!' Betony said.

'Paved with gold, then, is that it?'

'Paved with history,' Betony said.

Briefly, she felt embarrassed by what she had said, but Mr Bream's 'Bravo!' and Mr Lumbe's 'Hear, Hear!' set her mind at ease, and she saw that among these civilized people, a little flamboyance would not come amiss.

'Well, Miss Wilkings?' said Mr Lumbe. 'How were things at the market this morning?'

'There's a glut of narcissus,' Miss Wilkings said. 'Specially jonquils. Don't ask me why.'

'Oh, but I must!' said Mr Lumbe, with his plump-faced smile. 'I simply must ask why jonquils are glutting!'

'Early spring, no frosts,' Miss Wilkings said. 'Pass the bread, Mr Lumbe, please.'

'Mr Thorsby, you aren't finishing your soup,' said Mrs Bream.

'Yes, I am,' said Mr Thorsby, coming out of a dream and resuming his soup-spoon. 'It's very good. Very good indeed.'

And those, Betony noted, were the only words Mr Thorsby uttered throughout the meal.

Later that night, when she was preparing to go to bed, Edna came up to the attic room.

'What do you think of Mr Thorsby?'

'He's very silent,' Betony said. 'Rather stern. Rather reserved.'

'He's always silent, except when he and I are alone together. Then he talks. Oh, heavens, yes! But he *is* reserved with other people, and he's often thinking about his work.'

'Yes, of course.'

'Don't you think he's handsome, Betony?'

'He is. Very. But, Edna, isn't he rather old for you?'

Edna nodded. Her face was tragic. There were tears in her eyes.

'He's twenty-one years older than me, and he feels it dreadfully, poor man. That's what stops him, you see.'

'Stops him?'

'Well, if I had my way, we'd be married tomorrow!' Edna said. 'And I don't care who knows it! But Edward doesn't see it as I do, unfortunately. Oh, he's never said so, but I can read him like a book. He has such pride! And an iron will. He'd sooner deny himself every last chance of happiness than risk exposing me to gossip.'

'Does your mother know?'

'Well . . . She wants me to marry Rodney Lumbe. But I couldn't! He's soft and pudgy and wears yellow spats.'

'Has Mr Lumbe proposed to you?'

'No. I won't let him. But he follows me round all the time and he's always trying to get my attention. Had you noticed?'

'Yes, I had. He hangs on everything you say.'

'Edward is much more reserved,' Edna said. 'It makes me want to cry sometimes, knowing how he suffers underneath. But I've got faith and I know everything will come right for him and me in the end. Don't you think so?'

'I'm sure of it,' Betony said, with warmth.

'Oh, you are such a friend!' Edna exclaimed. 'I'm so glad you've come to live with us!'

At nine in the morning, Betony presented herself at the High School, and met the headmistress. The school was a square, clean-looking building, its white ashlar façade successfully hiding the absence of architectural style behind it. Inside, it was rather dark and smelt of polish, except for the head's room, which smelt of hyacinths and daffodils. Miss Telerra was a sombre-looking woman, her face loose-boned, her hair jet-black, and her skin swarthy. She looked very foreign, but her speech was as English as any Betony had ever heard.

'Are you settled comfortably in Matlock Terrace? I'm so glad. I'm sure you'll be happy with Mrs Bream.'

'I'm sure I shall,' Betony said.

'The school is not large,' Miss Telerra said. 'One hundred and eighty pupils, twelve to eighteen, all of them day girls.

'Mostly, they are not ambitious, but there are two scholarship girls of exceptional ability, one of whom may go on to university.'

'Florrie Smith?' Betony said.

'You know her?' Miss Telerra asked.

'No, but I happened to meet her father yesterday, when I arrived.'

'Florrie is an exceptional child, although coming from a poor home. You'll know her by her red hair and her hot enthusiasm for work.'

Miss Telerra smiled, thus transforming her dark face, and Betony liked her.

'Well, Miss Izzard, there are many things I must tell you about the school and your place in it, and then, when the rest of the staff arrive, I want you to sit in at our meeting. I trust it's convenient for you to stay?'

'Oh, yes! I'm looking forward to it.'

At ten o'clock, however, when the room filled with staff and the meeting began, Betony knew a moment of panic. She counted fourteen people in the room, and thought of the hundred and eighty pupils arriving next morning: how could she memorize so many faces and names at once? And the subjects now under discussion: how could she master the endless elaboration of administrative and academic detail?

But as the meeting went on, and she learnt the identity of each of the staff, she became calmer; and by one o'clock, when the meeting ended, she was cheerful again. The rest would come. She must give it time. And each new problem must take its turn.

Miss Telerra had introduced her in a general way, with a little speech welcoming her on to the staff, but now, as the meeting ended, most of them left without a glance in her direction. Only two young women, Miss Crabbe and Miss Horslam, spoke to her as they walked to the gate.

'I hear you're special,' Miss Horslam said. 'A personal friend of the King of Spain's Daughter.'

'Horse means the head,' Miss Crabbe explained.

'But I've never met her before today. Miss Telerra knows my headmistress at Chepsworth, that's all.'

'I expect you're cheap, then,' Miss Horslam said.

'Horse,' Miss Crabbe said apologetically, 'is not so delicate as her name suggests.'

'I meant no offence,' Miss Horslam said, meeting Betony's gaze with sleepy composure. 'You may be a super-excellent teacher for all I know. But you aren't an M.A. Cantab., are you?'

'Indeed I'm not,' Betony said.

'I am. And Crabbe hails from the other place with almost equal distinction. Which means we'll be out neck and crop as soon as cheaper substitutes can be found.'

'Oh, surely not!'

'Don't worry. It's a cross we career women have to bear. The school must pay its way and it's only common sense that the head should staff it as cheaply as possible.'

'Are you with the Breams?' Crabbe asked. 'Yes, I thought so. Your predecessor was there too.'

'Watch out for Edna,' Horse advised. 'She's a handful, that girl, and stuffed with morbid romantical nonsense.'

'So, having cheered you up to the best of our not inconsiderable ability, farewell!' said Crabbe. 'We meet in the morning – loins girded for the new term.'

They were at the school gate, and from there, the two young women went in one direction, Betony in another.

From The Panting Hart, she travelled on top of an open bus to the city. Edna was spending the afternoon with her dressmaker, and would not be free until four o'clock. She had asked Betony to wait for her, but Betony, glad of a chance to be alone, had made excuses. She wanted time to think and absorb; to drift according to her own inclination.

The day was damp, mild, and fitfully sunny. She leant against the rail of the bus, and, looking down at the traffic in the roadway and the lunch-time crowds filling the pavements, she felt a little drunk and dreamlike, enjoying the noise of the motor engines, excited by everything she saw.

She saw a tiny liveried page run down the steps of a large hotel and go weaving through the crowds and traffic. She saw a horse and dray drawn up outside a public house, and the draymen rolling barrels into the cellar. And she read the hoardings everywhere; the billboards on buses; the sandwichboards: Pear's Soap; Nestle's Milk; Hope and Parker's Menthol Snuff; Brand's Essence; Bawley's Beers.

Suddenly, more light, more space – the buildings pushed back – trees, fountains – pigeons in flight – and there was Nelson on his column in the sky. Betony blinked. She could not believe it. She looked at the passengers sharing the deck, and thought they must all be slumbering. She wanted to rouse them: 'Look! Behold! It's Nelson's column, Trafalgar Square!' But their eyes, amazingly, were open. It was only their souls that had gone to sleep, lulled by custom. She alone sat up and burned, looking down on London city, laid out so casually for any passer-by to see.

When she alighted, she was setting foot in a place built of dreams; a concrete chronicle of past and present: legend manifest in mortar, brick, and stone; where people even now were treading out the aching human fates that would make tomorrow's history.

She walked and walked, without knowing where she was going, and because she gave herself up to the city in this manner, it sprang its surprises upon her again and again. Here was the river, and a tug-boat folding its funnel to pass under London Bridge. Here was the Monument and its ball of fire. And here was the Tower, perfect and lovely; the Middle Ages seen at a glance, with scarlet pennants aflame in the wind.

She walked and walked, this way and that, through narrow passages and little courts; through Black Bear Alley and Playhouse Yard; Griffon Buildings and King Pin Walk. She saw pans of sausages frying on gas-jets in a café window, and was made hungry by the smell of soup coming up from a grating in the pavement. She went in, down the steps, into an underground room full of people. She ate sausages, onions, and mashed potatoes, and afterwards drank a cup of coffee, made from coffee-beans ground in a little machine on the counter.

She walked again, and came on another space between buildings, and there was St Paul's: the phoenix cathedral; the great covenant forged from fire; the City of London's act of faith; its dome moulded to the shape of the heavens as seen by the human eye.

'Look,' she said, to a newspaper-seller standing nearby. 'There's St Paul's!'

'Gorblimey, where?' he said, wheezing.

'There,' she said, pointing. 'Up on that hill.'

'Ho, yus! That's been there some time. Well, ever since I can remember, anyhow.' He looked at her with sharp eyes, unsmiling, straight-faced. 'Don't you touch it!' he said hoarsely. 'Or you'll have the king's horses and all the king's men after you. Ho, yes! The whole Magna Carta!'

As she journeyed home, the day drew in and the lamps were lit along the streets. She saw the lamplighters going about, busy with their long poles, and once she saw one of them poking a tuft of dry grasses out of a lamp where birds had begun to build a nest. All the lamps entranced her. The evening became a beautiful thing. The fuzzy rounds of pale splintered light were everywhere, dancing and glancing in the damp air, all the way home to Stanton Rise.

At dinner-time, when Betony entered and took her place at the table, Mr Bream greeted her with a sigh of relief.

'Well, Miss Izzard! You're back at last. We were worried about you, out alone in the great city. We feared you might be lost.'

'*Were* you lost?' Mr Lumbe inquired.

'I was, for a while, this afternoon, in a maze of little entanies behind St Paul's. But only on purpose, to see the city.'

'Lose yourself,' Mr Lumbe agreed, 'and you get to know the heart of a place.'

'Entanies?' said Mr Thorsby, looking at Betony with an interest so unexpected that it made her jump. 'What are entanies exactly?'

'Yes, whatever are they?' Edna asked.

'An entany is a narrow passage. It's what we always call it at home.'

'Ah, a dialect word,' said Mr Bream.

'A nice word, entany,' said Mr Thorsby. 'It sounds exactly what it is.'

'How did you get on with the King of Spain's Daughter?' asked Edna.

'She was most kind and helpful,' Betony said.

Mr Thorsby, next to Edna, looked at her with a dark frown.

'I think it's unbecoming in you, young woman, to speak of your headmistress by anything but her proper name.'

'But everyone calls her the King of Spain's Daughter! Even the staff!'

'You are not staff,' Mr Thorsby said.

'No,' said Edna, suddenly chastened. 'I ought not to say it, and I shan't again, ever, I swear.'

Edna's forearm, on the edge of the table, lay touching Mr Thorsby's sleeve. Betony noticed it, and the way Mr Thorsby, after a moment of deep thought, gently withdrew his arm from the table and turned to speak to Miss Wilkings. She noticed, too, how flushed and happy Edna was for the rest of the evening.

CHAPTER THREE

The attic room was a pleasant place to be in the evenings, when she had lessons to prepare, or her diary to write, or a letter home. If she sat at the window, she was able to catch every last gleam of light from the north western sky, and when she could no longer see to write, she often sat watching the sunset colours changing. She watched the first stars getting up, and the last birds flying home to roost, and when darkness really filled the room, she got up and lit the gas bracket on the wall by the door.

In her letters home, she wrote of the things she did and saw. 'Last Saturday, Edna and I went to the museum. Next Sunday, we go to Kew.' But, somehow, she could never write about the school, or the pupils, or her work as a teacher. And there were things about the Bream household, too, that she preferred to keep to herself.

One of the first things she did was to buy a diary, but three weeks went past before she found time to write in it, and by then her memory was playing her false. Only the first day at school remained perfectly clear in her mind, and two lessons clearest of all.

The first was with a class of the fourth standard, girls of

fourteen and fifteen years old, though they seemed older. They were quick and sharp, eager to know if she were flesh and blood, and one girl, Leonie Siddert, led the rest in a little trial.

'Oh, heavens! We're not still on that boring Middle English? I thought we'd done all that with Miss Scott.'

'Can't we get on to something exciting? Like "Moll Flanders" or "Tom Jones"?'

'Or something modern, like "Ann Veronica"?'

'Or Elinor Glyn!'

'Or "The Woman Who Did"!'

Betony, wincing under the onslaught of noise, was extremely angry.

'Be quiet at once!' she said fiercely, and, having surprised them by the trenchancy of her voice, she went on coolly: 'I shall give the lesson I have prepared, and if the material is already familiar, well, you'll be doubly sure of it when writing your essays in a few days' time.'

The lesson continued without further disturbance. Leonie Siddert appeared satisfied. And Betony had learnt how useful it was to have so much of her mother in her.

Later that day, she gave a history lesson to a class of older girls, and among them she found Florrie Smith, whose father had carried her travelling-box the day she arrived. Florrie was sixteen, a plain girl with ginger hair and a flat, freckled face, her plainness redeemed by wide-awake eyes and an easy, unaffected smile.

The lesson worried Betony, for whenever she sought to stimulate discussion by asking questions, Florrie Smith was the only one with anything to say. The others were silent from start to finish, though they listened intently enough, and made endless notes. After school, meeting Miss Crabbe on the stairs, Betony mentioned the matter to her.

'It's Florrie Smith,' Miss Crabbe explained. 'They look down on Florrie and won't demean themselves by competing with her.'

'Are they so special, for goodness' sake?'

'Their fathers are all great men, you see, such as stockbrokers or importers of tea.'

'Great men?' Betony said.

'To themselves, certainly, and to their daughters, for they Pay Fees while Florrie Smith is a scholarship upstart without two pennies to rub together.'

'But aren't they ambitious? Don't they *want* the education they pay for?'

'Their greatest ambition is to marry as soon as possible after leaving school, to pay a visit here in a motor car, and to flaunt their wedding-rings in the faces of their former school-friends. As for education – it's the done thing. They expose themselves to it just as they go every year and expose themselves to the sea air at Brighton or Clacton. The polish education gives them is on a par with the tan they get from a fortnight's sunshine, also paid for by their doting papas.'

'So we just won't get them to take an active part in discussions?'

'There's a golden rule,' Miss Crabbe said. 'Never ask: "Can anyone give the cause of the Luddite riots?" because Florrie's sure to answer and the others will just look down their noses. Instead, you point directly to a chosen victim and say: "Louisa, relate the events preceding the Repeal of the Corn Laws." '

Betony smiled.

'I've learnt more than I've taught on my first day of term.'

'Is it only the first day? I feel I've been back a lifetime already!'

Miss Crabbe and Miss Horslam were Betony's friends. Sometimes she went to tea with them in their rooms in Oldbourne, but they would never come to Matlock Terrace, because, they said, they knew from her predecessor that Mrs Bream frowned upon visitors. Betony liked them better than anyone else on the staff, and was soon calling them Crabbe and Horse.

'Not Horse and Crabbe, because Horse never really pulls her weight,' said Crabbe. 'And that's a hackneyed joke if you like!'

'I warn you,' said Horse. 'Friendship with us carries certain penalties. Miss Sylke will automatically detest you.'

'I don't much care for *her*. She's always so sneering about the other staff. Why does she call Miss Tweet and Miss Snubbs the Twins of Lesbos?'

'Izzard,' said Crabbe, 'you have a nice mind.'

'Have I?' Betony said, surprised.

'Well, compared with Sylke, certainly.'

'To Sylke,' said Horse, 'relations between the two sexes are disgusting, and relations between the same sex are more disgusting still. It's all in the eye of the beholder, and Sylke's eye is full of disgust.'

'She's quick to put people in the wrong,' Betony said. 'I've offended often.'

'I told you,' said Horse. 'You're friendly with us.'

Betony first offended Miss Sylke by mounting the school platform before her one morning at assembly. Next, in the staff-room, she offended by sitting in Miss Sylke's chair. And next, most serious of all, she dared to say that King Charles the First was an obstinate man. Miss Sylke, it seemed, was devoted to Charles.

'As head of the history department, Miss Izzard, I am the one to pronounce on such matters.'

'Divine right,' Crabbe murmured.

One day Miss Sylke came storming to Betony with a piece of paper in her hand. Again it was in the staff-room, for she liked an audience when she staged her scenes.

'This notice you put on the board, Miss Izzard, concerning the visit to Windsor Castle. It reads obscurely and I don't understand it. "Girls to apply to Miss Sylke by May the six-teenth, bringing their fare of one-and-sixpence and a packed lunch if they so wish." Am I to expect, Miss Izzard, that I shall be inundated with packed lunches to be kept from the sixteenth to the twenty-ninth?'

Betony took the piece of paper and rewrote the notice on the reverse side.

'There,' she said, handing it back. 'Now it's plain even to the meanest intelligence.'

Miss Sylke flounced out, and the staff-room door slammed behind her.

'You've done it now,' Crabbe said. 'You'll never be asked to see Sylke's collection of birds' eggs.'

'Did she lay them herself?'

'No, no, the dear little robins and wrens did that. It's the one touch of nature Sylke permits, and that's only because she thinks it's done by parthenogenesis.'

'I must speak to her,' Betony said, 'on country matters.'

She might have been lonely at school, sometimes, had it not been for Crabbe and Horse.

Sometimes, in the room below hers in Matlock Terrace, Mr Thorsby played his violin. He played Mozart and Mendelssohn, and old folk tunes like 'Barbara Allen' and 'Afton Water'. Once, meeting her on the landing, he asked if his playing disturbed her, and when she said no, that on the contrary, she enjoyed it, he went into his room and closed the door quickly, as though afraid she might follow him in.

Once, when Edna was with Betony in the attic, he played 'Drink To Me Only With Thine Eyes', and Edna was dreadfully overcome by tears.

'He knows it's my favourite, and he knows I'm up here with you, listening. Oh, dear, you'll think me so silly! But he does make me sad.'

Another evening, when Betony went out to the post-box, Edna was standing outside Mr Thorsby's room, listening to him practising scales. The girl shrank back, into the shadows, and Betony, pretending not to have seen her, went on down the second staircase and out of the house. When she returned, Edna had gone, and Mr Thorsby was playing a Mozart sonata.

On Whit Sunday, she and Edna walked in the park. There was hot sunshine. The holiday-makers were out in crowds, and among them, walking dreamily by the duck-ponds, Edna perceived Mr Thorsby.

'There's Edward!' she said, and, taking Betony by the arm, hurried her towards the ponds. 'I thought he might come. He knows I like to hear the band.'

Mr Thorsby was coming towards them, but gazing absently all around. As Edna and Betony drew near, his glance flickered briefly towards them, and then away, to where some children were chasing a ball. And he walked past, his hands behind him, his head in the air.

'Oh, really!' Edna exclaimed. 'Edward is very trying some-times. To walk past like that, – sulking – just because I'm not alone! It's always the same, you know. – If anyone's with me, he turns away.'

Betony walked along in silence. To her, it seemed Mr Thorsby had not even seen them. His thoughts, as always, had been elsewhere.

'Edna,' she said, after a while, 'are you quite certain of Mr Thorsby's feelings?'

'Certain?' said Edna, stopping abruptly and staring at her. 'Do you think I've been telling lies?'

'No. I thought you might have been mistaken.'

'Then you think me a fool, obviously!' said Edna, and her white-gloved fingers kept twisting the parasol on her shoul-der. 'I must be one or the other! – Either a liar or a fool! I don't see what else you can mean.'

'Please don't be silly,' Betony said.

'I won't!' Edna said. 'I won't be silly another minute! You can walk by yourself, you school-ma'am, you!' And she hur-ried away up the green slope, towards the south gateway and Matlock Terrace.

Briefly, Betony considered following, but then she shrugged and walked on. Edna's problems must wait until later. The day was too perfect to spend indoors.

Up on high ground, three children were flying a kite, and she stood and watched it, a bright yellow shield, now strain-ing its string as it rose on a current of hot air, now falling and swooping as the air failed. And then suddenly it was caught in an oak tree.

Not far away, a young man was also watching. He spoke to the children and went to the tree. He climbed up into the branches, out on a limb, among the thickening foliage, and down again, bringing the kite safely with him. The children took it and ran off, away to where there were fewer trees, and the young man collapsed on to the gras, bent double as though in pain.

Betony went closer and looked at him. He now lay flat on his back, his hands folded over his stomach. His eyes were closed, his thick black brows met in a scowl, and his thin face was covered in sweat.

'Are you all right?' she asked, just above him. 'Or are you ill?'

He opened his eyes, and sat up slowly.

'I climbed a tree and gave myself a bit of a stitch.' He stood up, wiping his face with a grubby handkerchief. 'It's over warm for such exertions today,' he said.

He was quite young, probably in his early twenties, though his hair was unusually streaked with grey. He was very thin, and his shabby brown clothes hung loosely on him, as on a scarecrow. His voice was strange, with an accent she had heard once before, and which, somehow, made her smile.

'What's funny, then?' he asked.

'It's the way you speak. I think you come from Yorkshire.'

'Where else?' he said, and stood with his hands in his jacket pockets, looking at her with a straight, steady stare. 'Runceley!' he said. 'And I doubt if you've even heard the name.'

'Runceley,' she repeated, and thought for a moment. 'West Riding town, on the River Tibble, Worsteds, woollens, corduroys. Population 45,000. Annual rainfall 86 inches.'

'Good God!' he said. 'You must've had the blue ribbon in geography when you were at school.'

'Quite the reverse. I was inattentive and the teacher made me write up the towns of Yorkshire as a punishment.'

'The old bitch!' he said roundly. 'Why Yorkshire?'

'She came from Bradford.'

'Eh, she can't have been too bad, then. And where are you from?'

'The three counties,' Betony said.

'What, all three?'

'My home village, Huntlip, likes to boast of having a foot in all three. But our nearest big town is Chepsworth.'

'Chepsworth,' he said. 'Cathedral ... River Idden ... Leather gloves.'

'*Three* rivers,' Betony said. 'The Idden, the Ennen, and the Naff. And three big brooks, the Swiggett, the Derrent, and the Shinn.'

'It sounds a very watery place.'

'It can't compare with Runceley for rainfall.'

'Why should it indeed?'

While talking, they had walked together down the slope to the central gardens, where lay the last of the three duck-ponds. Now Betony leant on the railings and looked at the ducks.

'Why must there be fences round every pond?' she asked in exasperation.

'To stop the foxes getting the ducks,' he said.

'Foxes? Here? Right in the town?'

'The town's grown up round them, and a few survive, getting their living as best they can. Three weeks ago, a fox ran out from under the band-stand, and a lot of daft folk chased it right across the park. Didn't you read about it in The Gazette?'

'No, I didn't. But surely a fox could dig down under these railings?'

'Nay, they were sunk deep on purpose to stop him. It was all in the paper a while back.' The young man leant on the railings beside her. 'Don't you ever read The Gazette?'

'No,' she said. 'But you evidently do.'

'Aye, well, I help to write it.'

'You're a journalist, then?'

'If you call it that. – Writing up band concerts and foxes seen in public parks.'

'Why do it if you don't like it?'

'I'm serving my time. An apprenticeship, like. But one day, I'll write for a paper with something to say for itself, and choose the subjects that really want airing.'

'Which subjects?' Betony asked.

'Children of twelve working in Runceley mills ... Conditions down the pit in the Yorkshire coal-fields. ... Girls in paint factories, dying of lead poisoning by the age of twenty-four ... I've a tidy few things to write about when I get started.'

'Will people want to read about them?'

'Nay. They prefer something pretty. And I shall oblige them! Oh, aye! I'll begin by describing Lord Soak's soirée, where the flowers alone cost four hundred guineas. Then I'll happen describe a Yorkshire collier, digging coal for a twelve hour stretch, up to his chest in poisonous waters.'

'You're a radical?' Betony asked.

'I'm a Voice,' he said.

Betony was reminded of Nancy Sposs.

'You're somebody's conscience, then, perhaps?'

'Aye. Yours for a start.'

'Why mine? I can't help it if people are poor.'

'That's what they all say!'

'It must be nice, being Conscience. Rather like being God.'

'God?' he said richly. 'I could run things better with my eyes shut and both hands tied behind my back! And don't look at me like that, woman! – You're no more shocked than those ducks and drakes on the water there.'

'How d'you know I'm not shocked?'

'You're too well founded. You're like one of those little lamps with a loaded bottom. – You might get knocked sideways now and then but you'll never go down. Aye, and you'll keep a trim wick and go on burning whatever happens, I dare say.'

Betony laughed.

'Only so long as my oil lasts out.'

'I've pleased you,' he said. 'You like the thought of yourself as a little lamp.'

'If you can be Conscience, can't I be Light?' Betony said, and then: 'Is Utopia possible?'

'It should always be the aim. A goal kept constantly in sight.'

'But surely there must always be poor people?'

'Why?' he demanded, and turned towards her. 'Why must there always be poor people?'

'I don't know.'

'Oh yes you do!'

'All right. I know what you want me to say. Because there are rich.'

'And you don't want to change it because it's what you've always been used to, and you've never known what it is to starve.'

'My parents have known poverty.'

'But not you?'

'No, not me.'

'That girl across there,' he said, nodding. 'She's staring at you. Is she a friend?'

Betony, looking across the pond, was just in time to see Edna walking away from the opposite bank.

'I must go,' she said. 'We had a disagreement, you see, and I want to catch her to put things right.'

'Aye. Well. Good-bye.'

'Are you sure you're feeling all right now?'

'So long as I don't climb any more trees.'

'Good-bye, then,' Betony said, and hurried off in pursuit of Edna.

'I came back to apologize,' Edna said, 'but found you otherwise engaged.'

'I apologize, too,' Betony said. 'Let's forget we ever quarrelled.'

'Who's your young man with the fierce eyebrows?'

'I don't know his name. We just got talking.'

'Shall you see him again?'

'I shouldn't think so. Unless by chance.'

'Was he romantic, Betony? Charming? Witty?'

'No, none of those things,' Betony said.

His name was Jim Firth. He was twenty-three, the youngest of six children, and the only one to survive childhood. His mother was dead, and his father lived alone in Runceley, publishing a weekly newspaper there.

'Doesn't he mind your coming to London and leaving him there all alone?'

'He sent me,' Jim said, 'to stir things up a bit here in the sawny south.'

'So you and he are two of a kind?'

'Rank socialists, the pair of us! Aren't you afraid of talking to me?'

At first, they met neither by chance nor arrangement. He came to the park every evening to escape his lodgings in Gasworks Grove, as he called it, and Betony, too, all through the hot May and June of that summer, could not bear to be indoors, but took to the park the moment she was free to do so. Each would have been there, anyway, but each, once there, looked out for the other. And so, almost always, they met. And, almost always, they argued.

'Why do you dislike your mother?'

'I never said I did.'

'She sounds a remarkable woman to me.'

'You and she would make a good pair!'

'Meaning something nasty?'

'You're both so cocksure that you know what's right.'

'Is that all that's wrong with her?'

'Well ... I've never understood why she married my father. I'm sure she doesn't love him.'

'What makes you think so? Is he unhappy?'

'No. He's perfectly happy. He's that sort of man.'

'Does he think your mother loves him?'

'I suppose so.'

'Well, he must know best. And there are five children. You can't all have been conceived in indifference. The trouble with you is, you never look below the surface.'

'It's a funny thing!' Betony said. 'I always make friends with people who tear me in little pieces!'

'They're the best kind, are friends of that sort, if you've the stomach for home truths.'

'Suppose I were to start on you?'

'Go right ahead. It's only fair.'

But Betony, though she tried hard enough, could find no fault in him. All the things that might have been faults, such as temper, impatience, the assurance that he was always right; his rough tongue and rude manner: all were so closely linked with one another, with his beliefs and essential being, they could not be considered faults at all. To censure him would be to censure a fox for its cunning or a wild bird because it had wings.

She tried to explain to herself why this should be so, but could think only of negative things, his lack of falsity, lack of self-interest. It was only later that she realized the positive thing about him: his love for everything on earth that lived.

'Tell me why you came to London,' he said.

'Because it's the centre of the world. Because it's romantic. Because there are so many things to see.'

'And what have you seen exactly?'

'St Paul's. The Tower. Westminster Abbey. Madame Tussaud's.'

'Is that all?'

'I think so.'

'By gow! I'll have to take you and show you the sights, for you've seen nothing yet, that's plain. How about Friday? I'll have a few coppers for a bus by then.'

'Friday, yes,' Betony said. 'But I'll pay my own fare.'

And so, now, they met by arrangement. They went by bus to the Edgware Road, and then walked, into a maze of back streets, this way and that. It was after nine o'clock in the evening, because Jim had worked until late that day, reporting a fire at Simsbury Junction. The night was hot, and they walked slowly, feeling they would melt at the slightest exertion.

'Where are we going? We've walked miles . . . We're leaving all the lights behind.'

'There's plenty to see all the same,' he said, as they turned into a long narrow street called the Fullway. 'Here, for instance. You've got an eye for architecture. Say what you think of the buildings here.'

'I suppose you're joking,' Betony said.

She looked at the cliffs of tall black houses, where many windows lacked glass, where cobwebs and dirt were the only curtains, and where, here and there, women and children sat out on the sills, exchanging remarks with others who sat on the doorsteps below.

'I don't believe these houses were built. They look as though they had festered from dirt-heaps. And they smell abominable.'

'Aye, well, there's only one tap in each house, shared between thirty or forty people, and the water's cut off at eight o'clock. And the drains, such as they are, run straight down into the footings.'

They turned again, into an alley, passing along the open back yards of shops and cafés. In one café yard, children were searching the dustbins for food. In another yard, in the darkness under the wall, a man and a woman lay on the ground, two bodies forming a single writhing shape, boots scrabbling against the cobbles, while other men waited nearby. And, in the alley itself, an old man, smelling of meths, went shuffling along, bent double, picking cigarette stubs out of the gutter.

Betony came to a sudden stop.

'Are these the sights you said I should see?'

'The romantic city!' Jim said. 'Wasn't that what you said?'

'Oh!' she said, raging. 'D'you think I've seen nothing at all in my life? We've got sights like this in Chepsworth! In my own village, too, if you know where to look!'

'Does that make it right, then?'

'I never said so! But what am I supposed to do about it?'

'You! With your miff-maff about romantic London! I decided you needed waking up.'

'Oh did you indeed!'

'Aye, and there's plenty more to see yet.'

'I'm not going another step!'

'Aren't you?' he said, amused.

'Not an inch!' she said, standing firm.

'Then you'd better return the way you came. *I'm* going on along here.'

He walked on, along the alley, towards the better-lit street at the end, and Betony stood uncertainly, clutching her purse against her breast. She knew she would never be able to find her way back. She could not even face it alone. And so, tight-lipped, she followed Jim.

He had turned the corner into Cord Street, and there, where the street-women paraded up and down, he was being accosted from all sides. A bone-thin woman, all frizzled hair and odds and ends of clothing, stepped out from a doorway; two girls, young and pretty, turned in their tracks and walked with him a little way; another stepped out from a crowd outside a public house; and to each of them, Jim politely raised his cap.

Betony, following a few steps behind, was hot all over with indignation. He knew she was there, for now, as well as raising his cap, he was speaking to each of the women in turn, making sure his voice would carry.

'Not tonight, chuck, thanks all the same ... Nay, not tonight, for I've had a hard day ... Aye, I believe you! – I'll tell my friends.'

But after a while, Betony began to laugh quietly. She couldn't help it. He walked in such a dignified manner, wearing his shabby clothes with an air, gallantly raising a cap much worn and frayed at the edges. She could not be angry. It was too absurd. And then he turned and caught her laughing.

'Well, fancy! You still here?'

'I could hit you!' she said. 'I could smack you hard.'

'You mustn't brawl in the street or you'll get clapped in gaol, and what'd they say at the High School then?'

They walked on together, and he drew her hand into his arm.

'There, the hussies won't trouble me now,' he said. 'They'll see I'm already suited.'

'Where are we going now?'

'Seeing you've come to my rescue, I'll take you to have a bite to eat. There's a place along here where you can get pie and potatoes and peas for fivepence.'

'I'll pay,' Betony said.

'Eh, you're a good lass, in your funny way.'

That was how it was between them. There was nothing loverlike about it. They had come together purely by chance; and because they were strangers in a strange country, each a long way away from home, they created another country between them, and thus were natives of a single climate, sharing a native kindness and warmth.

She would never let him spend money on her. More often than not, when they went about together, it was she who paid, for she knew he was poor, and she knew that all too often he was underfed.

Once, when they met at a bench near the children's playground, and he was eating his frugal lunch, a girl of nine or ten came and stared at him, watching every bite he took. He broke a bread roll, divided his cheese and pickles in two, and gave half to the eager child, who carried it in triumph back to the swings.

'Why d'you do it?' Betony asked, exasperated. 'Why

d'you give your money and food away? No wonder you're always so tired and worn!'

'Hush, woman,' he said mildly.

'She was begging shamelessly, the greedy thing! She's probably been taught by her parents to beg like that.'

'It's a parent's duty to teach survival,' he said, munching his own piece of roll. 'And that lass is passing the lesson on.'

The child had joined her small brother, and the two of them, sitting together on a swing, were sharing the bread and cheese and pickle. Each in turn took a small bite of bread, a nibble of cheese, and one lick of the pickled onion, then chewed slowly, making each mouthful last a long time. At the end, they shared the pickle, – one bite each and it was gone – and sat swinging gently to and fro, staring dreamily into the distance, preserving the memory to the last.

'I wouldn't call her greedy,' Jim said.

'You're very secretive,' Edna said.

'No, I'm not. There's nothing to tell.'

'You've never even told me his name, let alone anything about him.'

'Edna, pass that folder from the shelf there, will you?'

'I suppose I'm interrupting your work?'

'Yes. But I don't mind talking if you'll make do with half my attention.'

'As a matter of fact,' Edna said, playing with the curtain at the window, 'I happen to know his name is Jim.'

'There, now,' Betony murmured, still intent on her work, 'that's clever, I'm sure.'

'You'd be surprised what I get to know.'

'No, I wouldn't,' Betony said.

From the room below, came the sudden scraping of Mr Thorsby's violin, and Betony, glancing at Edna, saw the hot colour flooding her face. Mr Thorsby was tuning up. The harsh sounds continued a while. Then he began playing 'The Ash Grove'.

'Damn!' Edna said. 'And I've promised to go with my mother to a whist drive!'

'If you're passing a post-box, perhaps you'd post a letter for me?'

'Of course,' Edna said. 'Another letter home to Huntlip, I see. Oh, well, I'd better go down, I suppose, before mother begins to shout. Shall I knock on Edward's door and tell him you're working? – I'm sure the music must disturb you.'

'Do no such thing!' Betony said. 'It doesn't disturb me in the least.'

'Perhaps you enjoy it,' Edna said tartly, as she went out.

Betony wondered how Edna knew Jim's name. She had always avoided speaking of him, aware that even the most trivial detail would be magnified and shared with the other girls at school. But caution, it seemed, was no protection once Edna's curiosity was aroused, and the following day, when Betony was out in the school gardens, during morning break, two girls approached with a programme of well-rehearsed questions. One was Leonie Siddert, and the other, an older girl named Julia Temple, was Edna Bream's particular friend.

'Miss Izzard, is friendship possible between the sexes?'

'I don't see why not,' Betony said.

'But speaking from your own personal experience, Miss Izzard?'

'I took the question to be academic, Julia.'

'Well . . .'

'If not academic, it's very impertinent,' Betony said.

Julia was for a moment abashed, but, determined to impress the younger Leonie, recovered herself and tried again.

'Are you courting, Miss Izzard?'

'No, Julia.'

'Not even slightly?' Julia asked.

'Not even slightly,' Betony said.

The two girls, with knowing looks and a splutter of laughter, were turning away to rejoin their friends when Betony called them back and told them to follow her. Taken off guard, they obeyed without question, following her across the garden and through the french window into Miss Telerra's room. Betony knocked as she went in, and the headmistress looked up in surprise.

'I'm sorry to disturb you, Miss Telerra, but I'd like a moment of your time,' Betony said, and turned to Julia.

'Julia, you asked me a question just now. Will you please repeat it?'

Julia was silent, looking as though she would rush from the room.

'Well, Julia?' Miss Telerra said.

'It was nothing,' Julia muttered. 'Really. Nothing.'

'Come, come,' Betony said. 'You weren't so shy in the garden just now.'

'I only asked if Miss Izzard was courting!' Julia said, with a toss of black curls.

'I see,' Miss Telerra said. 'Well, Miss Izzard, if you will leave us, I will discuss the matter with Julia and Leonie.'

Betony returned to the garden, and when she next saw the two girls, they were careful not to meet her eye. But the damage was done, and Betony, foreseeing further annoyances, knew exactly who was to blame.

'Edna,' she said, when next the girl came up to the attic, 'you mustn't discuss my affairs at school.'

'Affairs?' said Edna. 'What affairs are those?'

'You know best what stories you've told.'

'I never told any stories at all! Why should I? D'you think I've got nothing to talk about but you and your peculiar young man?'

'Edna, I'm speaking to you as an adult person, so please don't behave like a stupid child.'

'It seems to me you must be ashamed of him, whoever he is. I can't think of any other reason for all this secrecy!'

'There are no secrets,' Betony said, 'because there's nothing to have secrets about.' And, as a gesture of peace, she put out a hand and touched Edna's arm. 'Come, now,' she said. 'We're friends, surely? Which means we must each respect the other's reserve.'

'But I'm never reserved!' Edna blurted, and great shining tears came squeezing out of her prominent eyes.

'Neither am I, really,' Betony said. 'It's a storm in a teacup, all this, so let's make it up and be friends, shall we?'

Edna nodded, smiling bravely through her tears.

'I know I'm silly,' she said, sniffing. 'I'll try to be sensible in future, I promise. Won't you come down for a game of whist?'

'Well – '

'Oh, do come, please! It gets so dull downstairs sometimes.'

'All right,' Betony said.

Whist was a passion with Edna and her mother, and because Mr Bream was so often out in the evening, they were always desperate for someone to make up a table. Mr Thorsby would never play; nor would Miss Wilkings, who claimed she could not tell aces from 'clumps or tubs or whatever they're called'; but the amiable Mr Lumbe would play, to please Edna, and Betony was often pressed into service as a fourth. She could never enjoy it, for Mrs Bream, who remembered every card that passed, would take her to task after every game, pointing out her criminal errors, and frowning at her flippancy in the face of loss.

'It's no good laughing, Miss Izzard. You'll never make a good card-player if you don't concentrate on what you're doing.'

'Oh, well, it's only a game, isn't it?'

'To some, perhaps,' Mrs Bream replied. 'To some, certainly. Just a game.'

Betony once described these games to Jim, and he laughed, saying Mrs Bream should meet Mrs Packle, his landlady in Gasworks Grove, who was also a demon for Norfolk whist.

'They'd make a pair, Mrs Packle and her. But, of course, your Mrs Bream would never be seen around Gasworks Grove. It's barefoot territory down there!'

'Is it really called Gasworks Grove?'

'Nay! Some wit went and christened it Borrowdale Gardens, and the streets across it are Wensleydale Grove and Malhamdale Avenue and such. Just imagine! Some of the wildest, sweetest country in the north and they name the slums of Simsbury after it!'

'But presumably it wasn't always a slum?'

'With the houses built back to back as they are, all round the gasworks, and as near the railway line as a cat can spit! – With inadequate water systems and inadequate drains! – Yes, it's always been a bloody slum! Right from the drawings on the board!'

'Don't you ever think of anything but social problems?'

'Sometimes I do. Sometimes I think about taking off like a gipsy and wandering forever in green places. Sometimes, especially these hot days and nights, I think about stripping and taking a bathe in a pool of cold water surrounded by trees. And I think of a cottage garden I know, miles from anywhere, down in Wiltshire, with an old leaning apple tree by the door.'

'Whereabouts in Wiltshire?'

'A place called Midlinger, under the downs. I take a bicycle and go there sometimes. It gets the smoke out of my lungs.'

'I can't believe you'd want to escape forever, though,' Betony said. 'I think you love your dark territory down in the slums.'

'Happen you do come to love a pain if it's with you long enough.'

'Pain? What pain?'

'That,' he said, with a wave of his hand, out towards the slums of Simsbury, lying under the smoke. 'The dark territory, like you said.'

Outside The Panting Hart, when she was buying a newspaper, a man came up and addressed her by name. It was Joe Smith, who had been her porter on the day of her arrival, and whose daughter, Florrie, was at the High School.

'I've been hoping to see you, miss. I wondered if I might ask a favour.'

'Yes, surely,' Betony said.

'It's this notice in The Gazette, about the High School wanting a groundsman. That's a job that'd suit me nicely. I've had some experience with gardening and that. So I wondered if you would put in a word for me with the headmistress.'

'I will indeed,' Betony said.

'Smith's a pretty common name,' he said. 'No one need know I'm Florrie's dad.'

But, in the morning, Betony found that Miss Telerra had too good a memory to be deceived.

'As I remember, Miss Izzard, from something you said previously, this Mr Smith is Florrie's father.'

'Yes. But does it matter?'

'I make it a rule never to employ anyone connected in any way with one of the pupils. And in this particular case, it would be most unwise.'

'Why?' Betony asked sharply. 'Because the family happens to be poor? Because Florrie is a scholarship pupil?'

'Miss Izzard, it's Florrie I'm thinking of primarily. You know as well as I do that the girls here come from middle-class homes and that there is a certain tone maintained throughout the school.'

'Snobbery, yes. I know all too well. But do we condone it, Miss Telerra?'

'Snobbery can't be eradicated by edict, Miss Izzard, and Florrie could be made extremely unhappy if her father worked here as groundsman.'

'I do see that,' Betony said. 'And I'm sorry if I was rude. But need the relationship be known?'

Miss Telerra gave her sombre smile.

'There are few secrets kept in a girls' school, Miss Izzard, as you have already learnt for yourself.'

'Yes, that's true,' Betony said.

At the first opportunity, she spoke to Florrie Smith alone, and explained the matter to her.

'It wouldn't worry *me* if dad worked here,' Florrie said. 'I don't care what the girls say. I'm used to their sneers.'

'Well, Florrie, I can't do much more,' Betony said. 'And Miss Telerra was only thinking of you, you know.'

Florrie gave a little smile, as if she placed no faith in Miss Telerra's solicitude.

'Thank you for trying, Miss Izzard. I'll tell my father.'

Some weeks later, when the matter of the Harriet Thame Prize came up, Betony remembered Florrie's sceptical little smile.

The prize had been founded by a former headmistress: it was given once every three years for the best history essay written by a senior girl on a subject approved by the staff, and consisted of a credit-note to be redeemed at The Study Book Shop. This year there were six entries, and Florrie

Smith's was unquestionably the best. Miss Sylke and Betony were for once in full agreement, and Miss Lazenby, head of the English department, also concurred. Their decision was delivered in a note to Miss Telerra, but nothing more was heard until suddenly, at the end of term, Miss Telerra announced during morning assembly that the prize had been awarded to Miriam Charcomb.

'Why, why?' Betony asked, in the staff-room, later. 'Miriam's essay was nothing at all!'

'Miriam's father is one of the Board of Governors,' Miss Lazenby said.

'It's not the first time,' Miss Sylke exclaimed, 'that something like this has happened here!'

'Isn't it?' Betony said.

'No,' said Horse. 'My predecessor resigned because of a similar piece of nepotism in the classics department.'

'Can't we complain to the head?' Betony asked.

'The King of Spain's Daughter,' Miss Lazenby said, 'would merely persuade us that hers is the only proper decision.'

'That woman is probably descended from Torquemada,' said Horse.

'Florrie Smith!' said Miss Sylke, still raging. 'The only girl in the school who has a brain and wishes to use it! And what use has Miriam Charcomb for a credit-note at The Study Book Shop?'

'None,' said Horse. 'Her father will probably have it framed.'

A bell rang, and Betony went to give a lesson. The afternoon seemed very long, and whenever she thought of Florrie Smith, her mind was darkly overcast. The school that day was dreary to her. She felt thankful the end of term was at hand; the long summer holiday lying before her.

'What will you do with yourself?' Jim asked, as they walked in the park one evening. 'Will you go home?'

'No,' she said. 'I'm staying here. There are lots of things I want to do.'

'Sight-seeing?' he said, to tease her.

'That's right. Why not?'

Every day, she left Matlock Terrace after breakfast and was out until supper-time, or even later. The feeling she had when exploring London was not so intense now as it had been. It was muted and calm. It was even tinged with melancholy, springing, she supposed, from her sense of smallness, her utter anonymity, as she walked the streets with the famous names.

One evening, when she went to meet Jim in the park, she found him asleep on a bench in the sun, and she sat beside him, watching the twitching of his eyelids, and listening to the tired little groans in his breathing. When he did at last awake, and saw her there, he struggled stiffly to sit up, stretching cramped shoulders, and looking sheepish.

'It's the heat,' he said. 'I've been shut up all day in the Magistrates' Court in Oldbourne.'

'Isn't it time you had a holiday?'

'You're right. It is. I'll have to see about getting a Saturday to put with my Sunday. Then I'll go down and see Auntie Jig.'

'Auntie Jig?'

'She's the old woman whose cottage I stop at, down in Midlinger.' He sat up straight, shivering, and pulled his waistcoat tidy in front. 'Have you got a bicycle? No? Well, happen you can borrow one for a couple of days, then we'll go down together. Saturday next. Or the one after. D'you think you can cycle so far in a day?'

'If you can, I can,' Betony said.

CHAPTER FOUR

She borrowed a bicycle from Margaret Crabbe. She met Jim at five in the morning, and they rode out of London in a soft white mist that lay shallowly over the land. After Twyford, they went by quiet country roads, avoiding even the smallest towns, and stopping often to rest, to eat, or to look around them.

It was September, and when the mist lifted, there before them were the harvest fields, some with corn-cocks still standing, and some quite empty, with the sunlight glancing along the stubble. In many places, especially further west, the stubble was burning, and when, on top of Rumble Hill, Jim and Betony sat eating their lunch, they looked down on ridges of thick black smoke, now and then lit by leaping red flames.

The smell of burning came up to them on top of Rumble. It was rough in their nostrils, and in their mouths, and it flavoured every bite of food. It was with them constantly when they travelled on, through Snifford, Lamsborough, Sneep, and West Hole: a smell from the very beginning of time; the smell of cleansing and purification; the smell of one earth-year as it died and of another earth-year in the offing.

'They burn the moors at home where I come from,' Jim said. 'They burn the old heather and gorse. Then the new comes up, bright green in the black ashes.'

He had not spoken much during the journey, and Betony, watching him now as they pedalled along side by side, saw that he was pale with fatigue.

'Shall we have another rest?'

'Nay,' he said. 'We're nearly there now.'

They rode through Midlinger village and out again at the far end. They came to a cottage, very small and crookedly built, with a lopsided thatch overgrown with moss, and with very small windows of old, dim, yellowing glass. They left their bicycles against the hedge, and walked up the path, and Jim knocked at the open door.

The old woman who came hobbling out was the ugliest Betony had ever seen. Her grey skin was shrivelled and none too clean; her upper lip had long silver hairs, like a cat's whiskers, sprouting from three or four little black moles; and she had one solitary yellow tooth sticking out from her upper jaw. She came in a temper to answer Jim's knock, and glared at him ferociously, but then, as she recognized him, she waddled out on to the step and dropped shapeless hands heavily on his shoulders.

'You, you villain!' she said, cackling. 'You haven't been near me for six months or more!'

'I'm near enough now, though! And you smell of tobacco, you old stove-pipe!'

'Stove-pipe yourself!' she said, shaking him roughly to and fro. 'Grudge an old woman her one bit of pleasure, would you? – You come-to-Jesus streak of sanctomy, you!' She humped herself round and stared at Betony with milky-blue eyes. 'Who's this you've brung with you?'

'This is Betony,' Jim said.

'Betony? I've got betony in my garden! It's good for all sorts of aches and pains. I make it up in ointments and such.'

'Aye!' Jim said. 'I'm well aware you're an old witch!'

'Don't shout! Godsakes! I'm not deaf, you silly fella!' Auntie Jig was still studying Betony. 'Betony,' she said. ' "Sell all you have and buy betony." – That's what they say. It's one of the bestest herbs there is. Did you know?'

'No, I didn't know,' Betony said.

'Betony tea! It'll cure you of death, or very nearly. And you, young miss! Are you any good for aches and pains? Eh? Are you? Are you any good for giving men their ease?'

'No, she's not!' Jim said loudly. 'She's a respectable girl, not a flighty piece like you, you old muck-wife! So don't be so busy trying to put her to the blush.'

'Hah! Cowpats! But you'd better come inside, I suppose.'

'We'd sooner go through to your back garden and sit under your old apple tree in the shade.'

'Please yourselves! Please yourselves!'

She led them through the dark little cottage and out into the back garden.

'Are you stopping the night? Oh, you are, are you? And what'll I give you for supper tonight? You tell me that!' She stood, hands on hips, and surveyed the chickens that pecked about where they pleased, in the house as well as the garden. 'I'll have to take a chopper to one of *them*.'

'No,' Jim said. 'There'll be no murder done on my behalf.'

'Nor mine,' Betony said.

'Then you'll have to have eggs. Eggs and cheese and a few potatoes baked in their skins. Will that do?'

'Couldn't be better,' Jim said.

He and Betony sat on the grass and looked at the apple tree leaning low, its old scabby boughs borne down by the apples, all ripening a rich russet red. Auntie Jig waddled to and fro, bringing tea and fruit-cake and plum tart with thick yellow cream.

'Auntie Jig's pastry is the best on earth,' Jim said. 'It's because she makes it with dirty hands.'

'You're a flaming liar!' the old woman said. 'My hands are spotless. Pink and clean as a baby's bum.'

'They come clean, making the pastry.'

Jim, when he had finished eating, stretched himself out on his back on the grass and was almost instantly asleep. Auntie Jig stood over him, looking down at his tired face.

'That's how I found him the first time he came. Him and that bicycle, all in a heap on the grass in the lane. I thought he'd fell off and cracked his skull. But he was just sleeping, that's all, and planned to sleep out all night, too, to save spending money on a lodging. So I brought him back here and put him to bed on my landing. He's been here often since then and he's always tired out like this.'

'He works too hard,' Betony said. 'And neglects himself. He's always giving his money to beggars.'

'Silly fool!' Auntie Jig muttered.

When Jim awoke, and raised himself on his elbows, he found the two of them sitting there quietly, Auntie Jig in a chair, knitting, and Betony, on the grass, winding up a skein of wool.

'I must've dropped off. Did I snore?'

'Snored your head off!' said Auntie Jig. 'The girl and me couldn't hear ourselves thinking.'

'Just as well, probably.'

'What d'you aim to do now? Have another nap?'

'No,' he said, getting up stiffly. 'I've brought a towel and I'm off to bathe in Luting Pool.'

'What, again? You did that last time you were here. If you're not careful, you'll wash yourself away, sloshing about in that old pool.'

'Betony, are you coming with me?' he asked.

'Of course she's going with you!' said Auntie Jig. 'She surely don't want to stop here with me.'

Sitting among the reedmace and rushes, while he splashed about, a white fish in the middle of the water, Betony felt herself soaking up the essence and texture of the place and the day.

The pool, so blue wherever it reflected the sky, so silver and gold when splashed up and broken catching the sun, so olive-black under willows and alders, so green-surrounded; the reeds so sweetly and greenly scented, cool harbours for morhen and duck, which plip-plopped quietly into hiding; and a lark singing from the ground somewhere not very far away: she was so full of all these things that she knew what it felt like to be a drop of water and flash in the sun; to be cool and green, a reedblade slenderly bending, giving way to the movement of ducks; and to be a skylark, – warm tiny body, warm tiny feathers under warm wings – sidling through the stubble forest, throbbing, throbbing, to sing from the nest.

'Don't look round!' Jim called, wading out of the pool into the reeds a short way away. 'You'll make me bashful.'

'Get yourself dried!' she called back. 'The sun's not so hot as you seem to think.'

She watched him drying himself with his skimpy towel. His nakedness was nothing to her, except that his thinness made her want to cry. Nobody should be as thin as that: the flesh so sparely stretched on the bones, and the bones themselves so sharp and frail, like the bones of a bird. Without his clothes, he looked as though he would snap in two. Even with his clothes, he was but a shadow compared with her sturdy brothers at home.

'I feel as good as new,' he said, coming and sitting down beside her, combing his hair. 'You going to bathe? Nay, it's awreet for you! You've plenty of water in Matlock Terrace.'

'Yes. The maid, Ruby, brings it up in a big copper jug. Silly, really, seeing the cistern is in the attic, right next to my room.'

'Ruby,' he said. 'Is she like a ruby?'

'Not really. Her eyes are red-rimmed and her hair is mousey.'

'Aye, well! I dare say Ruby is precious to somebody.'

'She is. The baker's boy is courting her. But they have to be careful because of Mrs Bream. So, if the coast is clear for him to stop and talk, Ruby gives his horse two lumps of sugar. If the coast is not clear, she only gives one. And they smuggle notes to each other in the basket with the loaves and muffins.'

'How do you know so much about it?'

'Sometimes, when Mrs Bream is not about, Ruby and I gossip together. Sometimes she asks me how to spell words for her letters to Matthew.'

'It's not the spelling that counts, tell her. And speaking of spelling, I'd a long piece on the subject of pensions published in Barcoe's last week.'

'You might have told me before this!' Betony said. 'Have you still got a copy of the paper?'

'No. But you don't need to read it. It's only what you've heard me say oftentimes before.'

'I'd like to have read it all the same.'

'Just because it was in print?'

'Because it was in a paper that goes out all over Britain. Surely you're pleased with yourself about it?'

'Well, it's a start,' he said.

Later, as they walked back slowly across the fields, she noticed how often he stopped to ease his back and shoulders.

'Aren't you stiff yourself, after cycling so far?' he asked.

'Not particularly.'

'You will be!' he said.

It was twilight by the time they returned to the cottage, and colder, too. Auntie Jig had lit the lamp in the kitchen, and there was a good fire in the stove. The kettle steamed on the hob, and the baked potatoes whistled and piped, buried in the ashes. The table, innocent of cloth, was set with yellow plates and mugs, a big round loaf with poppy seeds on its shining crust, and a wooden bowl of tomatoes and greenstuff from the garden.

'Are you hungry?' asked Auntie Jig, as she made tea.

'Aye, famished! There's nowt like a swim for making you hungry.'

'I'll take your word for that,' she said.

First of all, she brought them eggs, which she called co-cottes: eggs broken into a stoneware dish, into a pool of hot melted butter, sprinkled with parsley and pepper and salt, and allowed to set beside the fire. Then she brought the potatoes, still in their skins, which split open at a squeeze and revealed their crumbling white mealy middles, steaming hot and smelling like chestnuts, Betony said. And lastly, she pressed on them cheese and apples and rich raisin scones.

'No more,' said Jim, leaning back in his chair, 'or I'll have bad dreams.'

'That reminds me,' said Auntie Jig. 'Are you two sleeping together upstairs, nice and cosy, or sleeping apart with an extra blanket instead?'

'Apart!' Jim said. 'You wicked, immoral old woman, you!'

'Only asking, boy! Only asking!'

'You think everyone's as bad as yourself!'

'The trouble with you,' she said, poking him as she passed his chair, 'you don't eat enough, so you've got no good red blood in your veins.'

'Never mind my blood, woman. Just watch your tongue in front of a decent girl.'

'You young folk today! You're a strait-laced lot to my way of thinking. But if you prefer to die wondering . . .'

Later, she went upstairs, and they heard her rummaging about above.

'Don't mind her,' Jim said. 'She likes putting people out a bit, just to see what happens.'

'You seem more put out than me.'

'With my Wesleyan upbringing, what d'you expect?'

'Has Auntie Jig ever been married?'

'Off and on, I gather. *And* got some offspring scattered about.'

Auntie Jig came down with a load of bedding: a straw pallet, three blankets, and a linen pillow stuffed with hops. Jim got up to take them from her.

'Betony was asking if you'd been married.'

'Well, I've had a few husbands at different times.'

'Other people's, I suppose?'

'We can't all be fussy, boy!'

'I'll tell you this, Betony. — She's done pretty well out of her husbands, what with this cottage and its three acres, and another bit of land across the road.'

'Shows what you're missing, girl,' the old woman said.

'She's missing nothing,' Jim said, busy making his bed on the floor, 'for I'm as poor as a chapel mouse.'

'Damn fool!' said Auntie Jig. 'Damn fool, if you ask me!'

'Stop your noise,' Jim said. 'I'm ready for bed.'

Betony slept in a small bunk bed on the landing. Her pillow, too, was stuffed with hops, and she slept deeply. She awoke to full sunshine, and the distant sound of church bells, rung in changes. Midlinger church was famous for its bells, Jim told her when she got down, and for its ringers.

They had breakfast with Auntie Jig, and spent the morning helping her in the garden, gathering carrots, lettuce, and marrows, which she would take to market on Monday. At twelve o'clock, Jim said they must start back, and she packed great parcels of food for the journey.

'D'you have to go so soon?'

'It's a long ride.'

'Well, come again, and sooner next time,' the old woman said, grimacing at him with her one yellow tooth stuck out. 'And you!' she said to Betony. 'Bring him down once a month to be fattened up.'

'If I can, I will,' Betony said.

On the journey home, Jim was quiet, and Betony, knowing how tired he was, made sure they had long and frequent rests.

In the fields, the stubble fires were still burning, and the smoke drifted on all sides. When evening came on, the smoke vanished under darkness, and the tides of flame were seen instead. Jim and Betony, stopping to rest and eat their supper, sat in a field on the Snifford uplands, and, looking back the way they had come, could see a number of fires at once, burning in the distance, red tidal waves of flame on earth, just as, on the horizon, there were red waves of sunset flame in the sky.

Betony opened the packets of food: bread and butter, hard-boiled eggs, lettuce and radishes, screws of salt and pepper mixed. She opened a tin and found scones, tarts, and apple pasties.

The evening was cold. A sly little wind was blowing up. So she and Jim sat back to back, leaning against each other for rest and warmth, shoulders hunched, collars turned up against the wind. They sat together, eating their food and drinking tea from a stone bottle, hardly speaking, but watching the fires and breathing the smell of burning straw. There was great comfort in sitting back to back like this, and much warmth passed between them. They were two animals, wise in blood and bone, and sat in a warmth of their own making, under the wind.

'These are the times I dream of escaping,' Jim said. 'Going off for ever and ever . . . always free like this . . . never again imprisoned in towns.'

'I feel the same.'

'You? In love with the city as you are? You must be over-joyed at returning.'

'Not at this moment,' Betony said. 'At this moment, I don't want to go back at all. I feel as you do. I'd like to be free like this for ever and ever.'

When Betony got to Matlock Terrace, and was carrying the bicycle down the area steps, she slipped and cut her hand on the chain-guard. The cut was not serious but bled freely, and Ruby, having let her into the basement, went rushing upstairs to the sitting-room, shrieking out that poor Miss Izzard was bleeding to death.

The basement swiftly filled with people. Mrs Bream came down with Edna, followed by Mr Bream and the two male lodgers. Mr Thorsby took charge at once. He washed the cut with carbolic and bound the hand in a thick bandage. He scarcely glanced at Betony throughout. He was purely pro-fessional and utterly silent. But Betony, going upstairs on her way to the attic, caught a gleam of jealous anger in Edna's eyes.

A few days later term began and Betony was busy again. She scarcely thought of Edna at all. And then, suddenly, late one night when she was in bed, she was woken out of a deep sleep by a noise of shouting and screaming below. She got up, opened her door, and stood listening. Downstairs, Mr Thorsby burst from his room, strode across the landing, and hammered loudly on the Breams' bedroom door.

'Mrs Bream! Will you kindly come and remove your silly little bitch of a daughter from my room? Because if not I shall be obliged to drag her out by the hair!'

His voice was unexpectedly powerful. It could be heard throughout the house. Betony withdrew into her room and closed her door. She returned to bed and drew the clothes over her head, shutting her ears to the comotion below.

In the morning, Edna did not appear for breakfast. Nothing was said about her. The meal passed almost in silence. Mr and Mrs Bream pretended not to see Mr Thorsby, and he, although looking as if a single word would ignite him, ate with as good an appetite as ever and would not be hurried from the table. Edna did not walk with Betony to school that morning, but was there, in assembly, looking peaked and pale.

At supper that evening, Edna was present and her father took pains in making conversation, but Mr Thorsby was not there, nor was his place laid at the table. No one asked why. No one ever mentioned his name. He was not at breakfast the following morning, nor at supper again that night. The room below Betony's was now silent, and when she looked in, discreetly, on her way down one morning, she saw that all his things had gone.

The room remained empty week after week, and then, somehow, it became understood that Edna and Mr Lumbe would have it as part of a suite when they were married, perhaps at Easter.

Edna hardly spoke to Betony now, at home or at school. She had confided her secrets too freely and spoken contemptuously of Mr Lumbe, and she seemed to fear that Betony might repeat the things she had said.

'Edna, we all make mistakes,' Betony said. 'I don't see why we can't still be friendly.'

'I have nothing to say to you, I'm sure,' Edna said. 'But excuse me, please. I'm very busy at the moment.'

Betony smiled. She found it easy to forgive Edna's rudeness. She thought it a mood that would soon pass. But she was mistaken, and forgiveness was not so easy when, a week or so later, she found Edna in her room, reading her diary.

It was a Saturday evening in October. Betony had been to

the park to meet Jim. She had waited a while, but he had not come, so, as the evening was damp and cold, she had returned home unusually early. Edna was taken by surprise. She had no time even to put the diary back in the drawer, but stood with it hidden in her skirts, looking guilty and defiant.

'What are you doing here?' Betony said. 'I thought you had no time for me these days.'

'My mother wants to know if you need clean sheets.'

'Don't tell lies, Edna. You saw me go out. We passed each other in the hall. You've got my diary there, haven't you? And not for the first time, either, I think.'

'This!' Edna said, in a sudden temper, and threw the diary at Betony's feet. 'You needn't worry! I couldn't read your terrible scrawling writing, anyway!'

'Get out of my room,' Betony said, 'and don't come again when I'm not here.'

'I certainly don't want to come when you are!' Edna said, and slammed out.

Betony picked up the diary and looked inside. Edna had spoken the truth, she thought: the writing *was* a terrible scrawl.

From that time on, Edna's hostility became active, and it influenced a part of the household. Mrs Bream was barely civil to Betony now, and Mr Lumbe grew distinctly cool. Mr Bream behaved normally enough, but he was rarely at home in the evenings, and Betony was beginning to understand why. Only Miss Wilkings remained friendly, and Ruby, the maid, though she dared not speak now when passing Betony in the hall, would blink her sore eyes in a signal of sympathy and understanding.

At school, Edna was even more active. She and two friends, Julia Temple and Phoebe Davies, whenever they were in Betony's classes, made a point of sitting in front and staring at her throughout the lesson. They would look her up and down repeatedly, or stare at some particular part of her clothing. They would look very knowing, and they often whispered together, taking care that she heard certain words, such as *bicycle* and *week-end with friends*. And sometimes they mimicked the way she spoke.

'Where exactly do you come from, Miss Izzard?'

'Why, Julia?'

'You speak so very broad, Miss Izzard. We wondered what region your accent belonged to.'

'Is your father really a carpenter, Miss Izzard?'

'Confine your questions to the subject of the lesson,' Betony would say, coldly and calmly, in a bored voice.

But often, underneath, especially when they jostled her in the corridors, her temper was only narrowly held in check.

She had not seen Jim for almost a month, and because of the 'flu epidemic sweeping London, she was anxious about him. So, on a cold wet Saturday afternoon in October, she went down into the slums of Simsbury in search of Borrowdale Gardens.

The street was a long one, and she did not know the number of the house. All she knew, recalling remarks Jim had made, was that he lived on a corner and that the railway ran at the back of the house. It gave her a choice of six houses.

At the first corner house, when Betony knocked, the door was opened by a woman completely bald except for a single plume of long fair hair growing up from her smooth shining crown.

'Mr. Firth? No, not here. You've got the wrong house, dear.'

'Mrs Packle, then?' Betony said. 'She takes lodgers.'

'That's nothing. We all do round here. I don't know no Mrs Packle.'

At the next corner house, the woman who came to the door had a grey parrot perched on her shoulder, and carried a poker in her hand.

'No! There's no Mr Firth in my house. Nor I don't know Mrs Packle neither.'

'Somebody knocking!' the parrot screeched. 'Somebody knocking! Let the sod in!'

'Perhaps you've seen him,' Betony said. 'He's thin and dark-haired, with black eyebrows. He works as a reporter on The Gazette.'

'No,' said the woman. 'I don't know him. Try her next door.'

'Bloody trains!' the parrot screeched. 'Waterloo! All change for Watford!'

At the third house, there was a notice, Rooms to Let, in the window. The woman who answered Betony's knock was small and white-haired, with a tough, pugnacious nose and jaw, and sharp eyes.

'Yes? That's right. I'm Mrs Packle. Have you come about the room?'

'No. I wanted to see Mr Jim Firth.'

There was a silence, and the woman came out on to the doorstep.

'Gawd! Mr Firth! He's been gone these three weeks or more.'

'Gone?' said Betony. 'Gone where?'

'Dead!' Mrs Packle replied hoarsely. 'He was took ill all of a sudden, on the Friday, three weeks ago. Oh! But it was a terrible shock to me! I had to go and fetch Dr Sweeting. But it wasn't no use the ambulance coming. He was already dead when the doctor and me got back to the house. Appendix, it was. Peritonitis, the doctor said.'

Betony nodded. Peritonitis. Something that killed.

'They carried him out on a stretcher, dead, right through this door, like I'm standing now. Oh, I *was* upset, I can tell you! I was nearly ready to drop myself.'

'And the funeral?'

'Last Tuesday fortnight. His father came down as soon as I wrote him the sad news. Poor man! The last of all his children to go, he told me.'

'Where is he buried?' Betony asked, and was thinking three weeks ago; on the Friday; that would have been October the third.

'Why not come in?' Mrs Packle suggested. 'I can see it's been a shock to you. It was to me, I don't mind saying, but I think I could talk about it now.'

'Thank you, no,' Betony said. 'I won't come in. But could you tell me where he's buried?'

'Simsbury cemetery. Down the Junction. Such a nice little chapel of ease. Are you sure you won't come in?'

241

Betony was walking away. No, thank you. Perfectly sure. Simsbury cemetery and railway junction. Waterloo. H'all change.

The cemetery, acre on acre of white marble, chilled and appalled her: a lunar city, built in straight, sharp lines, hard enough to resist the working of time. The sharp lines threatened, as though they were knives, and the screaming whiteness was paralysing, shrilling coldly along her nerves.

At home, in Huntlip, the old churchyard was grey and green, quiet and restful to the eyes. The stones were sandstone and the weather soon ground them down at the edges. They sank comfortably into the earth, drew the ivy over their shoulders, and opened their grain in little fissures, to give the beetles and emmets a home. The churchyard at Huntlip, and those at Eastery, Middening, and Blag, were places where flowers grew and birds sang. They were places of rest, for those in the earth, and for those who tended the wilderness above.

But at least Jim's grave, when at last she found it, had no glaring marble slab. It was only a mound of dark earth, soaking up the soft small rain. Soon the grass would cover it over, and it would be green for evermore.

After leaving the cemetery, she walked about, hour after hour, going deeper and deeper into the region of chimney-stacks and cooling-towers; railway sidings and railway wharfs; the canal cutting and the sewage farm. In this dark region, the dwelling-houses were squeezed in, back to back, row upon row, wherever a space occurred between factories; between gasworks and power station; or round the smoking refuse dump. The rain went on falling steadily, and in this region it brought the smoke and fumes down with it, till the puddles all smelt of oil and sulphur.

The streets after dark made her think of things that crawled and crept, and she thought how, if the rows of houses were lifted by the hand of an inquisitive God, thousands of people would be revealed like maggots crawling on a heap of compost.

The darkness between the houses was more than just an absence of light: it had a texture of its own; it was like the corruption felt in the veins when the blood moved under primal compulsions; when there came a dark will to destroy; a will towards deeds of cruelty. It was like the feeling that came on seeing a flock of crows rise from their work of devouring carrion. It was like that dark territory in the mind, disputed by two conflicting forces; the will to survive at all costs, and the will towards self-destruction. The streets after dark were full of these forces; the houses, and the spaces between the houses, were sick and corrupt, yet full of squirming, pulsing life. This dark region was both the carrion and the crow.

She had walked herself into a weary stupor. Now she ached in every bone. She wanted to find a place to rest, but went on aimlessly, street after street, for her brain no longer commanded her actions.

A man was walking close behind her. She hastened her steps to shake him off. She took several turnings, but still he followed close behind. She hastened again, into a street where there were lights and traffic and noise. The man also hastened, coming beside her, his rubber mackintosh rattling and creaking as he walked. When she glanced up at him, into his face, he was grinning down at her, showing his teeth, a regular pattern of black and gold.

'Here are you, walking the streets,' he said softly, 'and here am I, feeling lonely, so what about our pairing up?'

'Go away!' Betony said.

'Now that's not nice. And you don't mean it. You've been leading me on for miles.'

'Go away!' Betony said.

'But you looked at me,' he said, injured, and put up a hand to take her arm.

On a corner, there was a public house called O'Leary's. The public bar was crammed to the doors, and a great many people were drinking outside, standing about in groups on the pavement, in the rain. One such group, seeing Betony pulling away from the man's grasp, spread themselves out to block her way, and one, a woman, screeching with laughter, pushed her into the man's arms.

'You two been having a bit of a barney? Well, let's see you kiss and make it up!'

Betony saw the ugly teeth: one black, one gold; one black, one gold; and caught the smell of the man's bad breath.

'Let me go! I don't know him! He's been following me!'

'That's different!' one of the women said at once. 'Hoi, let her pass, you drunken pigs! Can't you see she means what she says? And she's soaked right through, the poor little soul! Here, Queenie, get out of the way! And you, Clarence, – give that bastard a piece of your mind!'

They kept the man back, and Betony escaped at a run. She got on a bus and was carried towards The Panting Hart. She felt her clothes, which were indeed sodden with rain. She began to shiver, all through her body, and had to keep her teeth tight-clenched.

At home, on the way upstairs to the attic, Edna passed on her way down. She looked at Betony's wet clothes,

'Been to meet your paramour?'

Outside her room, Betony found a letter from home and the sight of it reminded her that today was October the twenty-fifth. It was her birthday. She was eighteen.

Winter set in early that year. November was a month of fog and frost. There was no fire-place in Betony's room, and the evenings there were bitterly cold. Mrs Bream had promised the loan of an oil-stove, but weeks went by and nothing was done, and when Betony mentioned the matter again, talking of buying a stove herself, Mrs Bream said she did not want the attic ceiling blackened by fumes.

'There's always a fire in the living-room, Miss Izzard. You're welcome to spend your evenings there.'

But Betony was not welcome. If she worked at the living-room table, Edna would play bagatelle with Mr Lumbe, and would jog the board, spilling Betony's ink on her papers. If she sat reading, Edna talked in a loud voice, passing repeatedly to and fro, leaning across her to open a cupboard, or making her rise so that her chair could be searched for a lost nail-file. So, however cold, Betony preferred to stay in her room, wearing a coat, and wrapping her legs in the blanket taken from her bed. And when it grew too cold to bear, she would put on her cape, her woollen scarf, and the thick leather gloves granna had made her, and go for a walk, quickly and briskly, until her blood was moving again and life came back to her hands and feet.

It was so cold at night that she went to bed wearing two nightgowns, and her woollen scarf wrapped round her feet. She had only one blanket on her bed, so she spread her coat and cape on it, and then the rag rug from the floor. Once she asked Mrs Bream for extra bed-clothes, and that evening, on going to her room after supper, she found one small blanket outside her door.

But it was during the evenings, when she had school work to do, that she felt the cold most badly. Her body, hunched against the draughts, would be stiff and aching. She would shiver inside, feeling the cold creeping down into her chest and stomach. She had to get up and move about, swinging her arms vigorously, and sometimes, when her fingers were cramped from holding a pen, she had to hold them close to the gaslight before she could open them out again.

One evening, when she was correcting test papers, some-one came up the attic stairs. She sprang to her feet, reluctant to be found sitting hunched in blankets, and moved about quickly before going to open the door. It was Mr Bream, all smiles, and he walked in carrying a small oil-stove, with a can of oil and a tin funnel.

'For the cistern,' he said. 'My wife is afraid the pipes will freeze.'

He opened the door into the roof-space, and, bent double, vanished inside with the stove.

'There!' he said, reappearing, brushing the cobwebs from his sleeves. 'That should safeguard us! We don't want burst pipes all over the place, do we? I'll leave the oil can with you, Miss Izzard. – Perhaps you'll superintend the stove and refill it when necessary? It'll save us a journey up the stairs.'

As he was going, he looked back, without quite meeting Betony's glance.

'It's cold up here, Miss Izzard. You will come down if you want to, won't you?'

'Yes, I will,' Betony said.

Later that night, when she was about to go to bed, she opened the door and peeped in at the little oil-stove, burning in the darkness under the roof. The sight was cheering; so was the faint breath of warmth in her face; but the smell of the oil was saddening to her, because it made her think of home. She closed the door and went to bed.

December came in colder than ever. Night after night there was hard frost. And one evening, so shrammed with cold that she contemplated swallowing her pride and going downstairs, she thought of the oil-stove in the roof. She went in, treading cautiously along the joists, and brought the stove back to her room. She turned it up high, to a big blue flame, and sat over it, reading a book, until bed-time. Then she carried it back to its place. When she undressed, the smell of paraffin was strong in her clothes, so she hung them close to the draughty window, hoping the smell would be gone by morning.

Every night after that she borrowed the stove for two or three hours and then returned it to its place. She felt no guilt, for the pipes and tank remained unfrozen, and every night she climbed on a chair to wipe the smudge from the bed-room ceiling. But then, one night, when she was in the roof-space, she lost her balance and put one foot through the laths and plaster between the joists, penetrating the ceiling of the room below.

The room was the empty one, once Mr Thorsby's, and when she looked in, quietly, on her way down next morning, there, sure enough, was the terrible hole in the ceiling, with the splintered laths sticking out like ribs and there was the plaster and dust on the floor. What a shame, she thought, to have made such a mess in Edna's future bridal suite! She closed the door and went down to breakfast.

'Ugh!' said Edna. 'You smell most dreadfully of paraffin! It quite makes me sick.'

'It's the stove in the roof,' Betony said. 'I filled it last night, as your father asked me, and perhaps it does make me smell, rather.'

'It's surely no trouble,' said Mrs Bream, 'for you to fill the stove, Miss Izzard?'

'None at all,' Betony said. 'It was Edna who complained of the smell, not I.'

In the school hall, now that Christmas was drawing near,

stood a model of the nativity, lit by candles in coloured glass jars. In front of the model stood a large open packing-case, into which the girls dropped gifts of discarded clothing, destined for the orphanage at Oldbourne Hill.

Betony, passing through the hall one afternoon, discovered a group of older girls, including Edna Bream and Julia Temple, gathered about the packing-case, rummaging through the bundles of clothes.

'Look at this!' Julia exclaimed, and held up a muff of grey astrakhan. 'It's positively *made* to go with my coat! It's just exactly a perfect match. My coat is grey and has grey astrakhan on the collar and hem. Whoever gave such a beautiful muff to the orphans? It's hardly been used!'

'If I were you I should keep it,' said Edna, running a hand over the muff.

'I shall, don't worry! It's absolutely made for me!'

'Julia,' said Betony, approaching the group, 'put that muff back into the box.'

'Why should she?' Edna demanded. 'Whoever gave it would just as soon Julia had it if they knew she wanted it so badly.'

'Yes, why should I?' Julia said. 'I'll never find anything so perfect again.'

'Put it back,' Betony said.

'No!' said Edna. 'Take no notice of her, Julia. She's not the headmistress.'

'Perhaps you'd like the head to be fetched?' Betony suggested.

'I don't care!' Edna said. 'I'm sure she'd agree to Julia's having the muff.'

'Yes, imagine an orphan in grey astrakhan!' said Julia. 'Whoever gave it was out of her mind.'

'Put it back,' Betony said, 'or I'll go at once and report the matter to Miss Telerra.'

'Oh, all right! You can take it and welcome and damn you so there!'

Furiously, Julia flung the muff back into the packing-case. Then, with a sob, she snatched it half out again, deliberately catching it on a nail and ripping a hole in the astrakhan.

'There!' she said. 'Now the orphans are welcome to it!'

Betony's own temper burnt hot and strong. Her hand flew up and slapped Julia's face.

Walking away, she felt divorced from everything around her, but for once it was the world that seemed unreal, not her own inner self. She went straight to the head's room, knocked in a rather perfunctory way, and walked in.

'I'm leaving the school,' she said calmly.

'I think you'd better sit down, Miss Izzard, and talk the matter over,' Miss Telerra said.

But Betony would not sit down. She had made up her mind and no discussion would ever change it.

'Nevertheless,' Miss Telerra said, 'I'd like you to give the matter some thought. Is it the Breams? Because if so, I could easily find you a more congenial lodging.'

'It's partly the Breams. But not them alone. It's everything, including the school.'

'The school?' Miss Telerra said, as though such a thing could not be believed.

'The prize that went to Miriam Charcomb. – It should have gone to Florrie Smith.'

'Miss Izzard, I believe you're going home for Christmas? Well, I suggest you think carefully during the holiday, and, if you feel the same when you return, I will then accept your resignation.'

'No. I won't be returning after Christmas.'

'But you must! A term's notice is obligatory. You know that as well as I do.'

'I don't care,' Betony said. 'I'm not coming back.'

Miss Telerra's face became very stiff.

'Are you aware that the school could sue for a term's salary in lieu of notice?'

'I'm still leaving, whatever threats you make.'

'You're lucky to be able to treat the threat so lightly, Miss Izzard. There are many people in the world too poor to share your rather casual contempt for money.'

'Don't speak to *me* about poverty.'

'I beg your pardon!' Miss Telerra said coldly. 'I think perhaps you've said enough.'

'I think so, too,' Betony said, and went to the door. 'But

248

there's one other thing you ought to know. – I've just slapped Julia Temple's face.'

During a lesson that afternoon, when she was looking through an Early English textbook, she came on these lines:

> Smale brids on plowed londe;
> A man sowing sede;
> Softe wind bryngen rain:
> God lette these abyde
> Till I come againe.

Small birds on ploughed land! She saw them plainly all the afternoon. The words were with her constantly, reminding her of home. A man sowing seed! Everything now made her think of home, and in four days' time, she would be there. God let these abide . . . till I come again.

On the last day, she took formal leave of the headmistress, a few civilities passing like splinters of ice between them. She sought out Crabbe and Horse, to say good-bye, and she sought out Florrie Smith with a farewell gift of books. The rest of the school she ignored completely. And her departure from Matlock Terrace was equally cold.

'I shall not be returning,' she said, as she settled accounts with Mrs Bream.

'Very well, Miss Izzard,' Mrs Bream replied.

'Good-bye, Ruby,' Betony said.

She wanted the train to hurry, hurry. She wanted the journey to be at an end. For now, travelling through the grey frosty landscape, she feared she might again be too late: that home and family, and everything belonging to her past life, might have been destroyed in some awful catastrophe. What proof had she that they were still there? Her letter home, giving the time of her arrival, had merely been an act of faith, and her thoughts now were a constant prayer. Let them abide . . . till I come again.

When the train ran into Chepsworth station, and she saw her father standing there, smoking his pipe, just as she had seen him last, it was as if the intervening months were only a long and complicated dream. Yet there *were* changes, for then his face had been long and glum, whereas now it was rounded out in smiles. Then she had actually *wanted* to leave him, whereas now his very existence was a marvel, and his great bursting smile was as warm on her as a burst of summer sunshine.

'I thought you was never coming!' he said. 'I've been waiting here I dunno how long.'

'The train was only five minutes late.'

'Was it? It seemed like hours.'

He shouldered her box, and they walked together along the platform. He took her ticket and give it to the man at the gate.

'My daughter here is home from London. Ah, London. That's right. She's a teacher there.'

The feeling that she was taking part in a miracle was with her still. The sound of their footsteps ringing out on the hard-frozen ground; the pony's little whicker of welcome and the way he nuzzled her with chaff-coated nose the instant his food-bag was taken off; the drive home, with a tartan rug over her legs, a hot stone bottle under her feet, and her father's warm solid body beside her; and his great importance at bringing her home through Huntlip, revealed in the way he sat up straight and made himself tall: all these things were a miracle to her, as though she had long been blind, and now saw; had long been deaf and dumb and unable to smell the pure cold smell of winter, and now had all these senses restored.

'Winter's put in early this year, freezing so hard,' her father said. 'But there! It's the best way, I always say. – Early winter, early spring!'

Sometimes, lately, she had wished with passion for it to be spring, with birds on ploughed land, and a man sowing seed. And sometimes she had wished it were summer, with the apple trees leaning low in the orchard. But now, knowing that spring and summer *would* come again, – her father had said so; it must therefore be true – she was content with the cold grey frost and mist, for the winter, too, was miraculous in its way.

'How long you home for, blossom?'

'For good,' she said. 'At least, I'm not going journeying again for a while yet.'

One day, perhaps. But not yet. One day, she would go to Midlinger and tell Auntie Jig that Jim was dead. One day, she would go to Runceley and see Jim's father. But now, at present, she needed time to rest and think and recover her strength.

'Not going back!' her father said. 'Why, wasn't you suited with things there?'

'No. That's right. I wasn't suited.'

'How was that, then, blossom?' he asked.

'I'll tell you some time. But not now. I just want to enjoy coming home.'

She could see that he was disappointed. His dreams had been vague, but dreams there had been, on her behalf, as she well knew, and in his heart, he had expected to hear her name come echoing out of the great city, to cause some stir throughout the land.

He said no more, but his feelings were plain in the way he kept looking at her, puzzled and frowning. He could not understand her, because she was changed. He felt that she had let him down. He thought she was shutting him out from things that mattered, and he was inclined to be hurt about it. The misunderstanding was saddening to her: the one smudge on the day's brightness.

But her mother, hearing she was home for good, asked no questions. Not even one. Her mother's eyes looked into hers, read something there, and remained perfectly clear and calm, as always. Her mother's nod was one of acceptance, and the things she said in her cool, calm voice were homely, practical, comfortable things that created a great feeling of safety. And to Betony, at that moment, her mother's acceptance was pure balm.

'It can't last,' she said to herself, 'but at this moment, I am good.'

'I wrote you a letter,' Janie said. 'On your birthday, two months ago. But you never answered.'

'I'm sorry, Janie,' Betony said. 'But now I'm here myself instead.'

'There's rabbit stew for supper,' her mother said. 'The boys went out for the rabbits this morning, because they know it's your favourite stew.'

'Did they? Did they?' Betony said.

Everything was exactly the same. Yet everything had a fabled beauty. And the kitchen became the heart of the world. The black beams overhead, the mellow red tiles underfoot; the fire so fierce in the stove when granna opened the damper; the smell of rabbit stewing with onions and carrots and parsnips and swedes and little dumplings flavoured with thyme; the blue and white china being set out, and the old horn mugs that had come from the Pikehouse; the light of the oil-lamp spreading out over the room; even the simple act of drawing the curtains, shutting out the cold grey dusk, shutting in the warmth and light: – everything was just the same, yet miraculously different.

And the boys, too, coming lumbering in from the workshop: all awkward grins and shyness at first; then all clamouring excitement and horse-play, eager to prove that they had grown to be men in her absence: they, though made of solid flesh and bone, were creatures lit by the beauty of fable. Even great-grumpa, clomping in, barking at her in his great voice, barking at everybody because he was growing a little deaf: even he brought a feeling of godlike warmth and safety. And Tom, hanging back from the rest of the boys, the odd one out as always: so dark and thin where they were all so blond and broad: so quiet, so still, watching her with his deep dark gaze: she had only to look at Tom to love him utterly, as her own, and to know that this love would be her punishment, evermore, for treating him cruelly as a child.

'Fancy not seeing the king and queen!' said Dicky, disgusted.

'Nor the lord mayor!' said Roger, laughing.

'Betony,' said William, 'I want you to teach me some geometry.'

'Betony,' said Janie, 'I want you as bridesmaid when Martin and me get married in June.'

'Seems to me you look thinner, blossom,' her father said. 'Your mother will have to fatten you up.'

'Have another dumpling,' granna urged.

The miracle lasted. She awoke every morning to find it intact. She went about, through the house and buildings, the orchard and the fields, and everything was precious to her.

Yet there *were* changes, especially in the workshop. Timothy Rolls had died, aged eighty, and Steve Hewish had retired, aged seventy-six. And the oak tree had gone from the workshop yard.

'Three hundred years,' William said, as they stood looking at the great stump. 'We counted the rings, Roger and me, and we both made it three hundred years.'

'Why was it felled? Was it dying?'

'No. Great-grumpa wanted to catch the timber at its soundest, so's we can use it and give it another life, as he says.'

She went with them and looked at the timber the oak had given, the trunk and great limbs, all piled up in a distant corner of the yard. Where would she be, she asked herself, when that timber came under the carpenters' hands?

'Shall you be here for the brandy-drinking, Miss Betony?' Sam Lovage asked her.

'Of course she'll be here!' great-grumpa shouted. 'She's come back home, where she belongs, and here she'll stay, you mark my words!'

She was home. She would stay. How good was great-grumpa's faith in the matter! Life itself was an act of faith.

On Christmas morning, she and the boys were out early, gathering holly from the hedges, mistletoe from the orchard trees. The house became as green as a forest, great-grumpa said, and the frost, melting from the holly on the beams in the parlour, dripped on granna's neck when she was busy polishing the table.

They carried in scuttles of coal and baskets of logs, and kept great fires burning all day, in kitchen and parlour. All morning, the house smelt of roasting goose and sage-and-onion stuffing, plum pudding and brandy-sauce. All afternoon, it smelt of roasting orange peel, which they toasted in front of the parlour fire and ate with brown sugar, just as they had when they were children.

Her present from her brothers and Janie to her was a new

diary, and a week later, sitting in her old place in the kitchen with her desk on her lap, she opened it and pressed down the first stiff clean white page. The miraculous feeling would fade in time, but, for the present, it was strong as ever, and had to be captured. There were so many things that were precious to her. She wished to record them; to have them down in black and white. So she took up her pen, licked the new nib clean of its grease, dipped it into the bottle of ink, and began to write.

'My great-grandfather, William Henry Tewke, was born in 1831, the year of King William's coronation, and the year the railway came to Chepsworth. He is now eighty-two.

'My grandmother, Catherine Rose Tewke, formerly Firkins, was born in 1853. My grandfather, John Tewke, was born in 1852, and died in 1885, killed by a horse on Huntlip common.

'My other grandfather, Walter Izzard, was born in 1833, and died in 1890. My grandmother, Goody Izzard, was born in 1837, and died in 1906, during the bad winter floods.

'My father, Jesse Izzard, was born in 1877, at the Pike-house, near Eastery, and my mother, Elizabeth Kate Izzard, formerly Tewke, was born in 1875, in a cottage on Huntlip green. They were married at Eastery in September 1894.

'I, Betony Rose Izzard, was born in October 1895, and my sister, Jane Elizabeth, in November 1896, both at the Pike-house. My brother, William Walter, was born in May 1898; Roger John in August 1899; and Richard Jesse in April 1900: all here at Cobbs. My foster brother, Thomas Maddox, was born in 1897: the exact date is not known, but we keep his birthday on March 1st . . .'

Betony paused, and dried the ink. She turned over to a new page, and wrote again.

'This book was given me by my sister and brothers, to keep as a diary. I here promise that all events recorded in it will be true in every particular, and written in a good clear hand; beginning today: New Year's Day, 1914.'

Mayflower Historical Fiction for your enjoyment

THE STUART LEGACY	Robert Kerr	40p	☐
THE WIND AT MORNING	James Vance Marshall	60p	☐
THOSE ABOUT TO DIE	Daniel P. Mannix	50p	☐
THE EAGLES: LAND OF MIST	Andrew Quiller	40p	☐
THE EAGLES: HILL OF THE DEAD			
	Andrew Quiller	40p	☐
THE PALADIN	George Shipway	35p	☐
THE WOLF TIME	George Shipway	50p	☐
IMPERIAL GOVERNOR	George Shipway	50p	☐
KNIGHT IN ANARCHY	George Shipway	40p	☐
THE VILLAGE OF ROGUES	Jeremy Sturrock	40p	☐
A WICKED WAY TO DIE	Jeremy Sturrock	50p	☐
GOAT SONG	Frank Yerby	75p	☐
THE SARACEN BLADE	Frank Yerby	75p	☐
PRIDE'S CASTLE	Frank Yerby	75p	☐
THE GOLDEN HAWK	Frank Yerby	75p	☐
THE DEVIL'S LAUGHTER	Frank Yerby	75p	☐
JUDAS, MY BROTHER	Frank Yerby	95p	☐

All these books are available at your local bookshop or newsagent, or can be ordered direct from the publisher. Just tick the titles you want and fill in the form below.

Name..

Address...

....

Write to Mayflower Cash Sales, PO Box 11, Falmouth, Cornwall TR10 9EN

Please enclose remittance to the value of the cover price plus:

UK: 18p for the first book plus 8p per copy for each additional book ordered to a maximum charge of 66p

BFPO and EIRE: 18p for the first book plus 8p per copy for the next 6 books, thereafter 3p per book

OVERSEAS: 20p for the first book and 10p for each additional book

Granada Publishing reserve the right to show new retail prices on covers, which may differ from those previously advertised in the text or elsewhere.